JACK CALDER

The Keeper of the Veil

Book One of the Veil Saga

First edition

ISBN (paperback): 979-8-9939224-1-6
ISBN (hardcover): 979-8-9939224-2-3

This book was professionally typeset on Reedsy.
Find out more at reedsy.com

Contents

Acknowledgments

To my daughter, thank you for sharing my love of storytelling, and for all those nights we spent watching shows so poorly written they should have been outlawed, yet became some of my favorite bonding moments.

To my boys, thank you for sharing my book with your friends and taking an interest in the world I've created. I'm deeply grateful that you still choose to spend time with your parents, willingly even.

To my wife, who has been steadfastly supportive of this writing adventure, even though it's "not really her thing," thank you for cheering me on. Your encouragement has meant the world to me.

To fellow author, Dina Galarza Mapes, the first person outside my family who read what I scribbled and actually liked the story. Your early encouragement mattered more than you know.

To the ARC readers, beta readers, and early supporters of *The Keeper of the Veil* series, thank you for taking a chance on an ancient warrior from Centerville, Ohio.

And finally, to anyone who occasionally needs a break from the real world, to share an adventure, and find out what might be lurking just behind the Veil, thank you for coming along. I hope you enjoy the journey with me.

1

Bread, Blood, and the Bishop (Sussex, England 1066)

The October sky hung low and grey. Smoke from burned steadings darkened the horizon. Northward, the road ran like a wound, a broad ribbon of mud churned by hooves and desperate boots. In the hedgerows, autumn's fire had dulled to rust and rot. Shattered shields littered the ground where men had fallen. Ravens hopped and picked, their work quick and efficient. The land twitched like a gut-shot beast.

For three days after Hastings, James Crable moved with a band of Saxons who couldn't stop moving. Men hollowed out by terror and fury, men who had watched their king die and denied the kingdom's death with every ragged breath. At first, they kept silent. They kept to deer paths, drank from muddy rills, slept in copses where the wind couldn't find them. On the second night, they talked again, coarse and bitter. By the third, laughter came back, the ugly kind that follows easy killing.

They called themselves survivors. Their knives grew quicker; their prayers thinned to whispers.

James kept to their edges. His clothes beneath the old mail shirt stank of blood and sweat. A round shield, scarred white by sword-cuts, dragged at his arm. A plain sword with a nicked edge and a seax at his belt was all that he owned in the world. He had fought because refusal meant a spear in the gut.

Prayer came now from rote memory, half habit, half stubbornness. Walking with them still seemed better than dying alone in a ditch, with only crows to bear witness.

That night, they built a fire in a hollow screened by blackthorn. Meager scraps of hunted meat sizzled on a spit. Sour ale made the rounds. Talk started low, then sharpened with hunger and bitterness.

"We go north," announced Wulf, a thick-shouldered man with a torn ear. "Through unguarded villages. We take what we need."

A few men chuckled, a dry, rasping sound. Leather-clad knees were slapped. Another voice cut through, blunt and flat. "The Normans will be hungry. So will we."

"Hungry," Wulf agreed, baring his teeth. "And thirsty. There's a church at the ford. I've seen a silver cup gleam on its altar. Priest preaches charity. He'll have some to spare."

Flames licked the blackening meat. James watched them climb and fall and thought of that church, of a priest with a child hidden behind his robes, of cups and candlesticks that meant more than their metal. Better to let the thought sit unsaid, so he held his tongue.

"You are quiet, Lundenware," Wulf's voice cut through the smoke, naming him by his birthplace. "Do you have a better plan? Or did they beat the courage out of you at Hastings?"

"They beat the folly out of me," James said, steadier than he expected. "Pillaging a chapel to fill your belly is a short road to losing your soul."

Wulf laughed without warmth. "I will keep my soul and the silver both."

A man nearer the fire leaned in, eyes glinting. "Our kingdom was destroyed on that field. I care nothing for those who didn't stand and fight with us. We'll show them the realities of battle."

They spoke of balance, though their scales were broken.

James rose, took his stale bread, picked out the weevils, and stepped beyond the circle of firelight. For a few heartbeats they watched him go; then their attention slid away. Stars pricked through cloud, cold and distant. Wind hummed low in the thorn. He ate standing, chewing slowly, each bite a prayer he couldn't quite form. If this was the remnant of his army, then it was truly lost. No looted cup would be added to the heap of his sins.

Dawn came thin and chill. A ragged line formed on the road, cutting through a tangle of hedgerows and scrub. Thick mud sucked at boots, greedy and cold. Crows lifted from the carnage as they passed, only to settle again in the wake of their march.

Near mid-morning, the road narrowed and dipped to cross a rivulet where alder trees leaned in. Ahead, a smudge of dust moved between the branches. Men. Horses. A small procession. The Saxons slowed. Nostrils flared. Eyes narrowed. Wolves scenting weakness. Wulf raised a hand, pointed two men left, two right. Bows whispered from their cases. A man's tongue darted out to wet his lips.

A choice descended on James, solid and heavy as a palm on his shoulder. He stepped into the hedgerow, letting bramble hooks catch and tear at his mail. His sword stayed in its sheath.

A carriage creaked into view, narrow and absurdly high on springs not meant for these brutal roads. Four riders flanked it, mail shirts dulled with grime, eyes sunk deep with exhaustion. Priests and clerks trudged alongside. Behind rattled two wagons piled with bundles. Sweat had shoved the driver's hat back on his head. Through a slit in the leather curtain, James glimpsed a woman's profile, pale, composed, her mouth a firm line.

Then arrows flew.

Arrows hissed from the banks. Two Norman riders crumpled in their saddles, bowstrings' song still hanging on the air. The carriage lurched as the driver yanked at the reins, horses fighting the bit. A woman's scream burst out and cut off, bitten back hard. A guard on the left spurred forward, shield high, only to flip backward as a shaft punched through his throat. Saxons spilled from cover with a roar, a raw-throated sound that meant men were about to die. James swore and moved.

Rather than charge with those he'd traveled beside, he cut across the ditch, taking the slope at a slant, shield coming up to meet a wild-swinging axe. The impact slammed through his shoulder; his legs slid in the churned mud. In an instant he was in it, that small, closed world where everything became noise and the fight shrank to hands and steel.

A Saxon with a boar's head painted on his shield lunged past, seax raised high, eyes gleaming with blood-fever. James met the man's wrist with the iron-bossed rim of his shield. Bone snapped. The seax clattered into the filth. Another fighter came in from the side. Steel shrieked on steel as James parried, then stepped in close and cut, a short, brutal stroke that opened the man's cheek to the ear. Warm blood sprayed across his face. He did not flinch.

Three archers held the bank on the far side. One sported a feather in his cap as if this were a hunt. James brought his shield up on instinct. A hammer-blow struck his forearm. An arrow punched through the linden planks, its point quivering a finger's width from his knuckles. He bit off a curse, snapped the shaft, and drove forward into the chaos.

The carriage groaned, one wheel sunk deep in a rut. The driver hauled at the reins and another arrow took him high in the chest. His body sagged. Horses panicked, eyes rolling white, harness rattling like chains.

Norman guards fought with the desperate knowledge that failure would cost more than their own lives. One took a spear in the belly, howling as if the pain had borrowed a throat. Another lost his sword, snatched up a fallen Saxon's axe, and swung in vicious, compact arcs that sent splinters flying from shields and ribs.

James reached the carriage as a Saxon scrambled up its side, fingers clawing at the leather, eyes fixed on the slit where the lady's face had been. He caught the man's ankle and wrenched. The Saxon hit his back with a grunt. A stamp crushed the wrist until fingers sprang open; the seax skittered away. When the man clawed for his knee, the shield boss slammed down against his temple. Limbs went slack.

A Saxon archer behind a tree fumbled to notch an arrow. James caught the movement, lowered his shoulder, and charged. The man looked up, eyes wide. James didn't break stride; his sword drove deep into the man's belly. A gasping, wet cry escaped the archer's lips as he collapsed.

Steel tore free just as three riders barreled into the clearing. Norman knights, coats of mail dark with muck, and with them a priest who carried himself like a king. One of the riders shouted a command toward the carriage.

A woman's voice answered, level and clear through the leather curtain, Norman French James couldn't follow, though the tone rang unmistakable, no panic, only control.

Riders swung down and closed around the carriage.

James stood at the edge of the clearing under the hard, measuring stares of the newcomers. From the tree line, Wulf burst forth. He howled, torn ear bright with fresh blood, eyes burning with betrayal. His blade feinted high and cut low. James barely caught the blow on the shield's rim. The jolt shivered up bone and sinew. Wulf hooked low, sweeping his legs out from under him. Mud grabbed at James's boots as he dipped and staggered. Wulf drove in, mouth twisted, teeth flashing.

Fingers loosened and let the sword drop. The seax's hilt met his palm as if it belonged there. A tight, vicious backhand carved along Wulf's forearm, not a killing stroke, but deep enough to make the hand forget its strength. Wulf's own blade skittered off mail; pain flared bright along James's ribs. He answered with his skull, smashing his forehead into Wulf's nose. Cartilage cracked, wet and final. Blood flooded Wulf's mouth and shirtfront.

"Go back," James spat, breath tasting of iron. "This is not our fight."

A thick, red gob hit the mud. Wulf laughed through it, the sound wet and ugly. "It is now."

They came together again. Wulf's sword skated along the shield and caught the leather wrap of the grip. Old stitches tore. Hold on, and the shield would be gone. James chose to surge instead, driving the heavy boss into Wulf's mouth. Teeth shattered. Wulf toppled and rolled through the mud. No need to chase him; the greater danger waited uphill. James turned back toward the carriage, toward the archers on the bank with their strings drawn tight.

"Down!" he shouted.

Arrows hissed overhead. One slipped through the leather slit; a sharp cry sounded from within. James stood in the open, raised his torn shield, and made himself the mark.

From the southern trees came a sound that could turn any fight: a clear Norman horn. Another answered it, nearer. On the far bank, Saxon archers let their bowstrings slacken, attention dragged toward the new threat. The hedgerow on the left bent, then spilled riders in mail, six, a dozen, swords up, faces set with the calm that only long drilling could teach. Men who'd been brave while arrows sang refused to wait for hooves. They broke for the thickets. Wulf rose, blood washing his chin, and ran with them, eyes throwing a promise of hate over his shoulder.

The riders let them go and swung around to secure the road and carriage.

A priest in a plain black robe vaulted the ditch with a grace that defied his years. Tall and spare, hair white at the temples, face kindly, eyes sharp as a newly honed blade, he took in the dead, the wounded, the stuck wheel, the pierced curtain. James came last in his survey.

"Lady," the priest called in French, voice carrying cleanly, "you are safe."

Leather shifted. The woman stepped down without waiting for a hand. Small, with a plain face whose steadiness gave it weight, she wiped her palms on her skirt like someone leaving a loom, not the inside of a death-trap. Soft, rapid French flowed from her lips.

Turning back to James, the priest said, "She thanks you, and asks your name."

"James."

"I am Bishop Geoffrey of Bagneux, and this is Duchess Matilda, Duke William's beloved. You have done a great service today. We were scouting the way forward when the carriage slipped ahead of its escort. If not for you..." He let the rest hang, the shape of William's wrath needing no words.

Matilda met James's gaze and spoke again. Geoffrey translated: "She says you stood where others fled. She is grateful for your honor."

A line tightened at the corner of James's mouth. "I chose not to be a thief. That is all."

"Sometimes a simple choice is everything," Geoffrey replied, eyes lingering on him.

From around the horses came another figure, helm shoved back, mail dark with mud, a face that might have been merry if not for the hard set to his jaw. As he took in the scene, the severity eased; his mouth was quick to a half-smile, his hands looked as though they had long practice with work. He weighed James in a single glance, then flicked his gaze to Geoffrey.

"James," Geoffrey said by way of introduction. "This is Arnaut St. Omer."

A nod from Arnaut, and then English, clear and well-shaped with a soft French accent: "You took quite a risk."

"I did what my conscience could bear," James answered. "That seems to have left me without companions and no place to go."

A low chuckle escaped Arnaut. He translated for Matilda in French, then repeated himself in English. "For now, come with us. Share our fire and a meal. We will talk. Then you can decide where you go next."

While riders worked the wheel free and righted the carriage, Geoffrey drew closer. Clean wool and wood smoke clung to him, a strange contrast to blood and muck. Long-fingered, unmarked hands held his robe clear of the mud.

"Assuming Arnaut allows you to leave, where will you go?" he asked. "Do you have a home to return to?" No trap lay in the words, only quiet interest.

Truth rose bitter on James's tongue. "Nothing that isn't ash. I was pressed to fight for Harold. I did. My kin are either long dead or went to ground long before the ravens settled. There is a barred door in Lunden that once opened for me. I doubt it opens now."

Geoffrey looked north, to where the road vanished behind hedges and a low rise. "The land is changing," he said. "Men who thought they were kings will find they are tenants. Men who thought they were nothing will be asked to carry more than they ever believed they could."

James stayed silent, listening to what moved beneath the words.

"There is work for a man who stands where you stood. A man that risks everything for what is right," Geoffrey went on, softer now. "Work that is not pillage and not flight. Work that needs a steady hand and a conscience still alive. Walk with us to our camp. Eat. Sleep. Speak with me again when the sun is up."

"Is this you as a man of God," James asked, "or you as a servant of your lord?"

A spark kindled behind the bishop's calm. "Both, if I do my office rightly."

Arnaut returned, wiping his hands on a scrap of cloth. "The wheel will hold," he reported. Once more that weighing look settled on James. "You have the look of a fighter who has learned when not to fight. That is rare in these times."

"Today seemed a good day to learn," James said.

Arnaut glanced toward Matilda, who had resumed her place not from fear, but because forward remained the only useful direction. "Her safety is our work," he said. "And work for more than soldiers alone. Come along, James. If you are a wolf, we will know it by morning. If you are not, perhaps you will find something worth following."

Dead Saxons went into the ditch, a rough crosspiece set over them. The driver found rest by the alder, the usual words spoken over him in tired voices. Archers who had tried to kill from safety left only black smears on bark where their hands had steadied. Ravens returned to their hop and pick, matter-of-fact as ever.

The procession formed again and moved. Ahead, Arnaut spoke low with the captain of the guard. Matilda's curtain lifted once, fell again. Mud clung to the road, to hooves, to boots, to hems.

He didn't know it yet, but the road he now followed had already bent beneath his feet.

Camp waited with fires already built, stew already bubbling, good soldiers preparing to live even on days they might die. Arnaut stripped his mail, set it on a peg, and drifted through his men with a word here, a hand there, quick to laughter now that the moment had passed, quicker still to sense who needed it. Geoffrey spoke to Matilda in tones that held both formality and kindness. James ate with his hands and warmth crept back into places that had been cold since the hill at Senlac.

Later, Geoffrey came to where he sat, cup in hand, and spoke without preamble. "If you walk with us, it will not be as a hired sword alone. There are things in this world that require a different kind of service. If you are willing to learn, there are men who will teach you."

James studied the bishop for a moment, then glanced to Arnaut in the lamplight, face open and bright once the grime was wiped away. Memory tugged, Wulf at the campfire two nights past, speaking of chalices as if they were meat; balance measured in theft and flame. Matilda stepping from her carriage without trembling. The arrowhead that had stopped a finger's width from his hand.

"I have nothing to return to," he said eventually. "What you are offering might be something."

"It is," Geoffrey answered. "And it is also everything."

Arnaut approached then, a torn loaf tucked under his arm, steam rising from its cracked crust. He offered it out. "Eat. Sleep. Speak in the morning. A man should never choose his path hungry."

James took the bread, hot, good, blessedly free of insects. A small, reluctant smile pulled at his mouth before he could stop it.

He had stood where arrows hunted him, bread in hand, blood on his shield.

2

Coffee, Cracks, and the Keeper (Ohio, Present)

I have lived in suburban Ohio for longer than anyone realizes. The anonymity is useful. People here are friendly, but they honor the Midwest's quiet code: you do not pry, you do not stare, and you assume every neighbor carries a past best left unopened. It suits me. Most days, that surface politeness is enough to keep old ghosts from stirring.

What I didn't know was that today, after years of peace and complacency, old ghosts would stir again.

The wrongness started as a pressure at the edge of my awareness when I awoke that morning. It was a faint tightening behind my ribs that was more than just a poor night's sleep. It felt like a storm gathering where no one else could see clouds. I decided to get out of the house and let my nerves settle in hopes that my mind would settle. Traffic moved, sprinklers ticked across manicured lawns, and the world pretended nothing was out of place. Habit told me to blend in. Instinct told me to watch the horizon.

As I showered and dressed, my mind turned to my roots, the ones that survived a millennium of battles. I find that when the stillness of this life presses too tightly, I return to Kew, a place not far from where I was born in the 11th century. I first placed temporary roots there when Tudor gossip still drifted through the halls of Richmond Palace. Courtiers schemed over religion and succession while pretending to admire tapestries. I listened, nodded at the correct moments, and made mental notes about which powerful men might one day cause trouble that required sharp correction.

I remained at Kew long after the palace crumbled into history, its red brick glimpsed like a fading memory through old oaks. I watched river fog swallow the outlines of towers that had once mattered very much and now mattered not at all. The land absorbed kings as easily as it absorbed rain.

I stood beside Princess Augusta as she sketched the beginnings of the gardens, her fingers stained with ink and soil, her mind a blend of calculation and wonder. She spoke of botany and progress. I spoke of something else. We shared claret in a small room while I murmured about the soul of a place, how a garden could anchor a people when the world shifted under their feet. She wanted science and beauty. I needed a sanctuary for something much older than either of us.

It was never truly about the plants for me. Kew had to stay green because something ancient lived there, a presence rooted in the first groves that once covered the area. The Green Man. His breath sounded in the rustle of leaves. His pulse moved in the slow drag of winter into spring. When I first sensed him, it felt like leaning against a tree and discovering that the bark could lean back.

I appointed myself his keeper long before I understood the full weight of that promise. He needed ground untouched by suffocating stone and smoke, a place where roots still remembered an older world. The gardens became his mask, a polished public face for a hidden reality that slept beneath the soil and woke only when the balance tilted too far.

Industrialists came later with plans and maps and confident little smiles. They spoke of progress and efficiency. They saw trees as numbers and paths as obstacles. One of them presented a proposal to reduce the grounds, to carve off a piece of Kew for housing. I met him at a dinner with port in his hand and ambition in his eyes. By the time dessert arrived, he no longer remembered why he had cared so much about that particular parcel. His attention drifted elsewhere. The land remained intact. The Green Man slept on.

America's call was faint at first, more resonance than voice. New nations bleed loudly. Old things hear that. The land across the ocean was wounded and restless, and it tugged at whatever sense of duty I still carried. Centerville became my base, or perhaps the city claimed me. Quiet. Unremarkable. A frontier when I first arrived at the behest of a friend. Now, a landscape of strip malls and subdivisions, where a man could live for decades without anyone asking why his face never changed.

I would stay just long enough before anyone took notice and then return to Kew, or travel for years until I came back after I was forgotten. I have been back in Centerville for a little over a decade now. I re-learned the local rhythms. Friday fish fries. Fall festivals that celebrated everything from sauerkraut to apple butter. I became one more regular at the grocery store and fell into a comfortable life. I blended in to a city where people were distracted by raising kids and work promotions.

Centerville and Kew became a metronome for me, back and forth every two decades or so for the last 300 years. The tide goes out. The tide comes in. My life stretched across an ocean and centuries, pulled by two guardians who trusted me to hold my corner of the Veil.

The morning looked calm enough as I pulled the BMW into a parking space outside Boston Stoker. A thin film of last night's rain slicked the asphalt. The SUV settled between a Suburban and a mud-flecked pickup, unnoticed in a town built around oversized vehicles and youth sports. In Centerville, the most serious battles most people knew involved crowded schedules and school politics.

Mine involved older, sharper things.

Boston Stoker stood apart from the nearby strip of chain restaurants and low brick offices. Its red brick and white columns once housed a local bank that had traded deposit slips for coffee. At night, its windows shone like a lantern set down in the suburbs.

I stepped inside and the air closed around me. The smell of roasted beans mixed with the sugary bite of flavored syrups. Wood floors creaked beneath my boots in a pattern I knew by heart. Students hunched over laptops, shoulders rounded, faces pale in the shallow blue of their screens. Retirees clustered together complaining about some new business that was opening and ruining the city aesthetic. The counter vibrated with the grind of beans and the sharp hiss of steam. Cups clicked. Voices rose and fell. The place thrummed with small, human rituals.

This was not a polished chain store experience. The walls held local art no one planned to buy. The chalkboard menu still had the faint ghost of last week's special beneath the new one. Parents collapsed into worn leather chairs, balancing strollers and lukewarm drinks with the hollow-eyed determination of people who had not slept a full night in years. The shop felt like part café, part chapel.

Its routine steadied me.

Places like this have been my refuge for centuries. I have leaned against sticky tavern tables lit by guttering candles, the air heavy with smoke and sweat. I have watched men in feathered turbans argue over tiny cups of thick coffee in Ottoman cities where every alley promised a deal or a knife. I have listened to philosophers in Parisian salons proclaim that ideas could reshape reality while they gestured with ink-stained fingers and spilled wine. The walls change. The furniture changes. The need for warmth and company does not.

In the end, it comes down to this: a warm drink, a familiar routine, and proof that other lives are still moving alongside your own.

Their conflicts have not changed either. Men once reached for knives over dice and spilled ale. Now, wars begin over empty chairs and power outlets. Someone spreads their belongings across three seats, holding them for friends who are perpetually ten minutes away. And if it's not the chairs, it's the sacred tables near the power outlets, the modern equivalent of a seat by the hearth, hoarded so our electronic familiars can feed before we do.

For someone like me, ordinary is rare. Fragile. Precious. And always temporary.

The door chimed behind me.

"Morning, James."

Avery's voice rose above the background noise. Her blond ponytail swung as she worked the register, hands moving through the practiced motions of buttons and bills. Home from Miami University, she still carried an open brightness the world usually beats out of you by the time you reach twenty-five.

Next to her, slouched at the espresso machine like a resentful statue, was Todd. He had dark hair, a perpetual scowl, and the general aura of someone for whom community college was less a stepping stone and more a life sentence. Sarcasm was his native tongue, wielded with the practiced ease of a man who found the world perpetually disappointing.

"Highlander Grogg?" he asked without looking up.

"As always," I said, sliding the folded Dayton Daily News onto the counter. "If I ever order anything different, assume I have been possessed and act accordingly."

Todd snorted. "Gladly."

"In that case," I said, "you have my permission to celebrate."

Avery shook her head. "He is cranky because he had to open."

"It is cruel punishment," Todd insisted, finally glancing up with a theatrical grimace.

"You were twenty minutes late," she said, smile tightening around the edges.

"Still cruel."

I shook my head, the corners of my mouth twitching. "I'll take a bagel too, but only if Avery toasts it. Todd burns them every time. I think he believes 'toasted' is synonymous with 'cremated'." I added a wink for good measure.

Todd scowled. Avery laughed, a sound like bells. And the familiar routine played out, a comfortable script we all knew by heart. Ritual. Comfort. A rhythm I had come to depend on more than I cared to admit.

Behind the banter though, that pressure in my chest kept rising. Something waited, patient and insistent, just beyond the edge of ordinary and something I couldn't pinpoint.

The truth is, I've grown soft. I came from a world of mud floors and a hunger that gnawed at your ribs like a living thing. I've spent nights wondering if I'd wake with a roof over my head or a blade at my throat. When you've lived like that, luxury isn't just comfort, it's armor. Every sip of good wine, every stitch of a tailored suit, every roar of a well-tuned engine is a silent declaration: I will never be that cold, that hungry, that powerless again. Maybe that makes me materialistic. A sinner of the flesh.

The reality is that money stopped being a concern centuries ago. Time teaches a man how to make it, hide it, and hold it steady while empires rise and fall. Swiss banks served me well for a while. Caribbean accounts followed. Property trusts with bland names came next, portfolios that could pass unnoticed in any audit. When people ask, I tell them I am a fund manager. It is not untrue. The fund simply has one very old beneficiary.

With wealth comes a different kind of account and I try and balance the scales between greed and charity. I give quietly. Anonymously. The food pantry at Incarnation receives more from me than anyone suspects. The shelves remain full even during lean years. After the Great War, I created a fund for widows and children who had nothing left but a folded flag and a picture on a mantle. Over time, you learn that guilt left to rot turns poisonous. Guilt channeled into action becomes something softer.

Eternity made me generous and greedy in equal measure. I crave texture. The feel of soft leather broken in by years, not months. The layered taste of a good Bordeaux. The precise weight of a well-made watch that outlasts the man who bought it. When you have watched every face you love age and vanish, small physical comforts become anchors. Then you write another check to the pantry and hope the math works out in some ledger you will never see.

Coffee entered my story in Yemen.

The Church sent Arnaut and me there, not to venerate relics but to break the Ottoman grip on trade routes. Our orders were clear. Weaken supply lines. Poison alliances. Turn powerful men by slipping questions into the right ears and coins into the right hands. This was work the Watch excelled at, the kind of history that never reaches official records.

We arrived in Aden half-starved and dust-choked, dressed as northern merchants with sacks of goods and letters of introduction. Coins handled most conversations. Our Arabic was passing and served our purpose. Markets teemed with color and noise. Spices. Salt. Sailors calling across crowded docks.

Arnaut thrived in that chaos. He laughed loudly, bargained hard, and rolled his r's with enough force to turn heads. My own speech was sharper, stripped down by old English habits and foreign tongues learned the hard way. The locals found the pairing amusing. Two foreign traders, one broad-shouldered and booming, the other lean and quiet. In a city where a smile could hide a knife, being entertaining was safer than being important.

One evening, we followed a rumor to a Sufi lodge near the edge of the quarter. The building looked plain from the street. Inside, lanterns cast shifting light on whitewashed walls. A slow, steady chanting vibrated through the floorboards. The sound felt less like song and more like the ground itself remembering a prayer.

The monks welcomed us without question. Their eyes held a steadiness that did not come from sleep. A young man with calloused hands handed me a cup of qahwa. The liquid inside was black and thick, bitter enough to scrape the tongue. It had been brewed in a dented copper pot over coals that glowed red-hot.

I took a cautious sip. Heat punched the back of my throat. My stomach clenched. For a heartbeat I nearly spat it back. Beside me, Arnaut choked and wiped his mouth with his sleeve.

"God preserve us," he said. "The Devil brewed this."

The young monk smiled. "Not the Devil. This is for those who want to see God clearly."

They drank it like medicine. They returned to their chanting with renewed focus. After his second cup, Arnaut nudged me, his gaze sharper than when we had arrived.

"If nothing else," he muttered, "this will keep us awake."

He was right. We talked with the monks until dawn. Faith. Empire. The strange, stubborn ways of men who would rather bleed than admit they are wrong. The drink held a harsh grip at first, but when the bitterness settled, it left a clarity that felt almost like a weapon.

We completed our task in Aden. Trade lines shifted. Trusted alliances frayed at their edges. Letters were intercepted, altered, and sent on. On paper, the Watch could mark another success. The Church praised the outcome. For me, the memory that stayed was not the victory. It was the ritual. The weight of the clay cup in my hands. The shared silence. The sharpness of thought that followed the burn.

Now, steam rose from my Highlander Grogg. The scent held nothing of Yemen, but the sense of alertness pressed at the back of my mind all the same. But the wrongness that had started as a quiet pressure now hummed with a stronger note. It felt like a signal.

I knew that my next stop was the park and to check on the Wendigo.

Its stewards once wove its presence into stories and rites. The Miami and the Shawnee spoke of a devouring spirit in the woods, a thing of hunger and winter. Outsiders heard warning. Insiders heard duty. The tales kept the careless away while the caretakers tended something powerful and timeless. Treaties and soldiers tore those people from their land. The bond between spirit and story broke like a severed nerve. The Wendigo was left alone beneath unfamiliar feet, stripped of context and care.

By the time I found it, the creature had turned inward on its own isolation. The hunger was not for flesh. It was for purpose. I felt that emptiness and knew it was a calling, and I knew that I would heed it.

It was not the only guardian on my ledger.

Across the ocean, the Green Man leaned against his trees in Kew. I have felt his moods ripple through branches when storms rolled over the Thames. I have listened to him settle back into stillness when seasons turned as they should. I pushed royal gardeners toward choices that served him without their knowledge. They believed they chose plants for science and fashion. I knew they were building a sanctuary for an ancient mind.

The Wendigo and the Green Man. Winter's hunger and summer's strength. Two guardians holding different corners of the same fabric. They are anchor points in a hidden structure that holds the Veil taut. Their magic binds them to the land, and that binding holds the Veil taut, like an anchor keeps a ship from drifting away. When the guardians weaken, the tension slackens. When the tension slackens, other things test the edges.

Most people believe the world is safe because it looks normal. They do not know that normal is a thin skin stretched over something with teeth and patience.

Those two are not alone. A hidden map of guardians threads through the world. In Japan, the kodama clings to cedar groves. In the Congo's dense green, the biloko lingers near old paths. In Iceland, the huldufólk watch from lava fields and hillocks. Others have passed from history due to neglect, and every loss threatens normalcy.

The ones that have survived do so with the help of keepers like myself. Some guardians are celebrated in festivals. Others survive only in families and orders who keep old stories alive across generations. Where memory holds, guardians endure. Where memory breaks, they fade.

The problem is that over centuries, human memory fades faster than bone.

"James. Bagel is ready."

Avery's call cut through the fog of thought. Her laughter followed, bright and untroubled. I forced my attention back to the present and walked to the counter. She handed me the plate with the casual grace of someone who assumes tomorrow will look very much like today.

The monks in Yemen poured their coffee with reverence and believed it brought them closer to God. The baristas here decorated lattes with hearts and leaves for social media posts. Different theology. Same ritual. Same need.

Back at my table, I left the newspaper mostly untouched and watched the room. Students hunched over screens, fingers moving in quick bursts. They reminded me of scribes I had once seen copying texts in cold scriptoria, hands cramped around quills, breath misting in the air. A mother balanced a stroller, a phone, and a cup, her expression a mix of bone-deep love and bone-deep exhaustion. I had seen that face in burned-out villages and refugee lines. A man in paint-stained jeans scrolled through his messages with the same distant focus I had once seen in masons studying a cathedral wall, searching for the next stone's proper place.

I picked up the paper and on the front page, familiar noise clamored for attention. Elections. Hollywood scandals. Local zoning fights dressed up as grand moral struggles. I skimmed it and then turned to the smaller columns, the places where editors shove the strange things that do not fit.

There, the patterns revealed themselves. A grainy photograph of a tall, indistinct figure in an Oregon forest. Livestock torn apart in a Japanese village with no tracks human or animal could explain. A tourist's account of floating lights in a German wood and the overwhelming desire to follow them off the path.

Most readers would roll their eyes and move on. I saw frayed threads in the fabric that held the Veil together.

Germany pulled up an older memory. A mission for the Church when the Black Forest earned its name and before the Brothers Grimm based their stories on what lurked in those woods. Villagers had reported strange lights at night, and friends and family were said to have vanished when they appeared. The order from Rome came through our bishop in three clipped words.

Investigate. Contain. Leave no trace.

The Apostles were not apostles in any biblical sense. They were the Custodes Apostolici, a circle of cardinals who believed they alone understood God's will. We called them Apostoli. Their decisions carried more weight than most kings would ever wield. When they spoke, the Watch moved.

On paper, we were the Vigilum Sacrum, the Sacred Watch. In practice, we were Gladii Dei, the Swords of God pointed at threats no one wanted to admit existed. We went where armies could not march, where bishops preferred plausible deniability. Our handlers, the Legati Sacri, the Sacred Envoys watched us from within the Church hierarchy. We called them the Oculi. The Eyes. They read our reports, pulled our strings, and pretended to wash their hands when things went badly.

The machine itself worked with brutal simplicity. The Apostles decided what needed to vanish. The Eyes passed that decision along. The Watch removed the problem. Then the Church encouraged the world to forget.

In those German woods, I wanted understanding more than swift action. Arnaut wanted the opposite. He always did. He was a blade given human shape. I was a tool with more than one edge.

The wisps came first. Pale blue lights drifting between the trunks, too steady to be fireflies, too fluid to be torches. Villagers began to walk. They left beds and hearths and crying children. They moved with the blank certainty of sleepwalkers, drawn out under branches that blocked the stars.

The forest swallowed them.

We watched from the tree line, breath clouding in the cold air. Arnaut's hand tightened around his sword hilt until the leather creaked. Magic gathered around him, hot and rough, a pressure that wanted to break loose. I felt it pressing against my own senses.

"Now," he said. "We end it."

"Wait," I answered, eyes on the lights. They did not drift randomly. They circled and pulsed, guiding the villagers toward a deeper darkness where the air thickened and sound dulled. Pattern reveals intent. Intent reveals nature.

We moved when we had seen enough to know where to cut. Branches slapped my face. Roots snagged my boots. I reached some of the villagers and dragged them back by force. Their eyes cleared slowly, fear returning as if poured into them. Others walked too far ahead. I called their names until our voices broke. They did not even turn their heads.

Arnaut charged in, magic flaring and a kind of war cry bellowing from him. The lights in the woods brightened at his approach and a flare of bright blue light shot from each of the tiny dots. Arnaut stumbled, but his wards and magic shielded him. The villagers that had already ventured too far into the canopy simply collapsed in a heap.

Fog then rolled between the trees, swallowing their forms. No screams. No struggle. One moment there were shapes ahead; the next moment there was nothing but grey.

Later, Arnaut spoke in a low voice, flat and hard. "If we had acted sooner, fewer would be lost."

I leaned against a tree and listened to my heart pound. "We lost more by your charge in," I said. "We had no idea what they were, or how to defeat them."

We both argued with deaf ears to the other's concern. It was the usual battle between the two of us, caution versus action.

The Watch did not hold funerals. We strangled rumors, redirected stories, convinced ourselves that carrying out God's will justified every silence. The

Apostles praised us for eliminating the threat and sent us on yet another mission. There was no thought to the plight of the villagers. No comfort provided to those that lost parents and children. We simply moved on to the next errand given us.

For me, trembling with both anger and the sense of loss in those woods marked something else. It was the first time I doubted the certainty of Rome's version of God's will. It was the moment I knew that the machine I served did not always care about the same balance I did.

The newspaper crackled as I folded it, the sound sharp in the warm murmur of the café. The threads in the news. The pressure in my chest. The old memories pressing at the edges of thought. Together they pointed to a truth I could not ignore.

Something was tearing at the Veil.

3

Fossils, Friends, and the Guardians (Ohio, Present)

The car ticked as if it resented me for killing the air conditioning and abandoning it to bake on the blacktop outside Normandy Elementary. Heat rolled off the asphalt in shimmers. I stepped out into the thick Ohio air with my to-go cup of Highlander Grogg in hand, the cardboard sleeve soft and warm against my palm. The coffee inside was black and bitter, the faint ghost of butterscotch and whisky just enough to take the edge off. After centuries of chaos, you learn to hoard these small rituals. Empires fall, kings lose their heads, continents trade flags, but there has always been something to drink in the morning. I will take coffee over mead every time. The hangover is less dramatic, and it does not attract flies.

I cut across the path next to an empty playground. School would be back in session soon enough. For now, it was quiet as the swings moved in a lazy arc from the breeze, chains creaking to a steady rhythm. A flat, forgotten kickball was half covered in the weeds, forgotten in the excitement of summer vacation.

Near the trail-head gate, I almost walked straight into a man in a tan uniform shirt with dark green epaulets. Cargo trousers streaked with dirt and pine needles. Wide-brimmed campaign hat throwing his face into shadow.

"Morning, James."

22

Ray Ennis. One of the park rangers, and one of the good ones. Mid-fifties, lean and tough as hickory. Sun had turned his skin to worn leather and etched fine lines around his eyes. Those eyes usually smiled, even when the rest of him sagged with fatigue. Normandy's kids practically worshiped him. He had that rare, patient gift, the kind that let him listen to a seven-year-old's story about a tadpole with the same intensity most men reserve for stock tips or confessions.

"Morning, Ray." I stepped aside and let the gate swing, metal rattling under my hand. "Thought you were out terrorizing second graders with poison ivy lectures."

"Soon enough. Kids will be back soon enough." His grin flashed, quick and genuine. "Besides, someone has to keep an eye on you old guys during the summer." He jerked his chin toward the parking lot. "That your new car? Looks like something I saw at a sci-fi convention."

"Just a car," I said. "You ready for the little savages to swarm back in the fall?"

His smile held for a heartbeat, then thinned. He glanced toward the tree line, where the trail disappeared into green, and the ease drained from his face.

"Be nice to hear the laughter again," he said quietly. "Gives the place its soul back."

He shifted his weight, then added, "You heading down to the creek?"

"As always."

This time his reaction was not a smile. Something in his shoulders tightened. He looked back at the woods, then at me, as if weighing whether to keep talking.

"Park's been strange lately," he said. His voice dropped a notch. "At night, mostly. Folks keep reporting howls from the woods. They think it is coyotes at first, but then the sound changes. Gets wrong. We do not have a resident pack here. Not really."

I felt a pit settle into my stomach.

"What do you think it could be?" I asked, keeping my tone neutral, casual. Just a neighbor with a coffee and time to kill.

He hesitated as if the trees might be listening. "I am finding things. Birds, rabbits, a couple of squirrels. Dead, but not torn up like a hawk or fox got them. No scatter, no mess. It is too neat. Like something took exactly what it wanted, and left the rest where I would find it."

"No dogs?" I asked. "Strays, feral, anything like that?"

"Nothing that fits." He shook his head. "No scat. No tracks that match the damage. I set a couple of trail cams near the old Reynolds place." A humorless huff of laughter escaped him. "Got wind, branches, a few deer, and one raccoon determined to die on camera. That's it. But it feels wrong. Feels like the woods are holding their breath."

His words slid neatly into the unease I had carried since I woke up, another weight added to the pile.

"Probably just coyotes pushing along the creek corridor," I offered. "They are better at slipping around people than we give them credit for."

"Maybe." The word landed heavy. He did not believe it. Not fully. He held my gaze a second longer. "You see anything strange, you call me. I mean it."

"If I do, you will be the first to know."

We traded a few more harmless lines about the heat and the school year, but the easy rhythm was gone. Ray lingered like a man who wanted to say more and could not find the right words, then shifted his pack and moved on along the fence line. I watched his back as he walked away, noted the tightness across his shoulders.

I have watched enough men carry burdens they could not name. I knew the look.

Grant Life Park stretched ahead, two hundred acres of stubborn green forced between subdivisions and arterial roads. Forest, meadow, wetland, all stitched together in a rough patchwork. The trees here fought a quiet war against vinyl siding and cul-de-sacs. From the right vantage point, you could stand in the woods and still see decks peeking through branches, hear the faint hiss of traffic. Civilization never quite shut up.

Holes Creek cut through the middle, shallow and clear, its limestone bed studded with fossils. For most locals, it was a scenic waterway, a place for field trips and summer walks. To me, it was a pilgrimage site. The creek bore the name of a man I had once called friend.

Dr. John Hole. Surgeon. Frontier settler. Reluctant mystic.

I met him in the American Revolution, in the middle of noise and blood and bad decisions. He was a calm in that storm, a man who boiled water and sharpened knives while everyone else prayed and hoped. I watched him dig a musket ball out of a soldier's thigh by firelight, hands rock-steady while the man bit down on leather and whimpered through clenched teeth. Other men begged God to intervene. John boiled his instruments and got to work.

We became friends the way soldiers do, in the wide, hollow silences between battles. It is easy to bond over shared fear. Easier still over the grim acceptance that you might not see another sunrise. Young men huddled at the fire talked about sweethearts and imagined futures. Some just slumped and slept where they fell. John and I talked about infection, herbs, and the way power moved through empires and left broken bodies behind.

One night, he studied me over the rim of a tin cup. "How do you know so much about the plants we pass?" he asked. "The other surgeons can barely tell poison oak from oak wood for the fire. You can name roots from Carolina, herbs from coastal marshes you have no business knowing."

"I have traveled," I told him. That much was true. I did not add that some of those travels had been aboard creaking Spanish galleons before his grandparents were born.

He did not press. That restraint told me more about him than any clever question.

Another night, with cheap whiskey burning our throats and cannon fire a distant echo, he tried again. "You talk about war like it is a habit the world cannot break," he said. "The lads think this one will change everything forever. You sound like a man who has already seen the next one."

I stared into the embers for a long time. "Because it will change things. For a while. Then another war will come, and another. Each one will be declared the most important in history, right up until the next one. I have seen the way monarchs, emperors, and clerics choke the life out of their own people for a convenient idea of the greater good."

He watched me with that surgeon's gaze of his, steady and unblinking.

"You sound," he said eventually, "like a man who has lived them all."

I shrugged noncommittally and gave no response. I did not need to. Some people are quick enough to add their own numbers.

What bound us was not just curiosity but the fact that he could look straight at the strange and not flinch. He trusted his senses and his reason, but he was honest enough to admit when both failed. Once, in the hush after a battle, he confessed he had seen wounds knit closed too quickly to be natural. Bodies without a mark, dead as if someone had plucked the life out of them with two fingers. He did not "believe in superstition," he told me. He just no longer felt comfortable laughing at it.

When the war burned down and the country staggered toward whatever came next, most men went home. I did not quite know how, and so I wandered for a bit. Distance and years stretched between us, but letters kept us tethered. His spoke of frontier medicine, of births and deaths far from cities, of a growing family. Mine spoke of travel and curiosities, trimmed carefully of anything that would drag him into shadows I wasn't sure he would believe. He never pushed. He simply left space.

True friends like that are rare. People who can look at you, glimpse the cracks and the impossible, and stay.

Around 1800, one of his letters found me. The paper was brittle at the edges, the ink faded, but the urgency rang clear enough.

James,

I have settled near a small settlement called Centerville in the western territory. My cabin sits near a limestone creek that cuts through the woods, a place the settlers remark upon for its strange fossils. In my walks there, I have discovered something unusual. It is not an illness, nor a natural wonder, but something of the sort you have long pursued, the hidden and the occult. I would not trouble you were I not convinced this is the sort of thing you seek. I cannot put it to paper without sounding mad, but I urge you to come. Follow the roads south of Dayton's new settlement and you will find me near the creek. I believe it holds secrets worth your attention, secrets beyond the reach of medicine or reason.

- Dr. John Hole

Back in the present, I followed the trail down from the school. The canopy closed overhead, oak and hickory stitching their branches together. Cicadas screamed from the trees, an unbroken chorus that felt more like pressure than sound. Sunlight broke into narrow beams that painted stripes of gold and shadow across the path. The air smelled of damp earth, leaf mold, and honeysuckle. To a casual hiker, it would feel peaceful.

To me, the forest hummed like a wire under current. The Veil was close here. You could taste it if you had the right palate.

The ruins of the old Reynolds place appeared ahead, where the trail curved. Two soot-stained chimneys still stood, clothed in ivy, the house that once joined them long gone. The Reynolds family had arrived hopeful, built a brick home and planted fruit trees. Winters turned cruel. Sickness came and did not leave. More children died than survived. The neighbors whispered about voices from the woods and animals watching from the shadows with a too-human stillness.

Then came the fire.

The tidy little placard by the trail now tells a sanitized story about pioneer families and generous land donations. It reads like philanthropy. The truth was closer to surrender. The land refused them. They had the sense, at the end, to listen.

The day after I first arrived in Centerville, John led me through bramble and brush to what was then called Silver Creek. The water ran clear and cold over limestone, its bed a crowded museum of ancient seabed. Even before we stepped into the open, I felt something. A pressure against my chest. A low hum in my teeth. The air thickened.

"Do you feel it?" he whispered.

"Yes." It startled me that he could. Most men feel only a vague unease and soon enough write it off.

We stepped out into a bend in the creek, a small clearing where the trees pulled back enough to let in a slash of sky.

That was where it appeared.

The creature emerged from the tree line as if it had always been there, waiting. Its limbs were long and jointed, more branch than bone. Antler-like spurs crowned its head. Its body blurred at the edges, haloed in a faint green glow. Its eyes were pale and fluid, no white, no clear pupil, just a steady, unsettling luminosity pinned on me.

Fear hit with the force of an avalanche. Not the sharp fear of an ambush or a drawn blade. Something older. Colder. It ran straight past thought into the oldest part of the brain that remembers what it is like to be prey.

My hand snapped to the sword at my hip. Even then, the weapon was already old-fashioned enough to draw looks. I had carried blades most of my life. Reflex spoke before reason.

Reason caught up.

I forced my fingers to loosen. The leather of the grip creaked in protest. Slowly, deliberately, I let the hilt fall away from my palm and lowered my hand. Then I did the only thing that felt right. I bowed my head.

Not as a supplicant. As one sovereign nods to another, when both remember what it costs to hold a line.

The crushing fear eased, thinning to something sharp and alert. The branches around us creaked. No wind moved them. The creature shifted its weight, joints crackling with a sound like dry bones rolling in a sack. For one heartbeat, its gaze deepened, and I saw a flash of something behind those pale eyes. Long winters. Hollowed bellies. Ice that never thawed. Hunger with no end.

We stood locked there, the three of us. Me. The creature. John, breathing shallowly at my side. Time stretched.

Then the creature turned. It stepped back into the shadows. Its form unraveled in the dappled light and was gone.

"John," I asked, my voice rough, "do you know what that is?"

He let out a long breath, the kind a man only releases once he is sure he has survived the moment. "Something older than us," he said. "I have seen it twice. Never this close. Always here. Always watching. I did not know if you would believe me."

I believed him because denying it would have required denying my own senses. I knew what it was as soon as my fear died and we formed a connection. I had encountered guardians of the Veil before, but never one left so completely on its own.

John explained that local legends told of a Wendigo that lived in the woods, but that it was only a superstition, left over from the times that the Native Americans held this land. I have never known if it was a name that the creature gave itself, but it worked for me.

That evening we sat on the planks of his porch. The heat of the day settled low and heavy. Fireflies floated above the yard. Crickets sawed and frogs croaked in a chorus that felt older than the flag that flew over us. John leaned back, pipe in hand, unlit.

"I have seen it twice before," he said at last. "Always near that bend. Always at dusk."

"It is bound to that place," I told him. "To the land, the water, the stories that once were told here. What you saw is one knot in a much larger net. The Veil is not a wall. It is a weave. Creatures like that keep the mesh tight. When they weaken, holes form. And things on the other side notice."

He sat with that awhile. Smoke from a neighbor's chimney drifted thinly through the air, carrying the clean scent of burning wood.

"So that is what you have been chasing," he said. "Not relics or miracles. Knots in the net."

"Among other things," I said. "This one has been left without a keeper. That makes it vulnerable. When one knot fails, the strain falls on the others. That is manageable, for a while. Too many fail, and the whole weave begins to sag."

"And what waits on the other side?" His eyes did not waver when he asked.

"Nightmares people pretend are only stories," I said. "Things the world is kinder to forget. I have seen demons with eyes like burning coal that walked out of breaches in old deserts. Vampires that emptied villages in forests where the sun never quite cut through. Spirits that wore the faces of the dead to drag the living after them."

Fireflies rose and fell over the grass like sparks from an unseen fire. He watched them in silence, then nodded once.

"You will stay?" he asked.

I let the quiet stretch. The choice pressed in, heavy as the humidity.

"I stayed once before," I said finally. "In London. For the Green Man.

Perhaps this place deserves the same effort. I have been wandering long enough. Perhaps it's time to set down roots again."

His mouth ticked at the corner. Not a smile. Something steadier. Approval, maybe. Or relief.

That night I told him more. About guardians scattered across the world.

He asked when I first understood any of this. I gave him the real answer.

"At the center of it all, Jerusalem," I said. "From a group of rabbis in the 1300s, men who had seen enough to know some laws applied on both sides of the Veil. It was there that I was first touched by the magic of the Veil. But the first time I fully understood that it was a weave that stretched across geography was in France, a century later, in the Dordogne."

I had drifted south after another war, following quiet roads and decent wine. In a market town, a monk I had met in my travels. He spoke like someone afraid to say the wrong word, asked me to come to a place the brothers had tended for generations.

They led me to a grotto where the forest leaned in so tightly the sun had to force its way down in narrow beams. A small chapel clung to the rock, a carved stag over the door. A spring trickled out of the stone, cold even in the hottest season.

At dusk the abbot took me into the trees. No chanting, no theatrics. Just waiting.

The air stilled. Birds fell silent in the branches. Then it came to the edge of the grove.

It had the shape of a stag in the way a masterful statue has the shape of a man. Accurate, but not confined by it. Light and shadow hung from its antlers like tattered banners. The air around it bent in a way that made the hair on my arms lift.

The monks dropped to their knees. They thought they saw an avatar of God. Heads bowed. Hands clasped.

I stood frozen. Not in worship. In shock.

When I found my voice, I asked the abbot about it, and about their care.

"This is a protector of God's will on earth," he said. His deep voice reverberated in the small space between the trunks. "It holds back the abyss.

Our order has tended this place as long as our records go back. If we falter, Hell walks."

Even then, the old Church loved drama. But buried under the rhetoric was a truth. They had been keeping watch over a guardian. Their faith kept them at their post. The guardian was one of many that held something far worse at bay.

He told me about woodcutters with fresh axes and a lord's contract who had tried to push into the grove. The sky had darkened in minutes. Wind rose from nothing and tore the tools out of their hands. Hardened men fled as if wolves were at their heels. The monks prayed for those men even as the storm raged.

Only later did I learn that attempted encroachment had coincided with a breach elsewhere. Threads tugged, knots strained, consequences rippled. That was the day I understood that civilization rests on more than laws and scriptures. It rests on things like that stag. On the Green Man. On the Wendigo. Guardians who do not care about titles, only balance.

On the porch in Ohio, I told John all of this. He did not flinch. He did not laugh. He simply listened, mind working behind his eyes.

Eventually I told him what the Wendigo had shown me.

Not in words. In flashes. In cold. In hunger. It let me feel snatches of memory. Winter rituals under bare branches. Smoke from fires that burned in dugout homes. Songs in languages this land has almost forgotten. The Miami. The Shawnee. Scattered nations who once tended the creature at the creek not with chains, but with respect and caution. Their stories cast it as something terrible and ravenous. Outsiders heard a threat. Insiders heard a warning and a contract.

Then came soldiers, then treaties, then ink on paper that took the land and called it progress. The tribes were pushed west. The line of stewardship snapped. The Wendigo was left alone. It turned inward, feeding on its own loneliness, its own fear. Eventually, its distress grew so sharp it risked showing itself to a man like John. That was not an accident. That was a cry for help.

In London, I had watched something similar happen to the Green Man.

Forests gave way to estates, then estates to streets. People stopped leaving offerings at the old oaks. They forgot the stories and kept only the metaphors. He would have faded entirely without the thin strip of green we managed to preserve and expand. A narrow victory, but enough.

John absorbed all of this without argument. That quiet belief made him one of the handful of people I have ever trusted completely.

The next day I went alone back to the bend in the creek, to both pay my respects, and to offer what comfort I could. The air thickened, as if someone had quietly shut a door on the forest and trapped all the heat and hum inside. The Wendigo showed itself to me again. It knew I was staying and I sensed a deep relief and thanks wash over me.

Now, centuries later, I stood by the same creek with that trust lodged behind my ribs like a piece of shrapnel that never quite worked its way out.

The trees ahead shifted as they had the previous day. Pale eyes glinted from deep shade, luminous and pupil-less. For a heartbeat, I felt a brush against my mind, light as a hand ruffling leaves. A flicker of curiosity. A hint of play.

Then everything changed.

The feeling snapped off, replaced by a surge of cold terror that was not my own. It hit like a spike of ice hammered into my spine. My heart stuttered, then slammed into a gallop. My knees threatened to buckle. The Wendigo shoved its fear into me, bypassing language. No nuance. No courtesy.

Warning.

The message was that simple and that absolute.

When something that has watched ice ages roll past feels fear, you stop and listen. I have ignored such warnings before. Villages burned because of it. Families died because I thought I knew better.

My mind jumped to the morning paper. To the odd little corner the editors use when they do not know where else to put a story. Grainy Bigfoot photo in Oregon. Livestock in Japan torn apart in ways no predator claimed. A tourist in Germany describing floating lights and a strange urge to follow them into the woods.

Most readers saw entertainment. I saw threads starting to fray.

The Wendigo retreated, its form dissolving into shadow, leaving nothing but the aftertaste of cold in my chest.

Downstream, the rest of the world carried on in its blessed ignorance. A family waded at a shallow bend. A father guided a small boy from rock to rock. A girl in bright shorts chipped away at the limestone with a plastic shovel, shrieking when she uncovered the spiral imprint of a fossil. Their laughter rang against the trees, bright and thin, like glass that does not yet know it will break.

They did not feel the pressure in the air. They did not taste the metal edge on the breeze.

I did.

The Wendigo had trusted me since the day John brought me to this creek. It had tolerated my presence, learned my scent, accepted my offerings. It had never pushed fear into me like that.

Until now.

I stood alone by the water with the taste of coffee and dread turning to ash on my tongue and wished, with a sharp, unexpected ache, that I could sit on that porch again with John. He would ask the right questions and, more importantly, he would listen to the answers.

Friends like that are a rarer currency than gold. I have learned to value them above wealth, above reputation, above the illusion of safety.

When guardians send warnings, the Veil is under strain.

And when the Veil strains, what pushes against it does not stay patient for long.

4

Eternity, Oaths, and the Nail (Rome, 1076)

Ten years had passed since Hastings, yet the memory still rode with me like grit trapped under a heel, never crippling, never gone. England carried its new masters now, patched over by decrees and fresh banners, but the men who had survived that field bore wounds no priest could absolve. I'd buried too many friends and watched a kingdom I barely believed in get folded into the margins of a conqueror's ledger. And now I, who had stood with the defeated, walked toward the heart of the Church that had blessed William's claim.

The road to Rome rose and fell under the heat. Summer baked the ruts until they bit into our soles, the stones sharp enough to punish any man who forgot his footing. Dust drifted from every passing cart. Pilgrims clutched relics in linen wrappings, merchants coaxed reluctant oxen forward, and monks whispered psalms as if silence itself might tempt something hungry.

I walked between two men who had shaped the last decade of my life. Geoffrey of Bagneux kept a steady pace ahead of us, robes swaying, his silver cross catching the sun whenever he shifted. Authority clung to him like a second garment. Behind me, Arnaut St. Omer whistled a tune that wandered every few bars, a soldier's melody without a home.

Somewhere past the haze over the Tiber valley lay Rome.

"Welcome to the heart of Christendom," Geoffrey said to us as the walls of the city appeared ahead of us.

"It's no heart, it's a stomach," Arnaut said. "It eats whatever wanders inside. Kings, bishops, sometimes men like us."

Geoffrey didn't turn. "Try speaking less when we arrive. You may keep your tongue that way."

Arnaut grinned. "You hear that, James? He's already preparing his sermon."

Despite the heat, I felt a smile tug at the corner of my mouth. Ten years with Geoffrey had taught me that humor was armor, and armor mattered. None of us wanted to name the truth: Rome marked the end of my apprenticeship. My oaths waited there. My anointing. Whatever the Church meant for me afterward.

We reached a priory outside Viterbo as the sun dropped. The walls smelled of herbs and smoke. A thin prior with ink staining his fingertips bowed low.

"Bishop Geoffrey, your rooms are ready. The Holy Father expects you at the Lateran by week's end."

"God willing," Geoffrey replied. "Provided my companions don't kill each other first."

The prior studied Arnaut and me for a beat too long. Arnaut swept into a bow.

"I'll try to die quietly, Father. Out of your earshot."

Inside, the brothers served olives, bread, and a stew thick enough to anchor a spoon. Geoffrey ate little. His mind drifted elsewhere as he and the prior murmured about Rome, Gregory VII's reforms, the Emperor's resistance, bishops who bought their miters and defended them with coin.

"The Church tears at itself," Geoffrey said. "Our Holy Father means to strip corruption from the root, simony, bribery, false crowns. Enemies rise on all sides."

The prior nodded. "Enemies in Rome. And elsewhere."

Geoffrey didn't glance at me, but the words settled like a weight. The world above fought for titles. The world beneath fought for something deeper. The Watch lived in the narrow space between.

That night, in the small cell they'd given me, I let the decade replay itself, less memory than scar.

Training under Geoffrey and the brothers at Cluny had worn down the raw soldier and carved cleaner lines in the space left behind. Latin and other new languages replaced the old battlefield curses. Brother Pascal taught me the shape of power, not the noise of it. His hands could steady a dying bird, and his voice had the stillness of deep water.

"Steel remembers fire," he told me when he handed me a nail. "To bind a thing is to remind the world of a truth it misplaced."

For weeks I strained against that scrap of iron, willing it to answer me. Nothing. Arnaut made sport of my efforts, hurling an apple at my head one afternoon.

"You don't need to bend the air," he said, "if you can hit what's breathing it."

I threw it back with enough force to make him duck. The brothers gave us penance for the noise.

Exhaustion finally forced patience. Instead of commanding the nail, I listened; I sensed the cold weight, saw the pitted surface in my mind, and heard the hush inside the metal. When I spoke to it again, it wasn't an order but a conversation. Light stirred along its edge, steady this time. Pascal called it a miracle, not for the brightness but for its endurance. Iron usually shrugged off magic. Mine held it.

Arnaut never took to that kind of persuasion. His strength lay in force, the bigger an explosion the better for him. We balanced each other, even when we argued. Especially then.

Pascal's last warning stayed with me. "Power follows the shape of your heart. Pride twists it. Mercy steadies it." I had the burns to remember what that meant.

We left Viterbo at dawn. By the third day the land leveled, and the line of the Tiber shimmered in the distance. Rome rose out of the heat like a hundred cities stacked together. The centuries created a city of historical contrasts; temples remade into churches, ruins bent into markets, but the constants were the banners of Pope and Emperor fighting for the attention of the people.

Arnaut shifted his sword belt. "Smells like power."

"Smells like sin," Geoffrey said.

"Same perfume."

Geoffrey let the comment die.

The north gate funneled us into a crush of bodies. Geoffrey guided us through alleys thick with voices and tension. Everywhere men whispered about rebellion, excommunication, loyalty, fear. Rome twitched like an animal ready to bolt.

Arnaut leaned closer. "If this place were any more nervous, it would gnaw through its own cage."

The Lateran Basilica rose ahead, the true heart of the Catholic Church. Inside, mosaics glittered in torchlight, saints and angels staring down with unblinking eyes.

Geoffrey paused at a bronze door. "Most men never stand beyond this point. The Watch begins on the other side."

He looked at me without any title, mentor, or expectation between us, just a man taking measure of what he had shaped.

"Tomorrow, you take your vows."

Arnaut clapped my shoulder. "Try not to embarrass us. Or wet yourself."

We laughed softly. Even laughter sounded small under that roof.

Sleep dodged me that night. Pascal's lessons drifted through the dark. So did Arnaut's warning. You can make holiness permanent. And damnation.

Morning bled gold through the shutters. A deacon in crimson led us down a corridor lined with frescoes. We stopped before a door bound in iron.

Inside, the room stretched long and dim. Narrow windows let in slanted light. Scrolls filled the walls. Three hooded figures worked at a central desk, quills whispering across vellum.

One lifted his head. "Bishop Geoffrey. You bring the candidate."

"I do. James Crable of Lunden. Pure in heart, firm in mind, steady in faith."

A quiet rustle of parchment. "You fought at Hastings."

"Yes."

"The Lord tempers His instruments," the scribe murmured. "That fire will make you strong where others fail."

He gestured toward a lectern carved with interlocking circles; a symbol and a warning.

Another scribe raised his eyes. Pale. Depthless.

"This is the ledger of the Watch," he said. "We remember what others would rather forget. The Apostoli command from the Lateran. We, the Legati Sacri, direct from the shadows. You enter as a blade. If the Holy Father sees edge enough."

A shiver ran through me, but I bowed. "May he find me sharp."

"Edges dull," the scribe said. "Faith keeps them honed."

He noted something on the parchment. The sound felt heavier than it should.

We were dismissed. In the cloister, Arnaut scattered crumbs for sparrows.

"They move like spiders," he said. "Holy ones, but spiders."

I laughed. "If that's heaven's bureaucracy, I see why Hell has no shortage of recruits."

"Careful," Arnaut said. "Mock them enough, and they'll promote you."

Near noon, the Pope's guard summoned us. Gregory VII stood beneath a canopy embroidered with crossed keys. When the chamber cleared, he stepped down from the dais.

Smaller than I expected, but presence isn't measured in height. His gaze pressed like a hand to the chest.

"Geoffrey says you can make God's power linger on iron," he said. No greeting. No ornament. "He says what you bless remains blessed. Is it true?"

"The grace is God's," I answered. "I am only His vessel."

"Men crack," Gregory said. "Iron does not. If faith can be made permanent, then the kingdom of heaven may be built in stone and metal, not just in men's wavering hearts."

He gripped my shoulder, strength surprising in its force.

"Do not let eternity seduce you, James. Even holy things can become idols."

He turned to Geoffrey. "Guide him. Sharpen him. Set him on the right path."

Geoffrey bowed. "As I have done for all entrusted to me."

Sunlight cut the courtyard as we stepped outside. Arnaut exhaled hard.

"He didn't strike you dead. Promising."

I rubbed my hands down my tunic. "He spoke as though eternity were a thing a council could own."

Arnaut shrugged. "It already believes it does."

Geoffrey's voice softened. "Do not mistake conviction for vanity. Gregory believes he stands between Christendom and ruin."

I stared at the Lateran's bright walls. For the first time I understood what they wanted from me. Not just service. Permanence.

Tomorrow, they would ask me to become eternal. To fight the horrors of the world that even the bravest of men feared.

And buried beneath all the ritual and certainty, a knot tightened in my chest, small, cold, and impossible to ignore.

The next morning began not with summons, but with silence. I awoke and donned a plain white tunic. No pretense, I would enter the ceremony stripped of everything but my faith. I spent the day in a small chapel. In quiet reflection of both what I had learned this last decade, but also in silent prayer for strength and wisdom. I fasted, prayed, and found strength in believing I walked the path of the faithful.

The weight of the coming vow was a physical thing. I knew that after today my life would no longer be my own. The hours crawled. I spoke words I had not spoken since childhood, and some I had learned only in the last decade. In between prayer and reflection, I sat in stillness, trying to understand the choice in front of me.

As the sun began to sink, a quiet knock broke the silence. A deacon waited outside my door, head bowed.

"It is time."

Geoffrey and Arnaut stood in the corridor. Geoffrey's face held no trace of the easy mentor I knew; the gravity of the day made him look older. Arnaut, usually irreverent even in sacred spaces, had gone still and solemn. He placed a hand on my shoulder and gave me a reassuring nod. It provided more comfort than I think he knew, or perhaps he did, having stood where I was many years ago.

Without a word, Geoffrey led us through the basilica's dim passages until we reached the inner cloister.

Night had swallowed the Lateran by the time we arrived. Candles burned in iron sconces along the walls, their flames bending inward as though pulled by some unseen tide. Hooded figures ringed the chamber, each holding a staff capped with iron. They watched in silence.

The stone floor had been carved with a vast pattern of complex sigils, interlocking circles and long curving lines etched deep into the marble, but it was the copper that stole the breath from my lungs. Not because of the gleam they reflected in the candle light, but from the power that surged from them. The energy from it felt pure. I could feel the power was in perfect balance with the world around us, as if it was focusing energy into the chamber. It was clean and pure. Thin strips of it filled every groove, hammered flush with the stone until the entire lattice shimmered like banked embers. Even without touching it, I could feel the quiet thrum beneath my feet.

A guard struck his spear twice. The far doors opened.

Pope Gregory entered, flanked by two Legati Sacri. In his hands he carried a reliquary, gold worked with thorn motifs, bound by a band of iron so dark it was nearly black. Every hooded figure bowed as he approached.

"James Crable," Gregory said. "Step forward."

I did.

"You have walked through discipline, silence, and testing," he said. "Tonight, you stand at the threshold of the Watch. You will carry a mantle laid first upon Christ Himself, the call to guard, to suffer, and to give your life if necessary. If you are worthy, God will grant you years beyond ordinary men, that you may keep watch as long as He wills."

The copper sigils flickered with a faint inner light, like something waking.

The Pope raised the reliquary slightly. "Within this vessel rests a nail of the True Cross, iron that pierced the Lord's flesh and carries the memory of His sacrifice. Through it, the breath of God flows into you."

A whisper moved through the hooded watchers.

"James Crable," Gregory said. "Kneel."

The stone was cold beneath my knees.

A cardinal of the Apostoli opened the reliquary. The nail inside was small, blackened, its surface pitted like cooled volcanic rock. When Gregory lifted it, the copper sigils brightened. A low hum moved through the floor.

He brought the nail to my head and touched my brow.

A shock tore through me, raw, piercing. Not fire, but memory. The copper flared, and I could feel a crescendo of energy pierce my body. I felt the weight of millennia. I witnessed Cavalry Hill and the people weeping. The weight of the Church's teachings washed over me. Mercy and wrath, eternity and anguish, all forced through a mind too small to hold any of it cleanly.

The copper flared again. Light surged along every channel. The hooded figures raised their staffs, and power leapt from the iron tips into the copper, rushing like water through roots, then into the nail, and into me.

My vision fractured. The chamber blurred. Pain roared up my spine like lightning. Geoffrey's prayers sounded distant, muffled, swallowed by the crackling energy.

Gregory's voice cut through it. "Rise as Christ arose. Endure as Christ endured. Let His mantle rest upon you. Let His strength carry you beyond the years of mortal men."

The nail burned in a steady, agonizing pulse. Something inside me stretched, felt near to tearing, and I could sense being tested. My will. My strength. My faith. I felt the power surge into place like a broken bone being reset.

I gasped and the world went black.

When sight returned, I was on the ground, palms flat against the glowing copper. Sweat soaked my tunic. My limbs shook.

Gregory knelt just enough to meet my eyes. "Rise, James Crable. By the authority of the Church, the blessing of the Apostoli, and the will of Almighty God, you are sealed into the Watch. Bound to its charge until your final breath, whenever that breath may come."

My legs trembled as I pushed myself upright. The chamber wavered. But I stood.

The hooded figures struck their staffs once more. The light in the copper dimmed slowly, reluctantly.

The Pope replaced the nail in the reliquary and closed it. The final click echoed like a closing verdict.

He turned back to face me, "In nomine Patris, et Filii, et Spiritus Sancti. Amen."

"Amen," I said in a tired whisper.

"Your life belongs to God now," he said quietly. "Walk with fear, and with faith."

We left the chamber. My steps were uneven. Geoffrey supported my arm without acknowledging it.

The sigils still pulsed faintly at the edge of my vision long after the doors closed behind us.

Whatever I had been when the day began, I was not that man now.

5

Chilies, Guns, and Shadow (Ohio, Present)

The scent of searing meat and hickory smoke was a welcome anchor in the strange, heavy weight that had clung to me this evening. A primal, comforting smell, a signal of community that cut through the static of my own unease. It led me, as it always did, through the side gate, the unofficially official "friend gate" in the wood fence that separated my manicured solitude from the vibrant chaos of Casey and Erin's backyard. Their little corner-lot ranch was the neighborhood's unassuming heart, and tonight it was beating a strong, steady rhythm of pure, unvarnished life.

Strings of lights were slung between the two old maples in lazy arcs, throwing a soft, buttery glow over a beautiful chaos of mismatched folding chairs and a long, heavily laden picnic table that seemed to sag under the weight of its own generosity. The air hummed with a dozen overlapping conversations, the rhythmic thump of beanbags hitting wooden boards, and the steady sizzle from the grill. In the center of it all, commanding a stainless-steel behemoth that looked like it could refuel a jet, was Casey Donahue.

Standing barely above five feet, she was a live wire in gray yoga pants and a faded navy t-shirt that read Tacos Are My Love Language, her long blonde ponytail pulled high and swishing every time she turned, a little banner of momentum. Compact and athletic, she lived by the motto a stranger is just a friend you haven't met. She wielded her spatula like a conductor's baton, flipping burgers and chicken thighs with a warrior's focus. She spotted me the moment I stepped into the circle of light.

"Crable! The man, the myth, the occasional legend! I was five minutes from sending a search party. We were worried you'd finally gotten lost in your own wine cellar."

"And miss your famous, possibly hazardous, marinade?" I said, setting a bottle of Pichon Longueville on a rare empty spot on the table.

"Damn right you wouldn't," she said, brandishing her spatula like a sword. "Cornhole rematch tonight. I've been doing wrist exercises. You're going down harder than the Bengals in a playoff game. It's going to be a historical collapse."

"That's a cheap shot, hitting a man where he lives," I said. "And for the record, I root for the Browns. I prefer my disappointment pure and unadulterated."

"Which is objectively a worse life choice," Erin stated, materializing from the kitchen with a tray of deviled eggs dusted with paprika and chipotle powder.

Erin Taylor was taller than Casey and narrower through the shoulders, her build more distance runner than weightlifter. Her dark, shoulder-length hair was pulled back in a low, neat ponytail, and her rectangular glasses framed sharp brown eyes that missed nothing. She adjusted the frames with one precise finger as her gaze swept the table like a hawk scanning a field. I could almost see her mentally inventorying the plates, the forks, the exact spacing of the napkin dispensers.

"Statistically," she went on, "choosing perpetual sporting disappointment is a fascinating form of self-flagellation. It builds character, I suppose, or at least a very high tolerance for pain."

Before I could formulate a retort, Casey leaned in, her voice dropping to a conspiratorial stage-whisper that carried perfectly across the patio. "So, Crable. The Garden Ninja. Did you get a sighting today? Any covert floral operations?"

A few heads turned. The Garden Ninja was our neighborhood's resident specter, a woman in her sixties who treated her immaculate corner lot with the grim, unblinking focus of a soldier defending a contested frontier.

"This afternoon," I confirmed, slipping into the ritual. "She was kneeling by the curb, surgical gloves on, attacking a patch of clover like it had personally offended her ancestors. I've seen less intensity in bomb disposal units."

Erin arched a perfectly shaped eyebrow, a knowing smile tugging at one corner of her mouth. "I swear she trims her boxwoods at two seventeen every Thursday morning. I heard the shears once when I was up reading late. It was methodical. Almost threatening."

"Maybe she's nuclear-powered," Casey mused, expertly flipping a row of chicken thighs that hissed in protest. "Or runs on pure, uncut spite toward poor landscaping. I think her lawn mower is just for show. I'm convinced she shears individual blades of grass with nail scissors."

Mid-conversation the patio door slid open and David Katz stepped out, looking slightly harried as he balanced a grocery bag in one arm and his phone in the other. David was lean, with narrow shoulders and long, restless hands that never seemed quite settled. His dark, unruly curls looked as if they'd given up on the idea of ever being tamed. A few permanent frown lines bracketing his mouth gave him a thoughtful, slightly worried look even when he was smiling. He didn't dress like a man who ran one of the largest privately owned cybersecurity companies in America; tonight, it was a soft black t-shirt and comfortably wrinkled jeans.

He offered a shy, encompassing wave to the group, his smile warm but distracted. "I saw her out in the downpour last week," he chimed in, setting the bag down with a relieved sigh. "No jacket, no umbrella. Just pruning in a torrential rain. Like she was in some kind of horticultural trance, or maybe proving a point to the weather itself."

"Retired Mossad," Erin said dryly, not looking up from arranging her deviled eggs into a perfect, geometrically sound grid. "The dedication is impressive. Security at my lab is tighter, but her operational patience is on another level. She's been 'gardening' that same hydrangea for three weeks. That's not gardening, that's a long-term surveillance stakeout."

"Please," Casey snorted, poking at the coals. "You'd audit her so fast her hedges would wilt from the sheer force of your spreadsheet. You'd find the receipts for the organic fertilizer and cross-reference them with her power bill.”

“True,” Erin conceded without a hint of irony. “I’d have a full cost-benefit analysis by Tuesday. Premium mulch doesn’t buy itself, and I’d want to see the ROI on that Japanese maple.”

David shrugged, a nervous grin spreading across his face. “If she has Wi-Fi, I could probably map her entire online presence in five minutes. Find out if she’s binge-watching gardening shows or downloading schematics for underground bunkers.”

“Everything’s a cyber-plot with you, Katz,” Casey laughed, shaking her head.

“I run a cybersecurity company,” he protested, shoving his hands into his pockets. “Professional paranoia isn’t just a hobby; it pays the mortgage.”

I joined in, falling into the easy rhythm. “If she’s a spy, she’s the most dedicated one I’ve ever seen. And I’ve seen a few. No one spends that many man-hours on begonias unless they’re hiding a body or, at the very least, a secret underground greenhouse.”

Casey, not one to be upstaged, pointed her spatula with a dramatic flourish toward a long, carefully organized series of display cases sitting on one of the tables. The bottles lined up there were a riot of color and menace, a library of liquid fire.

“Behold! The great re-organization of our spicy progeny is complete!”

Erin gave the shelf an appraising, critical look. “My re-organization. Let’s be precise. Sorted by Scoville units. The mild ones, relatively speaking, are in the green case. The yellow case is for ‘experienced enthusiasts.’ The red case is for ‘Casey, don’t you dare put that in the communal chili.’ And the black one with the skull sticker is for ‘liability waiver required.’”

“You rank-ordered hot sauce?” David asked, equal parts amused and horrified. “That’s simultaneously the most beautiful and terrifying thing I’ve ever seen.”

“Someone has to bring order to the chaos,” Erin said primly. “Casey collects them like Pokémon cards, but with more potential for gastrointestinal Armageddon.”

"We have over two hundred," Casey announced, beaming with the pride of a new parent. "Each one has its own personality, its own purpose. They're like my children. Spicy, unpredictable children that can clear a room."

"Children don't typically melt the enamel off your teeth," David muttered, eyeing a bottle with a label that featured a cartoon devil holding a fire extinguisher.

Erin adjusted her glasses again, the lenses catching a brief flash from the patio light. "That depends entirely on the child. Or the bottle. Last week, Casey tried to smuggle a ghost pepper extract into my five-bean chili. I detected the anomaly during the pre-simmer taste test. I nearly wrote her out of the will on the spot."

"And it was delicious," Casey declared, utterly unrepentant. "My taste buds have more courage than your entire circulatory system. Someone needs to uphold the spice standard around here."

A familiar, rumbling voice cut through the banter from behind me. "Evening, Jimmy. I see the circus is in full swing."

Charlie Mitchell stepped into the circle of light, and the mood settled around him as if it had found its center. He wore a simple dark polo shirt and jeans, but he carried himself with the grounded, unshakable authority of a man who'd spent a lifetime leading others. In his early-fifties, he was still powerfully built through the chest and shoulders, with dark skin and close-cropped black hair just beginning to give ground to gray at the temples. Fine lines radiated from the corners of his eyes, more from sun and responsibility than from age. His gaze, warm and deep, missed nothing.

He held out a six-pack of a local craft IPA. "Stopped by Arrow Wine and grabbed some local brew."

I took the offered beer. The bottle was cold and wet in my hand, and perfect for a hot August evening.

"Colonel!" Casey called, raising her spatula in a salute. "Glad you could make it! Ready to have your palate expanded?"

Charlie's eyes drifted to the hot sauce shelf, his expression shading into the kind of wary respect he usually reserved for live circuits. "Expanded, or exploded? That's not a spice rack, that's an arsenal. Landmines, every last one of them. I've faced down less intimidating artillery."

Erin grinned, a rare, full-wattage smile that transformed her usually composed face. "The green dots are scientifically verified as safe for human consumption. You're welcome, assuming you aren't colorblind. The rest are varying degrees of psychological warfare."

Casey, not to be outdone, gestured grandly at the grill, where a new burst of smoke rolled up. "Tonight's signature marinade is a state secret. Two limes, a truly disgraceful cheap lager, and three sauces Erin won't let me name because she says it 'biases the tasting' and 'violates experimental protocol.'"

"It does," Erin said, her tone flat enough to polish glass. "Also, last time you used one that promised 'instant regret' and had a warning label written in what looked like Sanskrit. We lost a good patio plant that night. It just gave up from proximity."

Charlie just shook his head, a slow, warm smile easing across his face. "I'm an electrical engineer, not a fire-breather. My job is to make sure things don't short circuit. Your job, apparently, is to make sure our insides do. I don't have the proper protective gear for your culinary experiments."

For a moment, I let myself believe this was all I needed. Friends laughing, charcoal smoke, good food, and better drink. The ordinary rituals of mortal lives.

Then the night changed.

A thin hush slid across the yard, so slight it might have been nothing more than the wind shifting. Conversations thinned for a heartbeat as people reached for drinks or plates. In that narrow gap of sound, it came.

A howl rose from somewhere beyond the houses; long, layered, and wrong for these suburbs. Not the yipping chorus of coyotes, but a deeper howl that is usually reserved for horror movies. It started as a low, singular call and climbed into something that scraped the nerves raw, lingering at the top just a fraction too long.

Cornhole matches froze mid-game. Laughter died. Every head turned toward the dark line of the trees beyond the fence.

"Uh," David said softly, the word barely more than breath, "tell me that's somebody's weird ringtone."

Casey's spatula stilled over the grill. "That's not coyotes," she said. The usual cheer in her voice had thinned; she sounded more like someone talking herself into not being bothered.

Erin, who believed in data more than superstition, frowned toward the dark. "I don't think we have wolves in Ohio. What the hell is that?" she asked, half rhetorical and half needing to know the answer.

Charlie had gone very quiet. His head tilted slightly, listening the way a man listens for mortar rounds in the distance. "Whatever it is," he murmured, "it sounds like it's pretty far from here."

Another howl answered the first, closer this time, the same coiled harmony of voices bending into one note. The sound pressed against us, a vibration more than a volume. I have heard my share of wolves, coyotes, and even hyenas, this was not something I had heard before. That certainly added fuel to my growing unease.

I kept my expression mild, my hand loose around my beer bottle, but inside something tightened, pulled taut. Predators test when the Veil thins. The Wendigo's fear that afternoon, the odd stories in the paper, Ray's nervousness, now this sound threading through a quiet neighborhood cookout, it did not feel like coincidence. I never really believed in coincidence.

Casey forced a laugh and nudged the grill lid closed with her hip. "Okay, cool, ominous wildlife symphony. Love that for us. Everyone relax. If something eats us, it'll at least get a good marinade first."

The group chuckled, but the laughter came out thinner, a little too sharp at the edges. People looked at one another, then back toward the trees, and only when the silence held did the volume of conversation begin to climb again.

Charlie's gaze met mine for the briefest of moments. There was no joke there, just a question, and beneath it, the readiness of a man long accustomed to taking bad news in stride. I gave him the smallest shrug, as if to say no clue.

The moment passed. Somebody cranked the music up half a notch. The beanbags began their slow arc again. The world pretended to uncoil.

David, perhaps grateful for the distraction, cleared his throat and opened his grocery bag with a flourish. "I come bearing gifts from the land of milk and honey! Bisli, Bamba, and a bottle of Tubi60, which I will admit is an acquired taste and may or may not cause hallucinations. All straight from Tel Aviv." I just got back. My firm is buying a data analytics company there. Still early days, but data is the future."

"Data is the past, present, *and* future," stated Erin. She was one of the country's top data scientists and worked for a firm that supported everything from environmental mapping to defense intelligence.

Casey dove for the snacks as if they were life-giving manna. "Oh, snacks I can't pronounce! You are my absolute favorite person today. Don't tell Erin. Are any of them spicy? Please tell me there's a spicy one."

David chuckled, his shoulders finally losing some of their tension. "Afraid not. All savory or sweet," he said, his ears turning pink with pleasure at her enthusiasm.

Then, with a showman's flair, he set a long, serious-looking cardboard box on the table. He opened it to reveal a brand-new IWI Jericho pistol, nestled in foam, its blued steel catching the string lights.

The group's attention snapped to it in an instant. Charlie let out a low, appreciative whistle, the sound of a man who knew his way around machinery. "Now that's a fine piece of hardware, David. A Jericho 941. Solid choice. You get a chance to break it in yet?"

David shook his head, his grin widening into something prouder and less nervous. "Just picked it up on the way here. Wanted to show it off first."

And just like that, the conversation pivoted, as it always did, with the easy logic of this group, from imported snacks to firearms without missing a beat.

Charlie thumped his chest lightly. "I'll always be a classic man. You can't beat the feel of a Colt 1911. It's history you can hold in your hand."

"Colt?" Casey scoffed, leaning on her spatula. "Come on, Colonel, this is the twenty-first century. It's like bringing a musket to a drone strike. Glock or nothing. It's simple, it's reliable, it's the Honda Civic of handguns."

"Glock for me, too," Erin affirmed, wiping her hands on a towel. "Though Casey just claims hers is better because it has more scratches, which she calls 'character' and I call 'evidence of negligent handling.'"

"Because it is better," Casey said, sparking a mock-marital debate that had the rest of the table grinning. "Your Glock is so boring it probably files its own taxes. Mine has stories."

I leaned against the porch railing, my shoulder brushing the weathered wood, and sipped the ale Charlie brought. Charlie was now holding David's Jericho, demonstrating its balance with an engineer's eye, his low commentary a steady bass line beneath Casey's exuberant storytelling about the time she nearly fumigated the house with her Carolina Reaper cornbread experiment. Erin listened, a dry smile on her face as she subtly readjusted a bowl of chips that had drifted out of alignment.

This was the ritual. This was profound and simple, not the grand battles or ancient ceremonies, but the sound of friends, alive and unafraid, framed by cheap string lights and fireflies.

Charlie eventually drifted over, nudging me with his elbow. "And what about you, Jimmy? Still carrying that fancy German pistol like you're auditioning for a Bond movie?"

"The Walther? Old habits die a hard death," I said, taking a measured sip of beer. "Besides, someone has to bring a little class and European engineering to the range. We can't all be banging away with plastic junk and museum pieces."

David looked up from his conversation with Charlie, a quick flicker of self-deprecating humor in his eyes. "As long as I can actually hit the target this time. That's my only goal. Hitting the paper would be a personal victory."

"Hit it?" Casey crowed, abandoning her grill for a moment to join the conversation. "Katz, last time you were at the range, you nearly gave the ceiling ten yards behind the target a new skylight. The range safety officer literally started praying."

"Easy now," Charlie said, his voice smoothing the edges off the teasing. "Recoil management takes practice. It's a skill, like anything else. We'll work on your grip and your stance next time, David. You'll get it. It's all about consistency."

"See?" David said, relief obvious. "At least one of you has a little faith in me."

"No," Erin said, without looking up from her meticulous condiment array.

"He just doesn't want you to accidentally shoot your own foot. Or, more importantly, his foot. My money's on the Colonel's podiatric safety being the primary motivator."

The night deepened, the sky above us settling into a steady indigo. The cornhole tournament raged with a mixture of fierce competition and spectacular incompetence. Casey threw with enthusiastic, wildly inaccurate power. Erin threw with the calm precision of someone who could probably calculate the arc and velocity in her head. David threw with hopeful optimism, his bags often falling short as if hesitation carried weight. Charlie threw like a man planning a beach landing, each bag landing with a soft, decisive thud.

Fireflies blinked in the hedges, little green-gold pulses among the shadows. The patio lights buzzed faintly overhead. Somewhere far off, a siren rose and faded, part of the normal soundtrack of suburbia. Nothing howled again. The silence between noises felt full of teeth.

I raised my glass in a small, private toast, accepted a splash of Tubi60 from David, a sweet, sharp herbal sour flavor that tasted like citrus cough medicine and bad ideas, and let their laughter roll over me: Casey's brash and unapologetic, Erin's dry and well-timed, David's quick and nervous, Charlie's deep and steady.

And yet, beneath the warmth, something in me stayed clenched. The wrongness I'd felt that morning, the Wendigo's warning at the creek, the strained note in Ray's voice, the twisted, too-harmonious howl in the distance; all of it lined up in my thoughts like pieces waiting to be named.

I told myself it was nothing, that the night would settle. But the feeling lingered, a cold thread woven through the edges of the evening. The sense that something was in motion, and that whatever had started would not stop at the property line, or the park, or the harmless pages of the *Dayton Daily News*.

The laughter around me felt, for the first time in a long while, less like simple joy and more like a dam. I could sense the pressure building behind it. The fear was not just for me; it was for them.

And that was a terror older, and far more potent, than any I had faced in many years.

6

Scotch, Home, and the Fear

The party had thinned out by the time Charlie leaned against the railing and gave me the look. The kids from the next street had already been dragged home by reluctant parents. The music had wound down to a soft playlist of country and yacht rock. Admittedly, Little River Band's Greatest Hits kept me around longer than I had planned. A couple of neighbors lingered at the cornhole boards, laughing low and steady, but the big energy of the night had passed.

David was still there, sitting cross-legged on the grass with Casey and Erin, all three of them finishing off the last of the Bamba like they were planning to declare snack bankruptcy. Casey was arguing that hot sauce improved everything, even breakfast cereal, while Erin countered that she was confusing culinary experimentation with a cry for help.

Charlie caught my eye, jerked his chin toward the friend gate, and I knew it was time.

We slipped out without much notice.

"Hey," Casey called after us, holding up a foil-covered tray, "you forgot the brownies I packed for you."

Charlie didn't miss a beat. "Last thing I need is a nuclear dessert that violates the Geneva Convention."

That drew laughter from the table and gave us the cover to slip away.

As we walked through the gate and into the backyard I had a brief feeling of dread. The backyard had a wrong rhythm, like a heartbeat out of time. The wrong didn't come from weather or nerves but from something brushing against the Veil where it shouldn't. I paused a moment, looked around, but the moment was fleeting and I was left thinking I was imagining things. I was afraid that there was something wrong with the Veil. Afraid the quiet wouldn't hold. Afraid this peace, this neighborhood, this life, was starting to crack in ways the others couldn't see.

Inside my house, the air was cool and smelled of old paper and cedar. I had built it about ten years ago, when it became clear it was time to shift roots again. I could never stay in one place for too long without questions being asked. Faces age, neighbors change, and eventually someone realizes that mine does not. So, I move from home to home, always circling back between Kew and Centerville, the two places I have anchored myself for more than two centuries.

When I built it, Charlie was still active duty and living with his daughter, Stasha. Charlie's wife had passed away a few years before I moved in and Charlie raised his daughter and put her through school on his own. When she moved out to college, I remember him telling me, "With kids, the nights are long and the years short." We became immediate friends as I was new and he no longer had a daughter at home to dote on.

I had designed this house with both security and comfort in mind. The bones were steel and stone, modern enough to pass unnoticed in the neighborhood but sturdy enough to endure anything. What the neighbors never knew were the wards I had set into the foundation and yard, subtle layers of protection woven into the very mortar. Nothing showy, nothing visible, just quiet boundaries that turned away curious eyes and dampened anything from the other side that might come too close, and gave me a bit of warning when I had visitors, especially unwelcome ones.

The living room was a mixture of the ordinary and the strange. Leather chairs, a scotch cabinet, a flat-screen TV that had been a concession to modern life. But the shelves that lined the walls gave me away.

Old volumes, spines cracked and worn. A bronze astrolabe. My trusty blade that hung over the fireplace mantle that reminded me of a different life and a different time. A framed letter from the late 1700s written in John Hole's hand. Small artifacts scattered like a private museum, though no labels explained them. Most people never looked too closely being overwhelmed by it all, or assumed I had a strong affection for Restoration Hardware and Sharper Image.

Below, in the basement, was where the truth of the house lived. My lab. Shelves lined with rare artifacts, both magical and mundane. Chests of tools, some that no blacksmith in this age could name, others that came from nothing more exotic than the local hardware store. Workbenches scarred with years of experiments, some gone wrong, some gone horribly wrong. That was where I refined my enchantments, tested theories, and kept the dangerous things locked away. Few would ever see it, and fewer still would understand it if they did.

The basement also held what was probably the most valuable wine cellar on earth. Bottles arranged with care, collected over centuries of travel. I had Latour and Haut-Brion from Thomas Jefferson's own cellars, dusty but still sound, at least I hoped. And tucked away, wrapped in cloth like a holy relic, was one of the legendary Forster Ungeheuer Rieslings from 1811, a vintage that had outlived empires. Still drinkable, still singing of a summer that ended more than two hundred years ago.

Someday I would have to leave this place too. Just as I had left others before it. And when that day came, I would leave more than bricks and mortar behind. I would leave friends. Good people who had welcomed me without knowing who or what I was. That was the price of permanence for someone like me. You never really get to keep it.

"You know," Charlie said, lowering himself into one of the chairs with a grunt, "you've got the weirdest damn living room in Centerville. Half Pottery Barn, half Smithsonian."

I poured two glasses of a rare 25-year-old Glen Garioch whisky and handed him one. "It keeps people guessing."

"Doesn't keep me from asking." He swirled the scotch, eyes on the astrolabe. "Where'd you pick that up? Yard sale?"

"Something like that."

A sort of yard sale in Alexandria, in the year 1124. But close enough.

He took a sip, let the silence hang a little. That was Charlie's trick. He didn't push, he just let space open up until you wanted to fill it.

"So," he said finally. "You faded in and out all night from your usual gregarious self to thousand-yard stares. Something's on your mind, Jimmy. There were times you looked…" He paused to select the right word. "Well, spooked."

I leaned back, enjoyed the tobacco and caramel flavor. "Spooked is a strong word."

"It's the right word." He pointed at me with his glass. "So, what was it? Because I know you. You don't drift like that unless something's grinding at you."

"I've been thinking about a meeting from earlier today," I said.

Charlie snorted. "Meetings don't usually put that look on a man's face. Unless it was with lawyers."

I didn't answer. Instead, I stared at the amber in my glass, remembering the stories. Animals torn apart in Japan. Wisps in Germany. The Wendigo's warning.

Charlie watched me for a long time. He had the patience of a man who had spent years in briefing rooms listening to people dance around the truth. Finally, he set his glass down.

"You don't have to tell me everything. But don't tell me nothing either. We've both seen what happens when you ignore your gut."

He's right. I've ignored my gut before. It cost villages. It cost friends. Yet here I sit, trying to protect my quiet little corner of Centerville as if I can wall the world out with cookouts and string lights.

I looked around my living room. The familiar lines of the chairs, the scent of the cedar shelves, the quiet hum of the air conditioning.

For centuries, I had no home. I wandered. A bed in a monastery one month, an inn above a tavern the next. A borrowed blanket on a campaign field. Always moving. Studying. Seeking. Chasing scraps of magic like a starving man chases crumbs. You learn to survive like that, but you don't live. This house, this street, these neighbors make it feel like I finally stopped running.

Maybe that's why the unease cuts deeper. Because I don't want to lose this.

Charlie broke the silence again. "Look, Jimmy. I don't need classified intel. But I've known you long enough to know when you're carrying something heavy. Whatever it is, don't carry it alone."

That's the trouble, Charlie. I've carried it alone for centuries. Who do you hand it to when no one else can lift it?

Before I could reply, a sound cut through the quiet.

It was soft at first. A bark, sharp and urgent. Then a shout.

We both froze.

Another shout. David's voice. High, strained.

We were on our feet before the glasses hit the table.

Out the back door, across the yard, through the friend gate. The night air hit me with the smell of cut grass and cooling charcoal. Casey and Erin were sprinting from their patio, yelling David's name.

David stood in my backyard, feet planted wide, arms rigid. The Jericho gleamed in his hands; muzzle pointed at the tree line. His shoulders shook with adrenaline.

"David!" Erin screamed. "What are you doing?"

"Something's out there!" His voice cracked. "It moved; it's watching us!"

The woods were still. Too still. The cicadas had gone silent.

Then came the sound. Branches shifting where no wind moved. A low rasp, like stone dragged over stone.

Casey skidded to a stop beside him. "Put the gun down before you shoot your foot off!"

"It's not loaded," David snapped, panic in his eyes.

He was right. No round chambered. The safety still on. All the bluster of a gun, none of the teeth.

Then I saw it.

A ripple in the shadows. A shape that wasn't a shape, too thin, too long, eyes catching the porch light and bending it wrong.

The fetchling.

It moved like smoke deciding to stand upright. Its skin, if you could call it that, shimmered between gray and black, edges blurring as though the night had not quite decided whether to keep it. Its eyes glowed, not with their own light but with everything they stole from the world around them.

It stepped forward. The air grew colder, a draft brushing my skin though the night was still. The smell of damp earth and old iron drifted with it.

David's arms wavered. The barrel tracked the creature like a compass needle spinning.

Casey pulled at his elbow, Erin grabbed his other arm, but he would not lower the gun.

Charlie's voice was low, sharp. "What the hell is that?"

Something that shouldn't be here. Something that belongs behind the Veil, not in a suburban backyard.

The fetchling tilted its head. A hiss, like wind through broken glass, slid from its throat.

It stepped closer.

David stumbled forward a half step, out of the grasp of Casey and Erin, the Jericho trembling in his hands. "Stay back!"

The creature twitched, its form flickering, half there, half gone. Each time it blurred, the shadows bent with it, as though the night itself were leaning toward us. He was approaching David; all menace and exuding raw terror.

My hand moved without thought.

A word, low and old, slipped from my mouth. My fingers curled into a shape I had not used in decades. The air thickened. Light bent.

The fetchling shrieked, a piercing sound that rattled windows and set dogs barking down the street. Its form snapped sharp for a heartbeat, every edge cut clear against the dark. Then it recoiled, twisting back into the shadows. Branches cracked as it fled, faster than any man could move.

Silence crashed down.

David stood frozen, gun trembling in his hands. Casey pried it away gently, Erin rubbing his shoulder, whispering to calm him. His face was pale; eyes locked on the trees.

Everyone had seen what I had done.

Casey's mouth opened, shut. Erin stared at me like she was trying to balance an equation that had no answer. David looked torn between gratitude and terror. Charlie's jaw was clenched tight, his eyes steady, sharp, and unreadable.

His look hit harder than I wanted it to.

Scared of me. No, scared of what I carry. Of what I am. And now my neighbors know enough to start asking questions I can't afford to answer.

I knew what it was the moment it stepped out of the dark. A fetchling. One of the Veil's creatures, half-shadow and half-thought. They don't belong here. They slip through cracks when pushed, never by their own choice. And they are never alone. Fetchlings are scouts. I've seen them used by demons, by warlocks drunk on borrowed power, even by one of the Apostoli in Rome who thought it clever to leash the shadows themselves and bend to the Vatican's will. They creep ahead of the real danger, eyes and ears for things that don't like to be surprised. They test boundaries, measure fear, and sometimes drag their masters in behind them like a hand pulling a thread through cloth.

They can't be fought the way other creatures can. You can't stab smoke or trap a shadow. They confuse the eye, cloud the mind, slip between the cracks of what's real. That hiss David heard was not its voice, but the echo of a place beyond the Veil pressing against the edges of this world. A fetchling doesn't kill. It scouts, it stalks, it whispers what it sees to the thing that sent it. And if one was here, more eyes are already watching. Always watching.

The last time I saw one, the Veil had been thinned by an order of warlocks in the 1930s. By the early years of World War II, they had bound themselves to a demon that answered to Berlin. The Nazis thought they were harnessing something new, but it was the same old hunger with a new uniform. The group was the Ahnenerbe, Himmler's pet project. Officially, they called themselves a research institute devoted to history and culture. In truth, they were grave robbers and fanatics, scavenging myths and relics to twist into propaganda and power. They dug through old bones and older legends, convinced that the right ritual or artifact could cement Nazi rule as destiny.

That demon used fetchlings to spy on Allied movements in Africa, Italy, Russia, and France. Camps would wake to find their sentries staring blankly into the woods, eyes glassy, minds still lost in whatever illusions the creatures had woven around them. A week later, those same camps were overrun with uncanny precision, as if every tent and trench had been mapped out in advance. It wasn't German intelligence. It was shadow work. I helped my old friend and colleague from the watch, Lucan, burn that coven out before the war's end, but the damage had already been done. Thousands paid the price for a few fetchlings' whispers.

And now, after decades of silence, one had walked into a backyard in Ohio. That was no accident. It meant something worse was already moving in the dark. And worse, someone or something knew where to find me.

The group's silence pressed in. The night waited with them.

I drew a breath, slow and careful. "Not here," I said at last. My voice sounded heavier than I meant it to. "Inside. All of us. We need to talk."

7

Neighbors, Secrets, and the Storm (Ohio, Present)

We filed inside and I knew that this would be a tough conversation. My friends were about to have their world turned upside down, assuming they haven't already.

As if on cue, the sky opened, finally cashing in the humidity's earlier threat. The night air followed us in, a damp mix of smoke and rain. David's hands still shook. Casey kept a steady grip on his shoulder while Erin hovered close, her eyes flicking between me and the window as if she expected the shadows to decide we were unfinished business.

My house had never felt so small. Every light seemed too bright, every corner too near. The scent of cedar pressed against the warm edge of the Glen Garioch I'd left open earlier, two centuries of habit colliding with one sharp moment of chaos. Charlie closed the door with the same deliberate care he used when he locked his gun cabinet, measured, final.

"Shoes off?" Casey asked automatically, because manners don't drop just because the world tilts.

"Leave them," I said. "Floor can take it."

They literally could. I'd enchanted the floors to withstand damage and the wear of time.

Nobody laughed. We moved toward the living room like people sheltering in a storm cellar. I flicked on a lamp; its light fell across the coffee table where two half-finished glasses of whisky waited from before everything had gone sideways. They looked almost obscene in their normalcy, like props left onstage after the play turned real.

"Sit," I said.

Casey and Erin claimed the couch. David perched on the edge of an armchair until Charlie's steady hand pushed him fully into it. Charlie stayed standing, broad shoulders squared, scanning the room as if he expected the enemy to pop out of a closet.

No one spoke. Silence pooled and there was an expectation hanging over my friends. They just witnessed something that didn't line up with their known world.

Erin broke it first. "What the hell was that?"

I topped off my scotch, more to give my hands a task than from any real desire for it. "Something that shouldn't be here."

"That's not an answer," Casey said. "We all saw it. That wasn't a raccoon with an attitude problem or some neighbor kid in a Halloween costume. The air froze, my phone glitched, and David tried to shoot a ghost with an unloaded gun. So start talking."

David winced at the word ghost. He hadn't unclenched since the thing appeared. "I didn't see any eyes," he said quietly. "No eyes. Just reflections."

"Yeah," I said, exhaling. I paused, weighing what to say and what to leave buried.

Their gazes locked on me. Centuries never feel heavier than when ordinary people look to you for rules to a world they didn't know existed.

"All right," I said. "You deserve some truth. What you saw is called a fetchling."

Erin frowned. "That's not in any book I've ever read."

"No," I said. "It wouldn't be."

Casey crossed her arms. "Great. It's got a name. Now explain why there's a smoke-demon stalking the neighborhood barbecue circuit."

"It's not a demon," I said. "Not exactly. Think of it as a scout. It slips through when the barrier between our world and the other side gets thin."

"The barrier?" David asked.

"The Veil," I said. "It keeps what belongs here separate from what doesn't."

Charlie's voice came low. "And you've seen them before."

"Yes," I said. "More times than I'd like. It's never good news."

Erin leaned forward, voice taut but steady. "You said it shouldn't be here. So, what makes it cross over?"

"Someone sent it. It can't just appear anywhere. Something's pulling on the fabric," I said. "A breach, a weak spot. Pressure builds behind it until something cracks and things like that find a way through."

Casey threaded her fingers through her hair. "Fantastic. I just wanted burgers, beer, and eternal bragging rights. Not that."

"I didn't expect that here," I said.

She studied me. "You weren't surprised, though."

"I was," I said. "I should've been more observant."

Charlie drifted toward the mantle, gaze sliding over the shelves until it landed on the sword mounted above them. The runes on the scabbard caught the lamplight, silver lines a little too bright tonight.

Erin cleared her throat. "Crable, how do you know about these things? You've been here ten years. The weirdest thing I've seen in that time is our garden-obsessed neighbor. None of this makes any sense at all."

Her eyes behind the glasses were sharp, clinical, as if she was cataloging me based on a new set of data.

"I've been around a long time," I said carefully. "I study things most people file under folklore. Guardians, boundaries, the patterns that keep the world from tearing itself open."

"Like ghosts," Casey muttered.

"Not ghosts," I said. "But most would call it supernatural."

David rubbed at his temples. "So, reality has what, a perimeter fence, and something just cut a hole in it?"

"That'll do for a first draft," I said.

"Awesome." He gave a thin laugh. "Reality's got a security flaw."

"That tracks," Charlie said, deadpan.

For a moment, the absurdity cracked the fear, and I almost smiled. These were good people. Frightened, yes, but grounded in their own ways: Casey with sarcasm as armor, Erin with analysis, David with restless curiosity, Charlie with the calm of a man who's seen worse and prays not to again.

Casey swept her eyes around the room, the books, the relics, the sword. "You've been hiding in plain sight?"

"Both hiding," I said. "And guarding."

"Guarding what?" she asked.

I looked toward the rain-blurred window. "To use David's analogy, I make sure the security flaws don't happen, or that they get fixed. I protect the creatures that keep things like that out of our world."

Erin's gaze sharpened. "You keep saying 'things' and 'patterns' and 'boundaries.' You used something out there. A word, a gesture. That wasn't just a prayer. What was it?"

The room tightened by a degree. I took a slow sip of scotch, then set the glass down.

"Magic," I said.

David huffed out a disbelieving breath. "You're actually saying that word."

"I am," I answered. "You asked for truth."

Erin didn't flinch. "Define it."

"Of course you want a definition," Casey muttered.

Erin ignored her. "If the Veil is real and fetchlings are real, then whatever you did was an interaction with something. Define it."

"Fine," I said. "There are four main ways people like me work with the world.

"First, elemental magic. That's the oldest. It pulls directly from the earth, plants, water, animals, and so on. You're not summoning anything new; you're persuading what's already there to move differently. To use an analogy you will understand, think of the druids.

"You are saying you're a D&D character?" David said, part joke and part his need to lighten his own tension.

Erin gave him a look that implied she wanted no more interruption.

"Second, sigil and mathematical work. You work with patterns; geometric, numeric, symbolic, that shape how power flows. Think of it as writing equations on reality. Most people are familiar with sigils and sacred geometry."

I let my eyes flick down toward the floorboards, thinking of a few old scars in the lab.

"Third, enchantments on items," I went on. "Imbuing. You bind effects into objects, iron, wood, stone, copper, so they remember what you've told them. Make a blade stay sharp, a door stay locked, and so on."

"And fourth, the most common," I said, "You draw from the ambient energy that's everywhere, life, emotion, movement, heat. The air isn't empty. Someone trained can pull from that and shape it directly."

Erin's brow furrowed. "Which one did you use out there?"

"A bit of the fourth," I said. "I channeled from the energy around us and pushed it at the fetchling. Most people would call it a spell, but I always hated that term."

"Can anyone learn that?" David asked. His tone held equal parts hope and dread.

"Some of it can be taught," I said. "Not everyone is adept. It's like music. Most people can learn a few notes, maybe carry a tune. A few can conduct a symphony. And some should never be trusted near an instrument. The only magic that most anyone can do with training is sigil work. It's not that simple though. You need to understand mathematical properties, physics, and be trained. You can't just copy a sigil and expect it to work. It's far more complex."

Erin sat back slowly, digesting. The word magic hadn't broken her; it had given her another problem to solve.

"And how long," she asked quietly, "have you been doing this?"

I studied the amber in my glass. "Long enough that I stopped counting centuries."

That landed like dropped glass. Casey's mouth opened. David made a strangled sound that might have been a laugh in a kinder moment. Erin's eyes narrowed further, running odds her rational mind refused to accept. Charlie said nothing. He'd suspected pieces of this for years, but not the whole portrait. He took it in, steady as ever.

Casey broke the silence, wielding humor like a shield. "Okay. Say I buy that for the sake of argument. What now? Do we call an exorcist? Animal control? The mayor?"

"No," I said. "You go about your lives. Keep your routines. Don't go into the woods alone. And don't talk about this outside this room."

David frowned. "You're serious."

"Very."

Erin's voice softened. "You're still holding something back."

"I'm always holding something back," I said.

Her eyes flashed. "I'm not joking."

"Neither am I," I answered. "Some knowledge isn't a gift, Erin. It spreads. It pulls things toward it. You don't want that kind of attention."

Rain began tapping at the windows. Then harder. The gutters whispered. The steady sound filled the spaces our words couldn't reach.

Charlie poured himself a small measure of Glen Garioch. "If these things are scouts," he said, "someone sent it. You know who?"

"I don't," I said. "Not yet."

"But you're going to find out."

"Yes."

He nodded once, satisfied. Soldiers understand missions, even when they belong to someone else.

Casey blew out a breath. "I vote we call it a night before my brain melts."

"That's the first sensible thing you've said since the cornhole tournament," I said, managing a thin smile.

She smirked back. "You wish."

David looked up, hopeful and hollow at the same time. "You mean we're just supposed to pretend this didn't happen?"

"Pretend? No," I said. "Ignore, yes. Let it settle. Fear feeds these things. Don't give them a feast."

"Awesome," he muttered. "I'll just feed it a buffet of anxiety."

Casey patted his arm. "You're a ten-course meal, sweetheart."

The laughter that followed was thin but real, like the first breath after choking. For now, it was enough.

They stayed another hour despite promising not to. No one wanted to be the first to step back outside. Small talk tried to paper over the tremor underneath and mostly failed. The air in the house felt charged, humming with the echo of whatever power I'd drawn earlier. None of them mentioned it, but I saw the hair on their arms standing on end.

When they finally stood to leave, the clock had slipped past midnight. The storm had settled into a mist that turned the streetlights into pale halos.

After we walked Erin and Casey back to their yard and made sure doors were locked and alarms set, David lingered just inside my doorway.

"You saved me," he said quietly.

I shook my head. "You weren't in danger, not the way you think. Fetchlings don't kill. They probe. But if it had stayed much longer, you'd have had a headache that made death look polite."

He blinked, unsure if I was joking. "That's oddly comforting."

"It's the best kind of comfort I offer," I said, giving him a quick wink.

A small, wobbly laugh escaped him, and then he stepped out into the mist.

Charlie waited until David's taillights disappeared. "You sure about keeping them close?" he asked.

"They're safer near me than out there alone," I said.

He studied my face, jaw working. "Then I'm sticking close too. Someone's got to watch your back."

"I'll drink to that."

He snorted. "You'll drink to anything."

I watched his pickup until it vanished down the street, the house going hollow around me. The wards, old and buried deep in the mortar, thrummed low and uneven.

I finished my scotch, set the glass beside the astrolabe, and turned toward the dark window. The yard looked normal again. Peaceful, even; a peace that knew how to hide its teeth.

I stood there longer than I meant to, watching the rain illuminated under the streetlight. The neighborhood had settled back into its careful quiet, a silence that felt deliberate, like the world holding its breath. Somewhere, despite the rain, a sprinkler sputtered to life next door, ticking steadily along. Domestic noise, layered over the memory of a shriek that didn't belong.

The world is very good at painting over cracks.

I shrugged on a jacket, grabbed a small flashlight, and stepped outside. The drizzle hung more than it fell, silver in the light. The grass slicked under my boots as I crossed the yard toward the trees where the fetchling had appeared. It had stood just beyond the line of my wards the first time I saw it, as if it knew where they were.

The air cooled as I left my manicured lawn and stepped under the first fringe of the woods. The cold felt wrong, not night-cool, but emptied, like something had drawn the warmth out and forgotten to return it. The mist thickened, swirling like breath hanging in the air. I swept the flashlight beam across the ground. No tracks, but I expected that.

Something brushed the edge of my awareness, soft and steady like a low note behind the ears. Not sound, exactly. Pressure. I crouched and laid a hand on the damp earth. The energy there was fractured, disturbed. The fetchling's passage had left a residue, an oily distortion I hadn't felt in decades. There were remnants of a portal, briefly opened and already closed.

I'd seen this same smear of distortion in Wales, when the Church had sent us to deal with druids who'd been less extinct than advertised. The Vatican had tried to harness that corruption once in an artifact that we carried with us, with predictable disaster. I'd hoped those days were finished.

The woods themselves felt wrong; too still. On any other night there would be frogs, owls, the rustle of something small going about its business. Now: nothing. Just the drip of water from leaves and my own breathing.

I turned back toward the house. From here, it looked small and fragile, a lantern set down on an empty field.

I'd grown careless. Time dulls sharp edges, quiet years teach you to mistake routine for safety. I had convinced myself that a little patch of Ohio could stay untouched if I just wanted it badly enough. Complacency is an old man's disease, and I have been old a very long time. If there in one lesson I have learned in my life, there's always a bill.

I knew the fetchling hadn't come at random. But why here? Was I being watched? Were my wards being measured? Was I a target, or just a particularly interesting flare on someone's map?

I went back inside. I locked the sliding door out of habit. The wards would hold for now.

The world strains, collapses, knits itself back together. The Veil frays, then tightens again. Every cycle shorter, every repair more threadbare. We patch what we can, but someday patchwork won't be enough.

I poured another half measure of Glen Garioch and stood by the window, watching water drip from the eaves. Streetlight pooled across the drive in soft gold, as if nothing in the world had shifted. But I could feel it: a faint hum running through the bones of things.

I turned away and headed for the basement. The air cooled with each step, stone and metal and dust wrapping around me like an old cloak. My lab waited in its usual organized chaos: books open to half-finished translations, relics laid out for repair, a long oak table scarred by years of experiments. On the back wall hung maps, old parchment, new printouts, each speckled with pins and lines. Breaches. Sightings. Failures.

I lit a lamp. On the workbench sat a shallow bowl etched with runes fine enough to vanish if you didn't know where to look. I poured water into it and traced the rim with one finger. The surface rippled, then stilled, then shimmered. I leaned in to inspect the water. The shimmer pulsed a few times and then weakened and vanished. It should have been a steady rhythm like a heartbeat. It should not have flared out. That was enough. The Veil here was thinner than I'd allowed myself to believe. Something was pressing against it, testing the seams. It was enough for tonight, but this was a clarion call and I had work to do.

Upstairs, the rain eased. Silence settled again. The wards hummed with a steady ease.

I went back to the living room, turned off the lamp, and let the dark take the room. My reflection ghosted in the window, the same face I'd worn since the Norman hills, barely touched by the centuries that had buried my friends. Outside, Centerville slept in its tidy grid.

I lifted what remained of the scotch, let it burn a path down my throat, and murmured to the empty room, "Tomorrow, then. We'll see what you are."

8

Geometry, Lectures, and the Rabbi (Ohio, Present)

Sleep didn't so much end as run out of excuses. By five-thirty I was by the window with a mug of cooling coffee, watching fog thread between the houses. The streetlamps glowed in the mist, each one a soft halo. For a moment it almost passed for peaceful, if I ignored the vibration under the floorboards where the wards pulsed reminding me of the day before.

I should've reinforced them years ago. Comfort dulls instincts, and quiet years teach you lies about safety. Last night proved I'd been coasting on luck.

A knock came at six. Three taps, steady.

Charlie.

He stood on the porch in jeans and a windbreaker, the half-awake squint of a man already regretting his morning. Two steaming cups from Boston Stoker hung from one hand.

"Morning, Jimmy," he said. "Avery says hello. Apparently, you tip like you're trying to buy the place. You're making me look bad."

"She exaggerates," I said, taking the cup.

"You're single-handedly funding her next semester. They're gonna name a table after you."

"I appreciate good service."

"Good service? She hands you caffeine and smiles."

"It's sacred work."

He chuckled and stepped inside, giving the room a slow engineer's sweep. His eyes, as usual, paused on the sword above the mantle, the morning light catching the edge in a silver thread.

He lifted his cup. "So. Ready to see what crawled through your yard?"

"Ready as I'll ever be."

Outside, the world smelled of wet dirt and that thin, clean scent you only get at daybreak. Rain clung to the grass, each droplet turning the first gray light into glitter. Charlie crouched near the trees where David sighted the creature at the end of my yard.

"See this?" he said. "Grass is brown in a perfect ring. Not burnt, just dead. Like something boiled the life out of it."

I crouched beside him. "Residue. Energy discharge. Portals push and pull more than whatever steps through."

He shot me a look. "That thing can teleport?"

"No. Someone, or something, brought it here. And the residual energy is too strong for a single visit. It's been here before. Longer than I realized."

He frowned. "You're saying David didn't scare it off? He spooked it while it was working."

"Exactly. Fetchlings linger only when they're gathering information. This one was keeping an eye on me. The question is, why? And for who?"

Charlie stood. "Fantastic. Monster stealth missions in suburbia. Sounds like a Netflix pitch." He glanced around the yard. "Any suspects?"

"That's the problem," I said. "It's old magic. Precise. Controlled. I haven't seen this kind of work in a very long time, and there aren't many left who could pull it off. Most of them are bones and dust."

He snapped a few photos with his phone. "If I hadn't been here last night, I'd swear someone spilled bad weed-killer."

"I'd prefer that."

He pocketed his phone. "You going to check the park? You mentioned the Wendigo being on edge. I'm guessing that's connected."

"It is. But not today. I need a couple days to prep, wards, readings, a full sweep. And my home protections need reinforcement."

"Like magical booby traps?"

"No. I'd rather not vaporize the Amazon driver. More like detection, think a security camera that notices intent instead of faces."

"You can read minds?" Charlie asked, half-joking, half-wary.

"No. Magic can't pierce minds. It can read the energy people give off. Like a bouncer watching a drunk get twitchy."

"A magical bouncer," he said with a laugh. "Fine. Just make sure I'm on the damn guest list."

He circled toward the drainage ditch and crouched again. "Hold up."

A smear of mud glinted in the morning light, metallic, wrong. He scraped a bit into a vial he had brought with him.

"Smells like someone soldered something," he said. "I've been around enough flux fumes to know that scent anywhere."

"You can smell solder?"

"Not the solder, rosin flux. Burning pine and metal." He looked at me. "You don't smell that oily tang?"

I knelt beside him. The residue shimmered with an iridescent streak. The smell was acrid. "That isn't man-made. It's the echo of the portal magic. Corrupted. I haven't seen this signature since..." I paused. "Since Wales, a very long time ago."

He capped the vial. "I can get this tested. Soil chemistry, spectrometry. Real science."

"Wright-Patt?"

He nodded. "Still know a few people at AFRL. Everyone jokes about Hangar 18 and aliens, but the truth's stranger. A few artifacts are stored there, Nazi hoards mostly. Metal fragments, carved bones, objects that didn't match any known cultures. Ancient. Wrong. I'll see if this matches any of their signatures. Still have my clearances. Couldn't hurt."

We stood there a while, listening to the neighborhood wake. Garage doors hummed. A dog barked at nothing. Sprinklers whispered across lawns. The ordinary world pushing forward, unaware of the prior night's drama.

Charlie tossed his empty cup in the bin and straightened. "I'll send the photos later. We'll hit the park in a few days when you are ready. Give you time to do your magic."

He glanced once more at the brown circle. "I've seen strange things on base, but last night?" He shook his head. "That was next level."

He nodded once, a quiet salute. "See you soon. Try not to let any more elves or goblins in the yard."

"No promises."

After he left, I started planning my next steps and what I was going to need. I spent the morning in the lab, checking tools I hadn't touched in years, reorganizing shelves, shaking off my complacency.

By mid-afternoon the fog had burned off. The street looked ordinary again. People going on about their business where their biggest care was spaghetti or pork chops for dinner.

I poured another coffee and sat on the porch, staring at the browned ring. Even in daylight it looked wrong. Not burned. Not diseased. Empty. As if life had been erased from a single point outward.

My phone buzzed. I checked the number, but didn't recognize it. I decided to live dangerously and answer anyway.

"Hello," I answered.

"James." The Israeli accent was unmistakable, Rabbi Eliyahu Ben-Ami. "I hope I am not catching you at a bad time."

"Never a bad time, Rabbi."

"Excellent, because I am in town and I would love to see you," he said with a warmth that came through even on the phone. "I was invited to lecture at the University of Dayton this Thursday. Once I accepted, I called. Old friends are like a garden; they must be maintained and properly tended."

"You have interesting timing," I said. "A portal opened here two nights ago. and the Wendigo at Grant Life has been restless for weeks. It isn't coincidence. We can go over all of it in person, but if you're here, I could use your advice and experience."

He paused long enough for traffic to murmur through the receiver. "I am afraid it is no coincidence either. We have noticed peculiarities at the Mount of Olives as well. We had no idea it extended elsewhere. We have much to discuss it seems."

"That is troubling," I sighed. "I don't know what it all means, though I intend to find out."

"Come to the lecture Thursday," he said. "I will leave your name at the door. Please bring friends, it doesn't help the reputation to speak to a half-full room. We can discuss after."

"I'll be there. Let's do dinner after. Thank you for calling. It is great to hear from you."

"Your dinner invitations usually mean I eat like a king. I will see you Thursday," he said warmly. "Shalom, my friend."

The line went silent.

Rabbi Eliyahu Ben-Ami was Shomrei ha'Adamah ha'Nitzchit. Keeper of the Eternal Earth, the most recent heir to an order older than Rome's aqueducts. Their work mapped the deep geometries that held the Veil taut, centered beneath Jerusalem, and laid down long before the Second Temple fell.

I first met members of the order in the 1300s, when plague and panic tore through Jerusalem and the Watch sent me to investigate rumors of sorcery accelerating the Black Death. The Keepers weren't warriors. They were listeners, engineers of resonance and proportion. Their magic was like architecture, exact and quiet. They changed my understanding of balance, taught me of the Veil, of what guardianship meant.

Eliyahu carried that same calm certainty. If he said things were shifting, the world was sliding toward trouble.

I called Charlie. He answered instantly.

"If this is about the soil sample..."

"It's not. A dear friend of mine is in town. He's a rabbi from Jerusalem and he is giving a lecture on Thursday. I'd like you to join me."

"A lecture? I get to spend my Thursdaynight listening to a speech on religion? I don't think I'll sleep until then in anticipation," Charlie deadpanned. "Is he normal? Or like you?"

I laughed at the quip, "It's not religion exactly. His specialty blends the arcane with math, symbolism, physics, architecture, and stuff. And I wouldn't call the rabbi normal. He is exceptional, and I'll let you judge for yourself. I guarantee you'll like him, and there'll be booze, probably."

Charlie paused. "I'm in. If only to learn more about all this mumbo jumbo and for the meal."

"Great, meet me here and we'll take my car."

"Sounds good," Charlie said. "Want me to loop in David?"

"Great idea. The invitation was open."

He sighed. "I swear man, if this turns into a three-hour theology lecture, you're buying dinner."

"I always buy," I said. "Oakwood Club?"

"That'll soften the blow."

After we hung up, the sunlight tipped toward copper. For a moment, the brown ring in the grass shimmered, as if something unseen had lingered, watching.

I finished my coffee and got to work.

9

Plagues, Demons, and the Wall (Jerusalem, 1348)

The year was 1348, and Arnaut and I entered Jerusalem with a quiet purpose under the guise of physicians aiding Pilgrims struck by the Black Death. In truth, we'd been sent to investigate a healer rumored to offer curatives for the plague, elixirs whispered to be powered by forbidden magic.

The Mamluks ruled the city with efficient cruelty, suspicious of any foreigner but too desperate to refuse help. They allowed us limited movement through markets by day and hostels by night, warning us to keep clear of mosques and official quarters.

The plague had reached Jerusalem months before, carried by traders and rumor. It clung to fur, cloth, rats, and fear. By the time we entered through Damascus Gate, even the soldiers posted there wore scarves over their faces. The air smelled of lime and rot. The scent was made worse by the thick smoke of burning pyres.

The streets were narrower than I remembered from a previous visit. Stone walls exhaled heat back into the evening. Water gutters carried runoff and worse. Spices and questionable meat hit my tongue before we even reached the bazaar.

"Still smells better than Paris," Arnaut said, pulling down his scarf with a grin. His Norman accent just audible after a couple hundred years of traveling.

"At least here the incense has purpose."

"Paris never had this many flies," I said.

He swatted one. "Paris never had this many saints either. Throw a stone, you hit a shrine. A fine way to part naïve Pilgrims from their coin."

We passed undertakers pushing a cart of shrouded bodies. The call to prayer drifted from a nearby minaret, low and haunting. Two Eastern Christian nurses sprinkled vinegar along the stones while murmuring blessings. No one held another's gaze for long. Fear was as contagious as the plague.

Our contact met us in a hospice near the Church of St. Anne, one of the few places still open to foreigners. He was a thin Syrian deacon with sunken eyes and the tremor of a man who hadn't slept through a night in months.

"You came from the north?" he asked.

"From Antioch," Arnaut said, though we'd cut in from Cyprus to avoid questions.

"That road carries more graves than travelers," the deacon murmured. "They say a healer walks the lower quarter, curing some and killing others. He sells black powders that drive sickness away, or so he claims. Those who buy seem to die quicker."

"What do you know of him?" I asked.

"His irises are black," the deacon whispered. "Black like ink spilled across the eye. And he moves wrong. Too fast. Like a puppet jerked by an invisible hand."

Arnaut smiled. "Then we'll recognize him."

"You won't be the first to try," the deacon warned. "May you have better luck."

We left before curfew and headed south toward the Khan al-Zeit market. Brass trays caught the last of the light. Vendors shouted over the noise, selling what they claimed were exotic wares from the corners of earth. Most of the time the goods were nothing more than cheap trinkets designed to part the foolish from their coin. As we walked, a camel coughed behind a spice cart and a swarm of flies rose in a single dark wave.

Arnaut pushed through the crowd like a ship through water, broad-shouldered, sword visible, subtle as a hammer.

We stopped at an apothecary's stall. The old man behind it had milk-white eyes but worked mortar and pestle with practiced precision. Bundles of herbs hung from the canopy. Jars labeled in careful Arabic lined the shelves.

I asked in halting Arabic, "Have you seen a physician selling powders for the sickness?"

He spat. "A dog from the south, they say. He sells the breath of death in little bottles. Men who buy die laughing."

"Laughing?" Arnaut echoed.

"Like they've seen paradise," the man said. "Or remembered it too late."

When he reached for a jar, his sleeve slid back, revealing a trembling wrist streaked with yellow bruises. He caught my glance and gave a grim smile. "Fear not, effendi. God has taken my measure. I only owe the balance."

He turned again, and something behind him moved. A shadow lagged a heartbeat behind his body, twitching as if unsure of its shape.

Arnaut's hand dropped to his sword. "Back," he murmured.

The old man stiffened. His mouth opened, but only a hiss escaped. His skin blistered black from the jaw upward. He clawed once at his chest, then collapsed over the counter, crumbling into gray ash.

Screams erupted. We slipped into the nearest alley before the Mamluk patrol arrived.

Arnaut brushed ash from his glove. "You think that was our physician?"

"No," I said. "Too easy."

The Mughrabi Quarter lay southwest of the Haram al-Sharif, pressed against the outer wall of the Temple Mount. Narrow lanes wound between low stone houses. Roofs were tied together by beams for shade. Pilgrims from the Maghreb lived beside traders from Damascus. Smoke from olive oil lamps mixed with the sweet scent of dates frying in honey.

Even with plague gnawing at the city, it lived. Merchants shouted prices. Women bargained for bread. Copper rang as smiths worked in open stalls. Beneath the chaos, something older pulsed; the rhythm of a city that refused to die.

Arnaut muttered, "If hell has a bazaar, this is it."

He wasn't wrong. But beneath the noise I sensed something else, a dense, ancient presence folded over itself like hammered gold. A nexus of power. Whatever hunted here was bold or desperate.

We asked after the "black-eyed healer." Most spat and hurried away. One old woman whispered that she had seen him near the quarter's well.

"He preys on the desperate," she said. "Stay away from that shaytan."

She hobbled off before we could ask more.

Arnaut checked his sword. He always checked his sword first. "Ready?"

I nodded, though not fully convinced this wouldn't get us killed.

The well was easy to find. A half-circle of people gathered around a figure in dark robes, face half-shrouded. His voice was soft and raspy as he passed out tiny vials. Buyers paid quickly and retreated faster.

Arnaut brushed my arm. "Do you see it?"

I nodded. The man's eyes were ink-black circles. His movements snapped too fast, too sharp, like joints wired wrong.

Arnaut approached as the last buyer stepped back. Using the Arabic honorific for physician, he said, "Tabib, the governor requests confirmation of your credentials."

The figure cocked his head at an impossible angle. "I serve no governor," he said, voice thick and scratchy.

"That's unfortunate," Arnaut replied. "The governor serves eviction notices."

The figure laughed, a deep rasp and raised a hand to Arnaut.

Arnaut, never one to lean on diplomacy, lunged.

His blade sliced through cloth that burst into smoke. A swarm of flies and dust blew outward. Beneath it stood a gray-skinned thing with a slit for a mouth and black teeth gleaming like obsidian.

The crowd scattered.

"Demon," Arnaut growled. "It's mine."

"Wait..."

Too late. Arnaut struck. The creature caught the blade barehanded. Steel hissed like water on fire as the blade's sigils flared. I murmured a binding. Light rippled. The creature recoiled for a heartbeat, then laughed, a grinding sound that made my teeth ache, and fled into the alleys.

Arnaut shouted, "After it!"

We plunged into the maze of Jerusalem.

The demon fled with jerking speed, its shadow lagging behind like a delayed echo. Arnaut barreled forward, shouting for people to clear the way. Vendors dived aside. Grain spilled. Pots shattered underfoot.

We chased it through a butcher's lane where skinned lambs swayed on hooks. Blood and brine burned the air. Arnaut vaulted a cart and toppled a rack of cleavers.

"Arnaut!" I shouted. "Don't drive it into the crowd!"

He didn't slow.

We broke into a narrow passage stinking of indigo dye and animal fat. The demon seized a merchant by the throat, lifting him clean off the ground. That delay was all Arnaut needed. His sword flashed like a strip of white fire and sliced deep. Black ichor sprayed the walls. The severed arm writhed before shrinking to ash.

The merchant bolted, leaving a single sandal behind.

I tried again to unbind the creature. The spell fizzled.

"You cannot unbind what isn't tethered," the demon hissed. Its voice echoed from the stones.

Then it vanished again.

We chased it up a staircase wedged between two houses, emerging onto the rooftops. Jerusalem spread beneath us, gold in the fading light. The Dome of the Rock gleamed like a fallen sun. Smoke from cookfires drifted up.

The demon bounded across rooftops. Arnaut followed with reckless speed. Chickens scattered. Clay jars shattered.

At the final roof, the creature paused, then dropped from the edge.

Arnaut leapt after it, using a short incantation to slow his descent.

I reached the edge moments later and saw them below, in a narrow yard pressed against the retaining wall of the Haram. Homes leaned right up against the ancient stones. Fig trees twisted among the structures. Even half-buried, the Wall dominated everything, massive, seamless, humming with its own quiet.

I followed Arnaut's lead and leapt off the rooftop. We approached the demon and trapped his escape. The two of us in front, and the Wall to its back.

The demon turned and with its remaining hand, traced patterns along the base, leaving trails of oily light. The pressure in the air deepened, like the moment before a lightning strike.

"Stop!" I shouted. "You're trapped!"

It turned, neck twisting far past anything human. "All walls crack," it rasped. "Even those built from faith."

Arnaut charged. The demon swatted him aside. He rolled, bleeding, and rose again.

"Arnaut! Don't..."

The creature pressed its palms to the limestone. The symbols flared. The air tore open with a backward-sucked breath.

A rift bloomed gold and black.

"Stop!" I shouted again, but he was already moving.

Arnaut ran straight into the light.

For one heartbeat he stood there, haloed. Then he was gone. The rift folded closed.

Silence hit like a blow.

I sank to my knees. "You damned fool."

The Wall loomed above, calm and indifferent. I pressed my palm to the stone. It was cool, steady at first, but I sensed something reach out to me. A power that I didn't understand extended from the Wall and into my body. I gasped and fell back, falling to my knees. It was over as quick as it started, but left me momentarily puzzled and stunned.

I heard hurried footsteps approach, as I knelt there trying to capture my breath.

Four men emerged from the shadows. Their robes were rough. Their staffs bore copper emblems. They moved with quiet confidence.

The first spoke in clear Arabic. "What happened here?"

I hesitated then stood and faced them.

He raised a placating hand. "Don't worry. We're friends." He looked at the wall. "Though it seems we have arrived too late."

I let my weight rest against the stone. "Something tore a hole in the Wall. My friend followed it through."

His gaze shifted to the scorched ground. "You touched it?"

"I was close."

"You're lucky to be alive."

"Doesn't feel that way."

He inclined his head. "I am Yosef ben Moshe ha-Cohen. We are the Shomrei ha'Adamah ha'Nitzchit, the Keepers of the Eternal Earth."

I frowned. "The who?"

"Guardians of this ground," he said. "We tend what lies beneath the stones, and protect what is atop them."

His companions stood quiet, faces weathered. Yosef continued, "We sensed the disturbance. The ground trembled. The Veil shifts here more strongly than anywhere else."

"He went after it," I said, voice thin. "Straight through."

"Zeal burns faster than wisdom," Yosef said. "It lights the way but warms nothing."

The others traced patterns in the dust, murmuring prayers. The glow along the Wall faded.

"What was it?" I asked. "Demon?"

"Yes, and an ancient one." Yosef said. "Arrived here as a reflection of despair."

"And the rift?"

"Beyond the Veil. A mirror of creation. Few cross it whole."

"Could he survive?"

"We know little of the other side other than what comes through," Yosef said, attempting some small level of comfort. "Perhaps."

"That's not an answer."

"It's the honest one."

He studied me. "The Veil touched you. It will remember."

"What does that mean?"

"Come, we will explain. Night is falling, best not to be out after dark."

"Where?"

"Up," he said, nodding toward the Mount of Olives.

We walked from the Kotel up the slope. When we reached the base of the hill a young Keeper met us and handed out torches. I looked back, Jerusalem glimmered below, domes catching moonlight.

Halfway up, Yosef said, "The two places are the twin lungs of creation, and the Temple site is the heart. The Wall and the Mount. One breathes faith, the other memory."

I was full of questions and concerns. I kept silent for now and kept walking.

Ancient graves lined the slope. Names faded. Stones cracked. The moon silvered them until they seemed to float.

I took a break from my thoughts and looked around as we walked. "It's beautiful," I said.

"It should be," Yosef replied. "Every stone is a promise that life continues."

Near the crest, we reached a grove of ancient olive trees. A limestone slab lay half-hidden. Yosef brushed dust aside and pressed his palm to it. Hidden sigils flared to life. The slab split, revealing a stair spiraling down.

"You have a doorway under a cemetery?" I asked.

"The dead do not mind," Yosef replied.

The passage cooled as we descended. The chamber below was carved from living rock, quartz veins catching the torchlight. A dais sat at the center, surrounded by six shallow channels forming a stretched star.

"We no longer have access to our Temple. So we do our work and prayer here. This is sacred to us, but kept hidden so that we may not lose more than we already have," Yosef explained. "Few have stood where you are now. Even fewer for those that are not of our order."

"What are we..." I started to ask before Yosef cut me off.

"Please, silence. You were touched by the Veil this evening. I can sense its presence in you. You need to learn what has been given to you."

The Keepers set their copper-capped staffs into place. The channels glowed amber.

The stone behind Yosef rippled.

A figure emerged.

Clay, dust, and molten-gold veins shaped into a giant form. Eyes like embers.

I stepped back. "What is…"

"Peace," Yosef said. "He is an Earth Golem. A protector and our charge."

The golem's presence filled the chamber. Not monstrous, inevitable.

"He has stood here since the first covenant was sealed," Yosef said. "There are others across the world that are echoes of him."

The golem studied me. The air smelled of rain on stone.

A low resonance filled the chamber, pressing meaning into my thoughts.

"He asks why you're here," Yosef said.

"I don't think I had a choice."

The golem rumbled again. Yosef nodded. "He says grief and doubt anchor you."

"Anchor me? To what?" I asked. My confusion growing.

"Allow me to explain."

Under Yosef's guidance, I learned of the guardians across the world, stag, serpent, wind-spirit, anchors that held the Veil in place. He taught me the nature of the Veil, and how the things I had fought were intruders from the other side. That his order, and others, carried out the task of protecting those that kept the Veil in place.

"What you fought was drawn here by despair," Yosef said. "The Veil is strong, but it can be damaged. Plague thins the Veil. Death, corruption, fear, all act as a chisel. When cracks emerge, things come through."

"And what if it breaks?"

"The guardians exist to prevent that."

The golem stirred, its veins glowing brighter, then dimmed.

"Why show me this?" I asked.

"You're part of the pattern now," Yosef said. "The Veil touched you. It will find you again."

"I never asked for that."

"No one does," he said. "But the world rarely asks permission."

He handed me a clay tablet. Its concentric rings glowed faintly.

"It records tonight. If you return, it will know you."

The golem reached out, its massive hand hovering over my chest. Warmth spread through me.

"A mark of recognition," Yosef said. "Not ownership."

I felt the same power that had reached out to me at the Wall. This time not an intrusion, but a comfort, as if something aligned inside me. Then the chamber dimmed. The golem merged back into the stone.

Silence followed.

"You cannot chase your friend," Yosef said. "But you can guard the path he took."

"If he lives," I said, "I'll find him."

"And if not, you'll still find his purpose. You will now be welcome here. This place is a part of you, just as it is for us. You will always find a friend amongst us. You are marked, and we will remember."

We climbed back into the night. Graves gleamed pale. The city shimmered below.

"I'll pray for your friend," Yosef said. "Some who vanish aren't lost. They're on longer roads."

"I'll hold you to that."

He bowed and vanished back into the chamber.

I stood alone among the graves. The weight of Arnaut's disappearance settled like a stone. Somewhere beyond the Wall, beyond the Veil, he was gone.

But whatever took him wasn't finished.

And neither was I.

10

Math, Cheese, and the University (Ohio, Present)

Charlie parked his truck near the Humanities Building just as the church bells on Brown Street tolled seven. Through the windshield, I watched students drift toward the Kennedy Union ballroom, most checking phones, a few clutching coffee like lifelines.

"Remind me why we're doing this?" Charlie asked.

I pointed at the banner above the doors: **THE DIVINE RATIO: MATHEMAT-ICS AND THE ARCHITECTURE OF BELIEF.**

"Because that rabbi I told you about? He knows things. And right now, I need to know what he knows."

Charlie killed the engine. "So, we're crashing a lecture to interrogate a holy man about supernatural geometry."

"When you say it like that, it sounds weird."

"That's because it is weird." He climbed out, slamming the door. "But at this point, weird is the new normal."

David waved us down near the entrance, his "Hello my name is" sticker sitting crooked on his polo like it had tried to escape. "Got here early so no one steals the back-row outlets."

Charlie clapped his shoulder. "Always thinking about the escape route."

"I prefer 'latency optimization.'" David held up a plate. "Also, free cheese cubes."

Inside, the reception buzzed with academic small talk. Faculty drifted with plastic cups of wine, eager students peppered them with preloaded questions, and a few priests mingled at the edges, polite and curious.

Across the crowd, Rabbi Eliyahu Ben-Ami stood slightly apart. Compact, stocky, black coat brushing his knees, wide-brimmed hat casting shadow across thoughtful features. His beard had the look of a man who trimmed it only when he remembered. The tzitzit at his belt moved slightly when he breathed. His rectangular glasses caught the light like polished steel.

He spotted me and broke into a warm smile. "James Crable. Eizeh kef lirot otcha!"

"It's good to see you too, Rabbi. Welcome to Dayton."

He clasped both of my hands. "The world still needs men who remember how to listen."

Charlie extended a hand. "Charlie Mitchell. Crable's long-suffering friend. If he invited me, it's because he needs a witness or a ride."

The rabbi brightened. "Then you are performing a mitzvah already."

"Looking forward to your talk, but I should warn you," Charlie said, "I'm a skeptic by reflex."

"The best kind of believer," Eliyahu replied.

David stepped forward. "Shalom Aleichem, Rabbi."

"Aleichem Shalom!" Eliyahu's smile widened. "Delightful. A member of the tribe."

David laughed. "My mom always gets on me for not being a better member, but yes."

"Your mother is a wise woman. Jewish mothers are undefeated in this area."

An usher guided the crowd inside. David handed me an extra napkin like we were heading into a picnic rather than a lecture.

The Kennedy Union auditorium tried its best, dark wood paneling and a cross high above a projection screen. Students filled the front rows, notebooks open. We took the three seats David had defended in the back, Charlie on the aisle, David in the center, thumb hovering over his phone.

Eliyahu began without notes.

"In every age," he said, "we ask the same question in different tongues: Why does the universe make sense?"

A professor in the second row leaned forward, pen poised. Eliyahu advanced to a diagram of the Vesica Piscis, two circles overlapping, forming an almond shape between them.

"The Greeks sought harmony through number. The Hebrews sought covenant through word."

Charlie's knee started bouncing. His thinking tell. I'd seen it when we played poker and held a mediocre hand.

"Both chased the same thing. Proportions. The balance between chaos and order."

The rabbi clicked to Fibonacci spirals, then cathedral blueprints. Each image built on the last, patterns emerging like a proof.

"Physics names it frequency." Wave-interference patterns filled the screen. "The mystics call it nigun, a vibration of the soul."

Charlie leaned in a bit more.

"Science and scripture are not enemies. They reflect the same light from opposite mirrors."

The rabbi moved to a slide of the rose window at Chartres. Colored light fractured across the screen, geometric perfection rendered in medieval glass.

"This window is a prayer in geometry. Each curve an equation of devotion. When sunlight passes through, matter and meaning become one."

David's chomping on his cheese earned a glare from Charlie who seemed to hang on every word. The lip smacking had taken Charlie out of his focus.

The rabbi walked us through golden ratios in Gothic arches, harmonic proportions in Hebrew letters, resonance patterns that appeared in everything from music to molecular bonds. Calm and unhurried, he spoke like someone explaining something simple but profound.

After an hour he wrapped up. The room sat in stillness for a beat before applause broke out.

As he stepped from the podium a crowd descended, professors, grad students, several priests. He met each one with patient attention, listening more than speaking. We waited near the back.

"He's like a rock star," Charlie muttered. "If engineers had this kind of charisma, we'd run the world."

"Give it a few centuries."

When the space finally cleared, Eliyahu waved us over.

"Now," he said, "someone promised me a proper Dayton dinner."

David grinned. "Oakwood Club. It'll convert you faster than theology."

Eliyahu laughed. "When you eat and are satisfied, you bless the Lord. Lead the way."

We stepped into the cool Ohio night. Streetlamps glowed amber along Brown Street as cars hummed through the dark.

The Oakwood Club smelled like money and tradition, dark wood paneling that had probably been there since Eisenhower, brass fixtures that needed polishing, and steak on every table. The kind of place where the waiters knew your drink order and acted offended if you changed it.

Our waiter materialized. "Mr. Crable. The usual table?"

I hadn't been here in six months, but Ted never forgot. "Perfect. And surprise us with the wine. Something for old friends."

Charlie raised an eyebrow as we sat. "The usual table?"

"I may have been coming here since 1952."

"Of course you have."

Ted returned with a bottle of 2015 Château Lamothe de Haux. As we tasted it, Charlie turned to the rabbi.

"That talk about alignment and pattern, part of me wants to reverse-engineer it. The rest is suspicious I might succeed."

Eliyahu smiled behind his glass. "Geometry is law. In every ancient symbol, we find a map of power. Ignore the pattern, you fall through the cracks."

"So how does your order use this practically?"

"We study number, shape, letter. The world was built on those things. Every ward, every boundary, every crossing, it is structure and symbol. We simply apply that to improving our lives and the lives of others."

Charlie laughed. "Oh, that's all."

Our food arrived. Ribeye for Charlie and David, pan-fried trout for the rabbi, walleye for me, a personal favorite. We talked through the meal about sigils, sequences, and guardians. By the time the plates cleared, the conversation had become a shared current, Charlie and David offering their own stories, the rabbi folding them into the larger pattern.

Eventually I steered us toward what had been gnawing at me all week.

"I briefly mentioned on the phone some of my concerns. There's something wrong, but I can't put my finger on it." I told him about the fetchling, the Wendigo, the growing sense that something was pulling at the edges of reality.

Eliyahu set down his wine glass with deliberate care. "We have been sensing odd pulses in Jerusalem. Not an attack on the Veil, but as if it is being probed. Tested." His eyes met mine. "I don't think your experience is a coincidence."

The waiter appeared to clear plates. We waited until he'd gone.

"This isn't the place to go into detail," Eliyahu continued, "but we need to discuss this properly. Compare notes. My next lecture is not for another few days."

"Come to my house," I said. "Tomorrow, if you can. We'll have time to talk through everything."

"Excellent." He thanked the waiter in a voice shaped by Jerusalem, softened by London, rounded by New York.

I paid the bill and overtipped. Ted smiled like a proud father and gave a small bow of thanks.

Outside, the air smelled of damp pavement. Streetlights shimmered on the wet road.

"Tomorrow," Eliyahu said, "I will come to your home. We must look closely at what happened and see how this is all connected. Tonight, the world will keep its silence."

As he walked toward his car, Charlie muttered, "Man's got gravitas."

David nodded. "My mother would love him."

The next morning arrived soft and gray.

Coffee brewed in the kitchen when Charlie knocked, exactly on time, holding a cardboard tray.

"Backup supply."

We sat in the quiet for a while, both thinking about the coming day.

"I'm anxious about what Eliyahu has to say. He's part of something older. People who've watched and recorded longer than both of us have been alive."

Charlie grunted his version of agreement.

At ten, Eliyahu pulled into the driveway in a dark rental sedan. He stepped out with two books, one small and leather-bound, one older and heavier.

"A gift," he said, handing the smaller one to Charlie. "Cheshbon Elyon, the Divine Calculation. You might call it a primer for our teachings."

Charlie opened it reverently, flipped through pages dense with diagrams and translated Hebrew text. "Thank you."

We sat. Eliyahu accepted coffee before setting his book and a notepad on the table.

"Show me where you saw the creature," he said.

We led him into the yard.

The grass looked normal until you knew what to look for. Then the wrongness became obvious, the brown circle, the faint curl of dead petals, the way the air seemed thinner, like standing near a vacuum.

Eliyahu crouched and held his hand six inches above the ground. His fingers moved in a pattern I didn't recognize, small circles, pausing at certain points, testing. After a moment he stood, brushing his palms together.

"Not a simple crossing." His voice had changed, less professor, more diagnostician. "This is a gateway. Opened here, but powered elsewhere."

Charlie frowned. "Elsewhere like... hell?"

"Elsewhere like Earth. Just tuned differently." Eliyahu walked the circle's perimeter. "Like two radio stations on frequencies so close they bleed into each other. The Talmud speaks of Kelipot; shells of shadow that cling to the living world when balance breaks. We call the other side the Sitra Achra."

I knelt where the impression remained in the soil. "Someone tore this open. Didn't bother cleaning up after."

"Which means they're either arrogant or desperate." Eliyahu looked toward the tree line. "The Wendigo you mentioned. It lives near here?"

"Few miles. A local park and nature reserve."

"I believe that the balance is shifting faster than I feared." He turned back to the circle. "When the barrier doesn't break cleanly, it frays. What crosses through carries traces of the other side. It warps them."

"That would explain why the fetchling felt wrong," I said. "Not just dangerous. Corrupted."

"Precisely. This required intent and power. And whoever did this wasn't worried about covering their tracks."

Back inside, I spread a map of Centerville across my dining table; ley lines hidden as utility routes, nodes marked as ordinary trees, intersections where the fabric wore thin.

Eliyahu pulled the map closer, fingers tracing intersections. His eyes widened slightly.

"Extraordinary." He looked up at me. "This mirrors Jerusalem. Not the modern city, the Second Temple layout. Same ratios, smaller scale."

Charlie moved to the other side of the table. "You're saying Centerville, Ohio has the same geometric pattern as ancient Jerusalem?"

"Not the same. The same type." Eliyahu pointed to Grant Park. "The center lies here, yes? Where you feel the strongest resonance?"

I nodded.

"In Jerusalem, that would be the Temple Mount." He traced outward. "These nodes would align with the Gates. Creation prefers symmetry. When sacred space is built, intentionally or by memory, it follows certain patterns."

Charlie grabbed his notebook, started sketching ratios and angles. "If I'm following this... it's like a CAD design. Stress points in a load-bearing structure." He paused, pen hovering. "God, I'm actually trying to solve this."

"That is wisdom beginning," Eliyahu said quietly. "We do not destroy imbalance. We rewrite it. The question is not whether the pattern exists. The question is: what happens when someone breaks it?"

The implications settled over us like fog.

"If someone's tearing holes in the Veil," Charlie said slowly, "and the Veil follows geometric patterns..."

"Then they're not attacking random points," I finished. "They're targeting the structure itself."

Eliyahu nodded. "And if enough stress points fail, the entire pattern collapses."

A few hours later, the map lay crowded with notes. Empty coffee mugs had turned to empty wine glasses over the morning and afternoon. When we felt there was nothing else to learn based on what we had at the moment, Eliyahu gathered his things.

At the door, he rested a hand on my shoulder. "You've carried this burden alone for a long time. Perhaps it is not yours alone now."

I glanced at Charlie. "I'm starting to think so."

Eliyahu smiled. "Tomorrow, we begin the real work."

Charlie watched his car disappear into mist. "For a man in a hat and tassels, he makes a hell of a lot of sense."

"Most prophets do. Just not right away."

He raised his glass with one last swallow left. "To patience, and not being vaporized by ancient geometry."

"Cheers," I said. "Best prayer I've heard all week."

11

Stones, Sigils, and the Corruption (Ohio, Present)

Charlie's truck skidded into my driveway at 7:05 AM, five minutes late, which for Charlie bordered on the supernatural.

He climbed out carrying a cardboard tray of coffees, eyes bloodshot, a slight slump to his shoulders. The kind of look he got when a problem had him by the throat and wouldn't let go.

"I know how they're doing it," he said, shoving a cup into my hands.

"Good morning to you too."

"The book Rabbi Eliyahu gave me. I was up until three reading it." He followed me inside without waiting for an invitation. "There's a whole section on prime numbers as structural elements of reality. Like the universe runs on code, and primes are the syntax."

"Dangerous bedtime reading."

"You have no idea. I had dreams about spirals." He took a long drink, grimaced like the coffee had gone cold despite the heat. "But that's not the important part. The important part is the patterns. The way the book describes reality-binding through mathematical sequences. Jimmy, it matches what we saw in your backyard. And I think I know how they're breaking the Veil."

He set his coffee down on my counter and pulled out the book, fingers rifling through pages. "See, it's not just theory. There's a whole section on prime numbers as structural elements of reality. Like the universe runs on code, and primes are the syntax."

He turned book to show me a page, text surrounding a geometric diagram. "See this? It's describing how reality maintains coherence through prime-number intervals. Every fundamental force, every stable structure, it all reduces to prime ratios."

I studied the diagram. The pattern was familiar. Too familiar.

"Now look at this." He pulled out his phone and swiped to a photo showing the circle in my backyard, the dead grass, the impression in the soil. "The spacing between the distortion points. Jimmy, they're hitting every seventh interval."

"Seven is prime."

"Exactly. And seven is the first prime that creates instability when you break it. It's not random chaos. It's surgical. They're not smashing the Veil open. They're finding the load-bearing primes and corrupting them one by one."

"Welcome to the deep end."

A sedan turned the corner and glided to the curb. Rabbi Eliyahu stepped out in full black wool despite the heat, looking perfectly comfortable while I was already sweating through my shirt. Long coat, dark hat, beard going gray at the edges. The tzitzit swayed as he walked.

"Good morning," he said, accepting a coffee.

"Late summer heat in Ohio doesn't get the press it deserves"

"I feel like I am in the Negev." He glanced at Charlie. "Still reading?"

"Finished it. Twice."

"Then you're on your way."

"To where?"

Eliyahu smiled. "To see if the math holds."

"OK, let's head out. I'll drive," I told them.

We piled into my car and the AC fought a losing battle with the humidity. I rolled down the block slowly, the smell of cut grass heavy in the air. August in Ohio, the kind where the air sits on your chest and the cicadas drone so loud you feel it in your teeth.

The Garden Ninja was out. No surprise. Black clothes, straw hat, shears flashing as she worked her flowerbeds with the precision of a surgeon. Not a weed in sight. Not a blade of grass out of place.

"There she is," Charlie said. "Our neighborhood enigma."

"You ever talk to her?" I asked.

"Once. I said good morning. She nodded. That was the whole conversation."

Eliyahu leaned forward, watching her through the window. His expression shifted, subtle but noticeable.

As we passed, she looked up. Not casual. Deliberate. Her eyes were green, sharp, and locked right on us for two full seconds before she went back to her pruning.

"You see that?" Charlie asked.

"I felt it," Eliyahu said quietly.

"Felt what?"

"The soil around her. It hums."

"Hums how?"

"Like it's listening to her," the rabbi said, settling back in his seat.

I watched her in the rearview mirror as we pulled away. She'd gone back to her pruning, but something about her posture had changed. More alert. Like she'd registered our attention and filed it away for later consideration.

"She's been working that garden since I moved in ten years ago. Every day. Same black clothes, same precision. I always thought she was just obsessive."

"Perhaps," Eliyahu said, and let that hang.

"She keeps our property values up," I said. "And who am I to judge a little eccentricity."

Eliyahu said nothing, but his eyes stayed on the rearview mirror longer than necessary.

When we arrived at Grant Park the air felt cooler. The trees arched overhead, old oaks and maples weaving together into a ceiling of green. The smell shifted from suburban lawn to damp earth and creek water.

Ray's truck sat crooked near the trailhead, one wheel up on the curb.

We parked and stepped into the shade. The cicadas thinned out. Water murmured somewhere ahead.

"This place always feels like it's watching," Charlie said, scanning the trees.

"It is," I said.

"That's comforting."

The path opened onto the Reynolds foundation, two brick chimneys standing in the grass like oversized gravestones. The air here felt heavier, thick with age and the weight of things long forgotten. Not bad. Just old.

Eliyahu set his coffee on a rock and pulled out a leather pouch. From it he drew ten smooth stones, each one carved with symbols I didn't recognize. He placed them in a circle, spacing them with the kind of precision that suggested measurement without tools.

Charlie crouched beside him. "Those marks, are those equations?"

"Older than equations," Eliyahu said. "But close enough."

"And the spacing." Charlie squinted, measuring distances with his eyes. "That's Fibonacci. Or close to it."

"Very close." The rabbi adjusted one stone a fraction of an inch. "The ratios that shape galaxies also shape this grove. When they weaken, balance fails. These restore the pattern."

I touched one of the stones. It was warm, and it vibrated faintly under my fingers. "How old are these?"

"Old enough that no one remembers who carved them." He finished the circle and murmured something under his breath. Not Hebrew. Not quite language.

The cicadas stopped. The breeze died. For three seconds, nothing moved. Then the world exhaled.

Charlie blinked. "Did the ground just..."

"Yes," Eliyahu said. "The Veil runs through here. We've aligned one node, but something's pushing back."

"Pushing from where?"

"Beneath." He studied the circle, frowning. "It'll hold. But not forever."

We followed the trail toward the creek. Sunlight broke through the canopy in patches, and the sound of water grew louder.

"This is where it watches," I said.

Charlie slowed. "The Wendigo?"

"Yes."

"Great. Nothing ominous about that."

The creek appeared, silver water curling over smooth stones. The air was ten degrees cooler here, and it smelled like minerals and wet leaves.

Eliyahu stopped at the water's edge. "The spirit, it warns of imbalance?"

"It just started."

"Then we need to find out what is causing it."

Charlie knelt and dipped his hand in the water. "Cold. Way colder than it should be."

"It knows we're here," I said.

Eliyahu closed his eyes for a moment, listening to something I couldn't hear.

We stood there in silence. The creek, the trees, the insects, everything moving in rhythm, like a song with no beginning.

The path continued along limestone shelves. Fossils curled in the rock, spirals frozen mid-turn.

"Look at this," Charlie said, crouching over a flat slab. "Perfect spiral. And the ratio..."

Eliyahu joined him. "Fibonacci again."

I knelt beside them. The spiral looked right, except it didn't. Something about it was wrong.

"This is amplified," I said. "The pattern's too strong."

"Someone carved this," Eliyahu said quietly. "Recently."

Charlie brushed dirt from the edges. "Why would someone carve math into limestone?"

"Not math," the rabbi said. "Magic. Dressed as math."

The breeze picked up. The creek's murmur deepened.

"You think this was intentional?" Charlie asked.

"I think someone knew exactly what they were doing."

Eliyahu pulled a small brass compass from his coat, Hebrew letters engraved around the rim. The needle spun wildly, then locked toward the clearing's center.

"There," he said.

We followed his line of sight. The ground looked normal, but when Charlie brushed away leaves, we found more carved stone.

"Foundations," he said.

"This is odd," Eliyahu said. "Too precise."

He whispered something and the carvings caught light, glowing faint blue for three seconds before fading.

Charlie stared. "What the hell was that?"

"Activation sigils," I said. "Someone's been here. Recently."

We knelt around the slab. The spiral carved into it wasn't Fibonacci. It drifted wrong, the pattern decaying as it turned inward.

"Every seventh rotation," Charlie said, tracing it with his finger. "The ratio breaks. On purpose."

"Corruption," Eliyahu said. "Someone bent this pattern to unbind instead of bind."

My stomach tightened. "The same signature as my house."

"Yes." The rabbi stood, brushing dust from his hands. "Whoever did this understands dissolution. And they've been probing the Veil."

Charlie pulled out his own notebook, the one he'd been filling with calculations all morning. "Why here?" he asked.

"Based on what we are seeing in Jerusalem I think they're testing multiple nodes," Eliyahu offered. "Looking for the weakest points in the global pattern."

"Or the strongest," I said quietly. "If you want to collapse a structure, you don't attack the weak points. You attack the supports."

Charlie pulled out his phone and started taking pictures. "Could this be connected to the disturbances at your place?"

"Has to be," I said. "Same fingerprint."

We spent twenty minutes measuring. Old-school pacing, depth estimates, angle calculations. Charlie documented everything with the methodical precision of a man who'd spent his career building systems that couldn't afford to fail.

"You know," Eliyahu said, watching us work, "it's oddly human to measure the immeasurable."

"If you can quantify it, you can model it," Charlie said, scribbling in his notebook.

"Then model this. Ten stones above, one spiral below. What number?"

Charlie looked up. "Eleven."

"And what is eleven?"

"A prime. One and one. Beginning and reflection."

"Exactly. Creation and mirror. But twisted," he tapped the corrupted spiral, "it becomes distortion."

The water upstream burbled louder, sudden and sharp.

Charlie closed his notebook with a look of slight confusion. "Someone used math to open something?"

"Math and magic. Subtle in some ways," I said. "But they left fingerprints doing it."

We rested on a fallen log. The forest breathed around us, patient and old.

"This place is hurt," I said. "Someone's been cutting into it like a surgeon. Except they're not trying to heal. Multiple small cuts though. They didn't want it to be obvious."

We turned back. The stone circle behind us hummed faintly, like a wound trying to close.

"I think Erin could help make sense of the data we collected," Charlie said as we reached the car.

"Good idea."

"She lives for pattern recognition. Show her what we found without context and she'll find the breaks."

Eliyahu nodded. "Truth prefers plain clothes."

Charlie sighed. "She's going to have questions."

"She always does."

"And then she's going to be pissed we didn't tell her sooner."

"Also true."

Back at the house, the air smelled like cedar and old paper. I put out wine, cheese, crackers. Charlie eyed the spread.

"No meat?"

"Rabbi Eliyahu's here. I'll put out meat or cheese, not both."

"I'm being spiritually oppressed."

Eliyahu smiled. "Suffer nobly."

Charlie groaned and grabbed three slices of cheese.

We spread out at the dining table. Charlie scrolled through photos on his phone while Eliyahu arranged his stones like relics. The rabbi produced a piece of vellum, unfolding it to reveal two spirals, one clean, one broken.

"This one sings," he said, tapping the clean spiral. "This one pretends."

Charlie leaned in. "Same seventh-cycle break. Same interference."

"Look at this sequence." Charlie spread his phone, my laptop, and three printed photos across the table in a line. "Your backyard. Distortion at the seventh interval. The limestone spiral. Breaks at seventh rotation. The stone circle at the Reynolds foundation. Ten stones."

"Ten minus three equals seven," Eliyahu said.

"Exactly. And here's the thing that kept me up all night." Charlie grabbed his notebook and flipped to a page dense with calculations. "Seven is the first prime where the pattern destabilizes. But it's also the number of days in creation. The number of seals. The number of…"

"The number that separates earth from heaven in most sacred texts," Eliyahu finished. "You break seven, you break the boundary."

I stared at the pattern spread across my table. "Whoever carved these knows sacred mathematics. They're not just powerful. They're educated."

"Or they were taught," the rabbi said. "This kind of knowledge doesn't appear spontaneously. Someone trained them. Someone with access to very old texts."

"Break time," the rabbi said, "and everything slides."

"Time," I said quietly. "Erin's phone jumping forward."

Eliyahu folded the vellum carefully. "Whoever carved that slab knew what they were doing. This wasn't exploration. This was preparation."

The house settled around us. Somewhere outside, a lawnmower started up.

"Are we safe?" Charlie asked.

"Safer than we were yesterday," I said. "The wards here still hold. But I got comfortable. Let things slide."

Eliyahu gave me a look. "Comfort is seductive."

"I got lazy."

Charlie stretched. "All right. I'll run the numbers tonight and get Erin a clean dataset. No magic, just math."

"She'll still ask questions."

"She'll demand answers. There's a difference."

Eliyahu stood. "I'm not leaving town yet. We'll go back tomorrow."

"Stay for dinner," I said.

He shook his head. "Promised I'd stop by the synagogue before evening services."

At the door, he paused. "James. The stones will hold for a while. But if the carver comes back, they'll know someone read their work."

"And if they notice?"

"They'll either stop or escalate. My money's on escalate."

I walked him out. The heat slammed back into us like a wall.

"You feel it?" he asked, looking down the street.

"Feel what?"

"The quiet between sounds. Like the neighborhood's trying to hear itself think."

"I've felt it for days."

He nodded and got in his car.

Inside, Charlie had already converted my dining table into a war room. Photos, measurements, angles, notebook pages covered in calculations.

"If Erin finds something concrete, she's going to kill us for not looping her in sooner."

"I'll bribe her with food."

"She'll take the food and stay mad."

I sent Erin a short message asking if she could spare time in the next couple of days to look over an odd dataset for me, nothing sensitive, just a pattern recognition puzzle that had Charlie stumped and me curious. I added a line about paying in ribeyes and crème brulee.

The three dots appeared almost immediately, then vanished, then reappeared, before resolving into:

If this is about Casey's brownies, I demand hazard pay. Send the data. I'll look tomorrow if my boss doesn't decide to invent a meeting.

Charlie snorted when I read it aloud. "See? Weaponized."

We worked for another hour. Photos printed, measurements recorded, arc lengths calculated, seventh-cycle drift annotated. Everything went into a manila folder labeled "Park Survey."

"I'll run analysis scripts tonight," Charlie said, standing and stretching. "Call me if the sky opens up or Casey burns down her kitchen."

When he left, I walked the house and checked the wards room by room. They hummed, steady and strong, but tuned to an old frequency. The frequency of someone who'd gotten comfortable. Who'd let himself believe that Centerville's quiet streets meant he was safe.

In the living room, I pulled my sword from the mantle. The runes along the blade caught the lamplight, still bright, still sharp. I'd kept the weapon maintained even when I'd let the vigilance slip.

Outside my window, the streetlamps flickered on one by one as dusk settled. Somewhere down the block, a dog barked. A car door slammed. The ordinary sounds of suburban life continuing, oblivious.

But underneath, beneath the cicadas and the distant highway hum and the air conditioners rattling in every window, something was pulling at the edges. Not dangerous yet. But insistent. Methodical.

Like someone testing a lock, learning its mechanisms, preparing to pick it clean.

I set the sword on the coffee table within easy reach and pulled out my phone.

Time to stop being reactive. Time to start hunting.

12

Pretzels, Aqua Net, and the Return (Ohio, Present)

The door to Kramer's swung open and I stepped into fryer heat and noise. The smell was immediate, spilled beer, something sizzling on the flat top, old wood polish worked into every surface. Kramer's smelled like every good bar I'd ever found, the kind that didn't change much and didn't apologize for it.

I'd been coming here for years. Every city I'd lived in had a place like this, somewhere that stayed steady while everything else insisted on evolving. The jukebox still took dollar bills. The beer taps outnumbered the wine options ten to one. The TVs were never too loud. You drank what you ordered, didn't start fights, and left your politics at the door.

The oak bar ran the length of the room, worn to a deep shine by decades of forearms and beer glasses. Neon signs buzzed red and blue against mirrored shelves stacked with bottles. The air tasted like hops and salt.

Behind the bar stood Barb, as permanent as the building itself. Somewhere in her fifties, face lined from years of cigarettes and late shifts, hair teased into an '80s wave that defied both gravity and good sense. Had to be half a can of Aqua Net holding that architecture together. She moved like someone who'd been doing this job for thirty years and could spot an empty glass from twenty yards in dim light.

The regulars were in their usual spots. Retirees near the jukebox arguing about the Reds. A couple mechanics at the bar nursing longnecks. Locals in ball caps whose laughter punctuated the background noise like familiar punctuation.

I'd felt off all day. That prickling awareness at the base of my skull, the one that said someone was watching. I'd caught myself checking over my shoulder twice on the drive here. Probably nothing. Probably just nerves after everything we'd found at the park.

But the feeling hadn't gone away.

I spotted my friends in the back corner booth under the framed photo of the '83 UD Flyers. Charlie raised his glass as I made my way through the crowd.

"You made it," he said. "Was starting to think you'd found something better to do."

"Got lost," I joked, sliding in. "After all these years in Dayton, that's my story and I'm sticking to it."

Casey leaned forward, elbows on the table. "We were about five minutes from ordering for you. Charlie said you'd want the usual."

"That predictable?"

"Consistent," Charlie said. "Better word."

Erin looked up from a folder, slight smile at the corner of her mouth. "He's right. You're gravitational. Reliable, steady, occasionally irritating."

I raised my glass. "I'll take it."

"Good," she said. "It was mostly a compliment."

The waitress arrived with the first round, pints catching the light, plates of fried bologna sandwiches, and two kinds of Smales Pretzels. The hard ones, twisted and baked to a dark bronze with burnt tips. The soft ones, fat and pale.

Erin pushed the soft pretzel plate toward me. "Want some?"

"I'll stick with the hard ones," I said, taking one and biting the burnt tip. "These have actual flavor."

"Snob," Charlie said.

"They're from Smales," I said. "Been making them the same way since

1906. You can taste the difference when someone gives a damn."

Casey pointed at me with a pretzel piece. "And yet you always order beer that sounds fictional."

"Because American lager tastes like someone's apology."

That got laughs. Easy, comfortable. For a few minutes it was just this, friends, pretzels, beer, the small mercy of normal.

The Reds game flickered silently above the bar. Barb dropped off refills without breaking stride. The light from the beer signs turned everything warm and slow.

Then Erin pushed her drink aside and opened her folder.

"All right," she said. "Here's what I found."

Charlie leaned in. "From the park?"

"From everything. The videos, the audio, the stills. I ran it through our analytics suite at work. Scrubbed it first. The AI doesn't know what it's looking at. It just hunts patterns."

Casey propped her chin on her hand. "Your top-secret lab can decode haunted forests now?"

"It deals with data," Erin said. "Which is scarier than ghosts."

Charlie smiled. "Fair."

Erin swiped through her tablet. "I started with audio. Isolated background frequencies from Charlie's recordings, ran a Fourier transform to separate ambient noise from structure."

Casey blinked. "English, please."

"She broke the sound into pieces to find patterns," Charlie said.

"Right," Erin said. "What I found shouldn't exist. There's a repeating pulse every 4.3 seconds. Too regular for nature. It's faint, buried under cicadas and water, but it's in every clip."

I frowned. "What kind of pulse?"

"Amplitude modulation. Like someone's pushing energy through the environment in waves. Gentle, consistent. Almost musical." She looked up. "And it's not just sound. The video shows the same thing."

Charlie straightened. "The trees?"

"Everything. I tracked movement frame by frame, reflections in the water, branches shifting, light scatter. All of it moves in the same 4.3-second rhythm."

Casey stared. "So, the forest is breathing?"

"In a way," Erin said. "But not naturally. It's like the park's stuck following a metronome that isn't its own."

The table went quiet. I felt it in my chest, the same pulse I'd felt standing by the creek.

"Could it be wind?" Charlie asked. "Groundwater?"

"Tested for that. It's not geological. The pattern's too narrow, too structured. Like feeding energy into a tuned circuit." She zoomed in on a graph. "And it's intensifying. I went online and found videos on social media from people that visited the park and don't keep their socials private. Ran that data too. It started around mid-June. Tripled in strength since then."

She pulled up a heatmap showing color gradients across the park. "The strongest readings concentrate near the Reynolds foundation. Right where you found that carved slab."

Casey tapped the screen. "Signal from what?"

"That's what I'm asking him," Erin said, looking at me.

I studied the rhythmic pulse on her tablet. "That's not communication. It's resonance. Someone's matching the frequency of the Veil."

Erin tilted her head. "Like sympathetic vibration?"

"Exactly. The Veil depends on harmony. Everything balanced. Drive it off-key and it starts to unbind. Slow, invisible, but it happens."

Charlie's expression shifted. "Like pushing a bridge into harmonic failure. Small, consistent force at the right frequency until it collapses."

"Except here it's the wall between worlds," I said.

Casey exhaled. "You guys know how to kill a mood."

Erin almost smiled. "If it helps, maintaining this signal takes massive energy. Whoever's doing it knows exactly what they're doing, but it's not efficient."

"Which means they're skilled but limited," I said.

Charlie tapped the screen. "Wait. You said 4.3 seconds. That's not exact.

There's drift."

"Right," Erin said. "Why does that matter?"

Charlie's face did that thing it had been doing lately since studying with the rabbi, confusion mixing with understanding. "If it were perfect, it would stabilize itself. Perfect ratios reinforce. But the imperfection introduces feedback. Like detuning an instrument on purpose to create dissonance."

"Corruption disguised as harmony," I said.

Casey shook her head. "You realize how insane this sounds?"

"My data doesn't care about sanity," Erin said.

I sat back, watching them. Erin's precision. Charlie's curiosity. Casey's humor keeping us human.

"There's one more thing," Erin said. She pulled up another graph. "I ran the audio through harmonic decomposition. Found subharmonics below hearing range. They don't match any geological source." She paused. "But when I compared them to the video Charlie took of your backyard that morning…"

She looked at me. "It's the same signature."

"Same entity?" Charlie asked.

"Or same power source," I said quietly.

Casey leaned back. "Let me get this straight. We've got haunted math, a breathing forest, and invisible frequencies trying to eat reality. Should we order another more beer or pints of holy water?"

Erin grinned despite herself. "Both. Cover our bases."

The humor helped. We needed it.

Charlie studied the data. "If this keeps going, could it spread?"

"Yes," I said. "But slow. Like rot in wood. You won't see it until something breaks."

He nodded. "Then we shore it up."

"I'll refine the model," Erin said. "Map the nodes. If we can generate counter-harmonics, maybe we can stabilize it. Science versus magic."

"I'll get more readings," Charlie said. "The Rabbi's teaching me ratio mapping. If we apply his sequences to the anomalies, maybe we triangulate the next stress point. I've got some old equipment in my garage that I can play with that may help."

Casey whistled. "Look at you. The King of Math and the Arch Mage of Centerville."

"Careful," I said. "We still need a court jester."

The conversation wound down. The beer got warmer. The pretzels disappeared. The Reds lost in the ninth and nobody cared.

I watched them, faces lit by neon, alive and laughing. I'd lived through empires. Seen cities burn. But this, friends in a bar, solving impossible problems over beer, this was worth protecting.

When the plates were empty, Charlie stretched. "I'll work the sequences with the Rabbi. See if we can find a counter-rhythm. Once I have something to work with, I'll see if I can modify my old field amplifier to the same frequencies. I have some ideas on how we might be able to use it to repair the inconsistencies Erin picked up."

Erin stacked her notes. "I'll feed more data to the model. See what else shakes out."

Casey raised her glass. "And I'll continue providing moral support and baked goods."

I smiled. "Don't sell yourself short. Weaponized capsaicin muffins may come in handy."

They laughed, gathered their things, and headed out into the cooling night. Their voices faded.

I stayed, nursing the last inch of beer. The tab hadn't come yet and I wasn't in a hurry. Barb wiped the counter, muttering about closing out. The Reds highlights played in silence.

That feeling from earlier crept back. The one that said I was being watched.

I scanned the bar. Same regulars. Same mechanics. Nobody looking my way.

But the feeling didn't leave.

The door opened. Someone stepped in, backlit by the streetlight outside. I couldn't see the face at first, just a silhouette, average height, deliberate movement.

Then he stepped into the light and my heart stopped.

I knew that walk. When you spend three hundred years with someone, you don't forget. Not the gait, not the posture, not the way they hold their shoulders.

Arnaut.

He hadn't aged. Not a day. Dark hair trimmed close, silver at the temples. Sharp features, the kind that looked carved. Same face I'd seen the night he vanished in Jerusalem. But his eyes were different. Darker. Not lifeless, too alive.

He saw me and smiled.

"James," he said. His voice was exactly the same as I remembered. Low, rich, unshaken. "It's been a long time."

I couldn't move. Couldn't speak. My brain was trying to process seven centuries of grief collapsing into a single moment.

"Arnaut." The name felt like breaking something open. "How…"

I half stood, caught between wanting to embrace him and needing answers. Ended up frozen awkwardly, half in the booth, half out.

He noticed, and his smile widened slightly. "Sit. I'll explain."

He slid into the booth across from me. The noise of the bar seemed to pull back, giving us space. The jukebox played on, glasses clinked, but it all felt distant.

"I thought you were dead," I said. "You vanished into that portal. I searched for months. Years."

"I know," he said. "And I was lost at first. What's beyond the Veil isn't like our world. It folds. Shifts. You lose yourself, then find pieces you didn't know existed."

"You were trapped?"

"At first." He shrugged slightly. "Then I realized it was only a cage if I saw it that way. Over time, I learned its language."

The way he said language made my skin prickle.

"You learned to control it," I said.

"Not control. Understand." He leaned forward slightly. "What's on the other side isn't our enemy, James. It's a mirror. What we see as darkness only reflects what we bring to it."

"That's not how it works," I said. "It's a boundary. Not a teacher."

He smiled, sad. "Still clinging to the certainty and optimism that Geoffrey taught us. Even after all this time."

"It's not dogma. It's experience."

"Then maybe your experience is incomplete." His eyes caught the light, too black, too deep. "The Watch told us the Veil existed to keep darkness out. But what if it's keeping something else in? Something divine that's been misnamed for centuries."

"You sound like the men we swore to stop."

"I sound like someone who's seen the truth." He leaned back. "You and I, what we were trained to guard against? We should have asked more questions. The Church twisted that purpose. But I can rebuild the Watch. Better. Purer. A fellowship of knowledge, not fear."

My pulse hammered. "You want to open the Veil."

"I want to perfect it," he said softly. "The balance isn't fraying by chance. It's calling. And we can answer. Together."

"You're asking me to throw away centuries."

"I'm asking you to consider that what we learned was wrong." He held my gaze. "Let me show you."

I studied him. Same face I'd trusted with my life. But now there was zeal behind it. His words were too smooth. His certainty too bright. The charm that once inspired men now hummed with something else.

"Why now?" I asked. "Why come back after all this time?"

"Because it's time. Because I felt the old forces stirring again. Once I returned, finding you was easy. You draw attention if you know how to look." He paused. "And because, old friend, you've grown comfortable. You've forgotten what we were."

"I haven't forgotten," I said quietly. "I've learned the cost."

He stood, resting one hand lightly on the table. "Think about what I've said. I'll find you again soon. You'll see."

Then he was gone. No farewell. No backward glance. Just the soft closing of the door, leaving me in the dim noise of the bar.

I sat there with a thousand unanswered questions rattling around my skull.

How did he find me? Why now? What does he mean the Veil is calling?

The abruptness threw me. What should have been a reunion felt like a sales pitch. Quick, rehearsed, strange.

Barb glanced my way, reading my face. "You good, hon?"

I nodded. "Yeah. Thought I saw a ghost."

"Tell me about it. My ex comes in here every Thursday." She chuckled and went back to her glasses.

I sat there until my beer went warm. The laughter, the clatter, the ordinary rhythm of the bar, it all felt suddenly fragile.

Arnaut was back.

And the world was holding its breath.

13

Orders, Druids, and the Relic (Rome and Wales, 1300)

Rome stank of pilgrims and money.

It was the Jubilee Year, Boniface's grand experiment. A year of absolution for anyone who came to Rome with coin in hand. They flooded in from everywhere, peasants, merchants, whores, thieves, all convinced forgiveness had a price and Rome was the only place selling.

The Watch wasn't what it used to be. When I first swore its oaths, we'd been guardians against things that crept at the edges of the world. Under Boniface, we'd become Rome's fist. Anything that didn't bend to papal authority got branded corruption. And corruption meant permission to destroy.

Arnaut loved it. He moved through Rome like he owned it, gold sword-hilt flashing, his laugh drawing looks from passing pilgrims. Three crusades had left him scarred and certain. He looked like salvation made flesh and believed every word of it.

I kept my head down.

We'd been serving under Bishop Alaric de Rouen for two years. The title sounded grand, *Legatus Sacri*, but it just meant leash with a crucifix attached. I'd outlived most of the bishops who'd held that office. Some were scholars, some zealots. A few, like Geoffrey, had been men of conscience. Geoffrey was centuries dead now, bones turned to dust under French soil, but I still measured every successor against him.

Alaric didn't measure up. Sharp where Geoffrey had been steady. Ambitious where Geoffrey had been careful. The kind of churchman who believed obedience was the highest virtue, especially when it was others obeying him.

When the summons came, I knew it wasn't social.

The audience hall was thick with heat and incense. Alaric stood beside a carved coffer, hands folded. Behind him hung Boniface's banner; two keys crossed over the world.

He didn't waste time. "James Crable. Arnaut St. Omer. His Holiness has a task for you."

Arnaut bowed. "Another heresy? Rome breeds them faster than we can burn them."

Alaric's expression flickered. "That's only because weeds grow in the most fertile soil. You'll act as envoys. The Pope wishes to extend peace to the druids of Anglesey."

Arnaut raised an eyebrow. "They're still alive?"

"Scattered. Hiding in the old forests." Alaric held up and opened a coffer. Inside, wrapped in silk, lay a dark splinter of oak bound in silver wire. "This relic was cut from the tree Suetonius Paulinus felled when Rome first conquered that island. Our holy mages have... enhanced it. It carries obedience now. Their earth magic will falter in its presence."

He placed it in my hands. The metal was cold, but it pulsed, like something alive trapped inside.

Arnaut leaned closer. "What did your mages do to it?"

"They bound power to it. Old power." Alaric's smile was thin. "Power that answers to Rome now. Think of it as insurance."

I turned it over. The pulse was wrong, slick somehow, like oil on water. "We're supposed to negotiate."

"You are." His smile widened slightly. "But if they refuse, you have the means to ensure compliance. I trust you understand?"

I bowed my head. "As you command."

Arnaut grinned. "We'll bring them to the light."

Alaric's gaze lingered on him, approving. "See that you do."

Outside, bells thundered across the city. Arnaut fell in beside me, adjusting his sword belt. "A diplomatic mission. No demons, no necromancers. Just peasants in the rain. Practically a holiday."

I looked at the relic wrapped in my satchel. It pulsed again, stronger. "If this is a holiday, why does that thing feel like it's watching us?"

He laughed. "Maybe it likes us."

The relic pulsed once more, and I could've sworn it was mocking me.

We left Rome before dawn two days later. No escort, just sealed letters with the papal crest and orders to report when we returned.

North through the Alpine passes, the air thin and knife-sharp. Arnaut sang old campaign songs while I pulled my cloak tight and envied his warmth. At Lyon we traded horses. At Calais we found a merchant ship bound for Dover. The captain took our coin and didn't ask questions. Men carrying papal seals were best left alone.

The Channel rolled gray beneath us. Arnaut leaned on the rail, watching England's cliffs rise from the mist. "You think the Church sends us where nobody else wants to look?"

"Yes," I said. "That's exactly why."

He grinned.

We rode north through London, chimneys and church spires stabbing at low clouds, then west along Roman roads toward Chester. The relic thrummed each night as we camped, responding to something in the soil beneath us.

By the time we reached the Welsh coast, the wind carried salt and rain together. Beyond it lay Anglesey. Green. Old. Waiting.

Arnaut's mood lifted with each mile. Mine sank.

Anglesey was a land caught between forgetting and remembering. The hills rolled like sleeping beasts. The sea whispered behind them. The air itself felt older than Rome would ever be.

We reached a village by dusk, smoke and thatch at the mouth of a shallow valley. A stream cut through it, stones black with moss. The people looked up from their work as we approached, faces weathered by wind and silence.

An old man stepped forward. "Rome?"

"We come with a message," I said in Welsh. "Questions, not swords."

He studied our armor, the cross at Arnaut's neck. "Peace. That word burns on this island."

He didn't bless us, but he let us stay. A cottage by the stream. Straw beds, cold bread, silence. More hospitality than I'd expected.

That night the relic hummed, softer than before, like it was listening.

Arnaut rolled over, one eye open. "That thing sounds guilty."

"It should be," I said.

He laughed quietly. "Then we'll get along fine."

The villagers didn't talk much, but they talked to me. A woman milking goats told me the druids still met beyond the ridge where the oaks grew thickest. A grove called Coed y Gwaed, the Blood Wood. Not a threat, she said. A memory. Where the Romans had slaughtered their ancestors centuries before.

"They gather at the full moon," she whispered. "They don't summon demons. They sing. Make offerings. The crops grow after."

I wanted to believe her.

Arnaut didn't. "A song's still a spell. And if it's not Rome's spell, it's heresy."

"We could wait. Talk to them properly."

He tightened his gauntlet strap. "You've gotten cautious."

"Experience teaches that."

"Experience teaches hesitation," he said. "Hesitation gets you killed."

Two nights later, the moon rose full over the hills. Even the village dogs went quiet. We left without being seen.

The path wound between lichen-crusted boulders, up through bracken and into forest. The oaks were massive, wide as houses, roots woven through the soil like veins. The air smelled like damp bark and crushed herbs and something I couldn't name.

The clearing opened under moonlight. A ring of standing stones glowed pale. Figures moved between them in gray and green robes, chanting in waves. At the center stood a low stone altar covered with oak leaves, feathers, and a bowl of water that caught the light.

The sound was beautiful. Not evil. Balanced. Preserved.

Arnaut didn't hear that. He heard defiance.

He shifted beside me, hand on his sword. "They're weaving power. Feel it?"

"Yes," I said. "And it's clean."

"That's how heresy works," he muttered. "Pretends to be holy."

The relic pulsed, steady now. I could feel it connecting to the grove, but there was something else underneath. Something slick. Foreign. Wrong.

We stepped into the clearing. The chanting stopped. Faces turned.

The leader came forward, tall and broad-shouldered, beard silver-white. "Rome walks far from home."

"We're here to talk," I said.

He looked at me, then at Arnaut's sword. "Your friend wants blood."

Arnaut smiled. "I want obedience. Blood's optional."

The druid's eyes came back to me. "You're carrying something that was ours. I can hear it."

I hesitated, then drew out the relic. Silver glinted like frost. "A token. The Pope sends this as a symbol of unity."

The druid's face twisted with something like pity. "That tree grew from this soil before Rome existed. You bring its corpse back and call it reconciliation?"

"Rome wants to end division," I said quietly.

"Rome wants submission." He looked at Arnaut. "Your empire will crumble like all the others."

Arnaut's jaw tightened. "Enough talk."

"Arnaut," I warned. "Not here."

He didn't hear me. His sword rang free.

The grove reacted instantly. The druids raised their hands as one, voices lifting in harmony that wasn't quite song, wasn't quite speech. The air itself seemed to thicken, pressing against my skin like water.

The leader spoke a single word in a language older than Latin, older than Greek. The ground beneath us trembled and split. Vines erupted from the soil, thick as a man's arm, moving with terrible purpose. They lashed toward us, thorns glinting in moonlight.

Arnaut met them with fire. His blade traced arcs through the air, each swing leaving trails of flame that cut through the vines like they were paper. They shriveled to ash, but more kept coming, faster now, learning.

I threw up a ward, golden light snapping into a half-dome around us. The vines hit it and recoiled, smoking. But I could feel the drain already, the constant pressure eating at my concentration.

A younger druid stepped forward, hands raised, chanting in that same ancient tongue. The stones at her feet began to glow, pale green light spreading through cracks in the earth. Roots broke through the ground, smaller than the vines but faster, seeking our ankles.

I stamped my foot and spoke a word of unbinding. The earth bucked beneath her, throwing her back. The roots withered. But three more druids had already taken her place.

Lightning crawled across the ground toward us, not the violent kind from storms but something stranger, pale threads of energy that moved like living things. They found Arnaut's armor and flared bright. He grunted, muscles seizing for a heartbeat.

Then he grinned, spoke a counter-charm our teachers had drilled into us decades ago, and the lightning reversed, flowing back toward its source. One of the druids screamed and fell, smoke rising from his hands.

"You'll need more than that to stop us." Arnaut shouted, and hurled a blast of concentrated light at the nearest standing stone.

The stone exploded. Shards of rock flew outward like shrapnel. I threw up another ward just in time to catch the pieces that would have torn through both of us.

The forest screamed. Not metaphor, the trees themselves made sound, a deep bass groan that I felt in my chest more than heard.

The lead druid's eyes went wide with fury. He thrust both hands skyward and shouted something that made my teeth ache. The wind reversed, sucking inward from all sides, crushing pressure that drove me to one knee. My ward flickered, dimmed.

Arnaut drove his blade into the soil and fire erupted outward in a perfect circle, tracing lines that glowed like molten metal. The wind hit the fire and the two forces ground against each other, neither giving way.

I could feel the relic in my pack pulsing now, faster and harder. That oily wrongness spreading outward like ink in water.

The druid's magic faltered. Just for a second. But a second was enough.

Arnaut's fire overwhelmed the wind and surged forward. The blast threw the lead druid backward with crushing force. He hit the ground hard but was already rising, blood streaming from his nose.

Two more druids joined him, standing shoulder to shoulder. They began a new chant, voices braiding together in complex harmonies. The ground between us split open, a chasm three feet wide that exhaled cold air and the smell of deep earth.

I leaped back, nearly lost my footing. Arnaut jumped the other direction. For a moment we were separated by that black gash in the world.

From the chasm rose something that wasn't quite mist, wasn't quite solid. Shapes moved within it, hints of antlers, of eyes, of teeth. Old things. Wild things. The druids were calling up the memory of what this land had been before Rome, before Christianity, before men decided the earth needed taming.

"Arnaut!" I shouted. "Pull back!"

He couldn't hear me over the roar. Or he chose not to. He raised his sword high and light poured from it, white and burning, the kind of holy fire the Church said came from heaven itself.

The shapes in the mist recoiled, writhing. Where the light touched them, they dissolved into nothing, screaming sounds that weren't quite animal, weren't quite human.

But for every shape that dissolved, two more rose from the chasm. The druids' chanting grew louder, more frantic. They were pouring everything they had into this working, calling up centuries of memory, of blood soaked into this soil, of their ancestors' rage at Rome's conquest.

I felt the relic pulse again, that sickening slick feeling intensifying. And suddenly I understood what the Vatican had done. They'd bound something to it, some fragment of power that fed on magic, that corrupted and weakened and undermined. Not holy. Not clean. Just efficient.

The druid leader felt it too. His chant stuttered. The shapes in the mist wavered, losing cohesion.

"No," he gasped. "What have you..."

Arnaut saw his opening. He leaped the chasm in one bound, sword blazing, and drove it toward the druid's chest.

I threw myself forward, hand outstretched, trying to bind Arnaut's arm. My spell caught him mid-swing. His blade froze six inches from the druid's heart, trembling with the force of Arnaut fighting my working.

"Stand down!" I shouted. "We can still..."

Arnaut's eyes met mine. There was nothing human in them. Just certainty, cold and absolute.

He spoke a word I'd never heard him use, something dark and guttural. Power exploded outward from him, shattering my binding like glass. The backlash threw me backward into the base of a standing stone. My head cracked against rock and the world went white.

When my vision cleared, seconds later, the lead druid was falling, Arnaut's blade withdrawing from his chest.

The others screamed. Their chanting broke into chaos. The shapes in the mist dissolved all at once, the chasm snapping shut with a sound like thunder.

But Arnaut wasn't done.

He turned on the remaining druids, blade singing through the air. A woman raised her hands to ward him off and he cut through her defense like it was nothing, fire following in his wake. An old man tried to run and Arnaut threw a spear of pure force that caught him between the shoulders.

I staggered to my feet, head spinning, and threw up a barrier between Arnaut and the fleeing druids. Golden light solidified into a wall.

He hit it full force. The barrier held for three heartbeats. Four. Then cracked down the middle.

"Arnaut, stop!" My voice was ragged, throat raw from breathing smoke.

He broke through, grabbed my collar, slammed me back against the stone. "You don't stop infection," he snarled. "You cut it out!"

He threw a blast of power in every direction, striking me and the druids with the same force. I stumbled and my vision blurred. By the time I could see straight again, he was already past me, pursuing the druids who'd fled into the trees.

I ran after him, legs unsteady, power gathering in my hands. I could hear screaming ahead, see flashes of fire through the branches.

The trees opened onto a small cluster of huts. Families. Children.

Arnaut stood at the center, arms raised, fire building between his palms. Not the controlled flames he'd used in the grove. Something bigger. Hungrier.

"Arnaut, NO!"

I threw everything I had at him. A binding strong enough to hold a demon, chains of light that wrapped his arms, his chest, his throat. For a moment he faltered, the fire dimming.

Then he looked at me over his shoulder. "You're making me do this the hard way."

He spoke another word from that dark vocabulary I'd never heard, and my bindings shattered like they were made of cobwebs. The backlash dropped me to my knees, gasping.

The fire left his hands.

It wasn't an explosion. It was a wave, rolling outward in all directions, consuming everything it touched. Thatch roofs caught instantly. Wooden walls blackened and collapsed. The air filled with smoke and screaming.

A girl, maybe six years old, stumbled from a doorway, her dress already burning. I lunged toward her, pulling water from the stream with a desperate working, throwing it across the distance.

But Arnaut's fire was too hot, too fast. It reached her first.

She fell without a sound, a small crumpled shape that would haunt me for centuries.

I seized Arnaut's arm, physical this time, no magic left in me. "You have to stop. Please. They're just..."

He shoved me away with casual strength. "They chose this when they chose heresy."

More fire poured from him, spreading through the settlement like a living thing. People fled into the forest. Some made it. Some didn't. The screams mixed with the roar of flames until I couldn't tell them apart.

I tried one more binding, weaker this time, desperate. It caught his left arm. He barely noticed, kept casting with his right.

A man with a child in his arms ran past me, both burning. I threw water at them but my power was gone, drained to nothing. The water evaporated before it reached them.

They fell together at the edge of the clearing.

When it ended, the sun was rising. Thin gray light filtered through smoke. The grove was a blackened shell. Standing stones scorched and cracked. The altar split down the middle. Bodies everywhere, in the grove, in the ruins of the huts, scattered through the trees where they'd tried to run.

Arnaut stood in the center of it all, sword dark with soot and blood, breathing hard. He looked exhausted. Satisfied.

"They refused grace," he said, voice hoarse.

"They refused Rome."

"Same thing." He sheathed his blade.

I couldn't answer. My throat was closed, my chest too tight. I walked through the devastation in a daze, looking for survivors. Found none.

The relic had gone completely silent. No pulse. No hum. Just dead weight in my satchel.

I spent the rest of that day and all the next gathering the dead. My hands blistered, then bled, then healed, then blistered again. I dug graves in the ash-choked soil. Stacked stones. Murmured words that felt hollow.

Arnaut watched from the edge of the clearing but didn't help.

When I finished, I knelt beside the graves in the center of what had been the grove. The air still tasted like ash and grief. I took the relic from my satchel, the power spent.

I dug one more hole, deeper than the others, and placed the relic at the bottom.

As I covered it with soil, pressing the earth down with my ruined hands, the wind stirred once. Soft and cold, carrying something through the dead trees. A whisper or a warning or maybe just the sound of the island exhaling.

When I rose, Arnaut was standing behind me.

"You're burying a relic," he said.

"I'm burying a mistake."

He shook his head. "You've lost faith."

"No," I said. "I've found the edge of it."

We left without looking back. The sun climbed through smoke, pale and distant. Behind us, the ruined oaks swayed like the island was exhaling grief.

We rode south under gray sky.

The road was mud between hills. Neither of us spoke for days. My hands still smelled like smoke no matter how much water I used.

Arnaut seemed lighter with every mile. He hummed. Talked to the horses. Recounted old battles like the last week was just another story. Whatever he'd done in the grove had made him more alive, not less.

I envied that. His ability to step over blood and keep walking.

Eternity doesn't make the soul stronger. It just makes the weight pile up.

By Calais, the sea air turned sharp and cold. On the ferry to Boulogne, Arnaut leaned over the gunwale, watching his reflection in black water.

"You'll thank me someday," he said.

"For what?"

"For finishing it. They would've come for us eventually."

I stared at the horizon. "I saw people defending their home."

He snorted. "Heresy doesn't get to have a home."

"What did you do, where did you learn that power? I have never seen it before."

He answered with a look in his eye I had never seen from him before. "While you were busy on your enchantments, I have been studying with Alaric's mages. They have uncovered a new source of magic, and they have been showing me how to wield it. What we have learned these many years pales next to it."

"It feels wrong Arnaut. Surely you can sense that."

"It is but another tool in our arsenal. One that will allow us to keep the balance in this world, and being the Word of God to those who oppose it."

I didn't answer. The wind cut through our cloaks. For the first time in centuries, I felt old.

Rome greeted us with incense and gold.

The Jubilee had turned the city into a carnival of salvation. Pilgrims flooded every street. Boniface's banners hung from every arch. The city smelled like fear and ambition mixed together.

We were summoned to the Lateran before we'd even stabled our horses. Guards led us through narrow corridors to a small chamber lined with frescoes of angels holding swords.

Bishop Alaric stood by the window, light behind him turning him to silhouette.

"You've returned," he said. "Alive."

Arnaut bowed. "The mission's complete. The grove is ash."

"Efficient." Alaric's gaze shifted to me. "And the cost?"

"Too high," I said quietly. "The grove burned. There were children."

His expression didn't change. "Regrettable but acceptable. The Church will call them casualties of purification. The Pope will be pleased."

Pleased. The word tasted like ash.

Arnaut straightened. "We acted under orders."

Alaric nodded slowly. "And you'll be commended. But understand, this is only the beginning. There are new heresies rising. New threats. The world doesn't rest."

He crossed the room, stopping close enough that I could see embroidery on his cuffs. "The Pope will receive you at week's end. He wishes to thank his immortal servants personally."

When he left, Arnaut exhaled and smiled. "Immortal servants. I like the sound of that."

"We're tools," I said.

He laughed. "Tools that never break. Rome rewards results."

"And what about conscience?"

"Conscience is for mortals." He clapped my shoulder. "You've gone soft, James."

I looked at him and saw something new behind his eyes. Not cruelty. Conviction. The dangerous kind.

Boniface received us three days later in the Lateran's private audience hall, a room drowning in candlelight. The Pope sat on a marble throne beneath a tapestry of Christ handing keys to Peter.

He wasn't stooped or weary. He was lean, sharp, every movement deliberate. The air around him felt charged.

"You return victorious," he said. His voice filled the room. "Anglesey is cleansed. The old gods sleep."

Arnaut knelt. "By your command, Holiness."

Boniface looked at me. "And you, Frater Crable? You seem less certain."

"I did what was required," I said. "But I question what was necessary."

His eyes narrowed. "Faith doesn't question. It acts."

"Faith built on silence is just fear wearing a cross."

The chamber went still. Alaric shifted but said nothing.

Boniface rose. "You speak as though you stand above the Church. Remember your place, Watchman. You are our instrument."

"Instrument," I said softly. "Like a blade."

"Exactly." He seemed pleased. "And a blade doesn't choose what it cuts."

Arnaut smiled. "May we always be sharp, Holiness."

The Pope's expression softened and he lifted a hand in blessing. "The Watch endures because it obeys. See that you remember."

We bowed and left, our shadows long on marble.

That evening, Arnaut found me on the terrace overlooking the Tiber. Rome glowed below, the river a dark thread through firelight.

"You shouldn't bait him," Arnaut said. "You know what happens to men who question Boniface."

"We're not men anymore. That's the problem."

He leaned against the balustrade. "The problem is you think too much. You've been given forever and you spend it doubting."

"I spend it remembering."

"Remembering what?"

"The cost. The boy who screamed when the huts caught fire. The girl..."

He frowned and looked away. "Collateral. Rome's purpose is bigger than any one life."

I turned to him. "That's what every tyrant says."

He met my gaze. For a heartbeat I thought I saw something human flicker there. Then it was gone.

Weeks passed. Orders came and went. Quiet exterminations. Whispered purges. Cults in Marseille. Revenants in the Rhineland. Witch covens in France. The Watch grew busier, more ruthless.

Boniface had made his vision real. We weren't Rome's shield anymore. We were its executioner.

And with each mission, something inside me wore away.

When we returned from the Black Forest, I found a summons in my quarters. Crimson wax. The Pope's sigil. Alaric wanted to see me.

It was never a request.

His study overlooked the northern wall, Rome's rooftops sloping toward the river. The city was waking, dawn haze clinging to domes and spires.

Alaric looked up from his desk. "James. You don't sleep."

"I used to. Before Anglesey."

He sighed and leaned back. "You did what was required."

"What the Church required and what the world needed aren't the same."

His shoulders sagged slightly. "You think I don't know that?"

"I think you pretend not to."

He stood and moved to the window. Rome spread below, banners and bells and pilgrims flowing like water.

"Every day men kneel and beg for absolution," he said. "They bring coins, prayers, tears. They all want the same thing, certainty. Order. The world has too little of both."

He turned back. "The druids would've brought chaos."

"I saw what we brought them."

His expression softened. "Yes. And that will stay with you. It should. But don't mistake regret for failure. The Church doesn't act without reason."

"Then why lie? We were sent under a banner of peace."

"Because peace opens doors that war can't." He poured wine into two cups, offered one. I didn't take it. "Sometimes you open the door before you cauterize the wound."

"You talk like we're physicians."

"In a way, we are. You're immortal. You've watched nations rot from within. The Watch preserves what keeps the world from Satan's grasp. Without Rome, everything collapses back into shadow."

"Do you trust Boniface?" I risked asking him quietly.

"I trust the structure. Popes come and go. Rome endures. The Watch must endure with it." He set down his cup. "That's why Geoffrey made you what you are. To stand when everything shifts."

"Geoffrey believed we were guardians."

"We still are. It depends who's wielding us."

Silence settled, heavy and uneven.

"I know this shook you," he said, gentler now. "But doubt doesn't make you faithless. It makes you careful. And careful men keep the world intact." He paused. "We are the nails that hold it together. Sometimes nails draw blood."

I swallowed. "And when the hammer falls on us?"

He smiled sadly. "Then God finds another hand."

That night I couldn't sleep. I stood on the balcony watching lights flicker along the Tiber. Rome murmured below, alive and unrepentant.

Alaric's words echoed: *We are the nails that hold it together.*

Maybe he was right. Maybe this was the cost of keeping the world upright.

But I couldn't shake the image of the grove. The way the relic had pulsed with that oily wrongness. The girl falling, dress on fire, her scream cut short. The change in Arnaut.

The earth remembers, even when Rome forgets.

And buried in that grove, wrapped in corrupted oak and Vatican ambition, the relic waited.

Quiet now.

But not gone.

14

Donuts, Deer, and the Cop (Ohio, Present)

I left the house and knew something was wrong.

Not storm-wrong or danger-wrong. Just off, like someone had retuned the world a quarter-step flat. The humidity pressed down hard on me, thick and close. Maples arched over Mad River Road, morning sun breaking through in patches. A mower droned somewhere. It looked like any other late August morning in Centerville.

But it wasn't.

Arrow Wine had called about my order, a case of '96 Lafite Rothschild. Good Bordeaux was ritual for me. After the last few weeks, I needed ritual.

Traffic thickened as I drove, parents running late, school buses stopping every block. School had just started and the city was finding its rhythm again. By the time I turned onto McEwen Road near Watts Middle School, traffic slowed to a crawl.

Then I saw them.

A dozen kids crossing the street. Not in a group. Single file. Perfectly spaced, three feet apart. None of them looked up. No earbuds, no phones, no backpacks slung sideways. They walked forward with their eyes open but empty.

I'd seen armies march with less precision.

The car ahead of me hit its brakes. Tires squealed. No horns followed. Drivers just sat there, hands gripping wheels, watching children step into

129

traffic without blinking.

A boy in a red hoodie walked in front of the lead car. It stopped inches from him. He didn't flinch. Didn't even seem to notice. Just kept walking, head tilted up slightly, mouth half-open like he was listening to something far away.

Another kid stumbled on the curb, caught herself, and kept going. Same blank expression. Same wide eyes.

They reached the far sidewalk, turned toward the school, and walked across the grass field. Still single file. Still silent.

I watched drivers look around the way people do after waking from a dream they can't remember. Then engines started and traffic moved again.

I drove on. My chest felt tight.

I'd seen strange things. Men turned to ash by their own spells. Cities that burnt under full moons. But this felt different. Small. Subtle. Worse because of it.

By the time I reached Arrow Wine, I'd almost convinced myself I'd imagined it.

Almost.

The store was mostly empty, just me and the manager at the counter. Cork and oak and lemon cleaner. I nodded and asked him about my order. He went to the back to grab it while I strolled the aisles to wait.

A man stood by the impulse-buy endcap, staring at a display of Beaujolais Nouveau. His lips moved but made no sound. Nobody is that interested in a cheap wine that has more marketing than flavor. This was not normal.

I stopped beside him. "Morning."

Nothing. Not even a blink. Just that slack look, like he'd forgotten why he was standing there.

I moved on.

The manager came back with the vase in his arms. He looked at the man and shook his head as I checked out. "Some mornings, huh?"

"Yeah," I said, paying. "Some mornings."

In the parking lot, a woman stood halfway between two cars. Not walking. Just standing. Her sedan sat with the trunk open, engine running, hazards ticking. A case of White Claw rested on the asphalt by her feet.

"Ma'am? You all right?" A driver called through his window.

She blinked hard, looked down, laughed. "Oh! Yes, sorry!" She grabbed the case, threw it in the trunk, and drove off.

The man from inside came out a moment later, walking like he'd just remembered how legs worked.

I set my wine in the trunk and stared at my reflection in the rear window. The glass bent in the heat, warping my face.

I pulled out my phone and called Charlie.

He answered on the second ring. "You're calling before noon. That's either a crisis or you want coffee."

"Neither. Something's wrong in Centerville."

"Wrong how?"

"Kids walking into traffic like they're hypnotized. People staring into space. A woman just stood in a parking lot for a full minute and forgot to move."

Silence. Then: "You think it's Veil-related?"

"I don't know. But I'm near the park and it feels like the edges are thinning again."

He sighed. "You want company?"

"Always. Bring your camera."

"Twenty minutes. You buying coffee?"

"Sure. If it's nothing, I'll buy lunch too."

"And if it's something?"

"Then we drink whatever's in my cellar."

"Now that's motivation." He hung up.

I started the car and cranked the AC. The world outside looked the same, sun, trees, neat lawns. But it felt like someone had twisted the tune half a note flat.

If experience had taught me anything, small wrong things never stayed small.

Charlie showed up exactly twenty minutes later. His truck rumbled into the driveway, engine coughing once before dying. He climbed out in jeans and an Air Force polo, thermos in hand.

"Morning," he said. "You look like you've seen a ghost."

"Not yet."

"You sounded rattled on the phone. What happened?"

I told him. The kids at Watts. The woman at the wine shop. He listened with his arms crossed, frowning.

When I finished, he said, "Maybe everyone's running on no sleep. School just started. Half the city's fried."

"It wasn't distraction. It was synchronized. Like something pressing on the same nerve."

He studied me. "You're sure?"

"Sure enough."

He sighed. "Fine. You're buying breakfast."

"Bill's Donuts?"

He grinned. "Now I know you're serious."

Bill's sat on Route 48 like it had for decades. The parking lot was full, work trucks, minivans, SUVs, a police cruiser. The smell hit as soon as we opened the door. Sugar glaze, fryer oil, hot coffee.

Inside, the air was warm and loud. Glass cases, hard plastic booths, photos of youth sports teams going back forty years on the walls. Shirley ran the register in a hairnet, powdered sugar on her sleeve. She'd worked here as long as I could remember.

We got in line behind a cop leaning on the counter, talking to the younger clerk boxing up donuts.

"Busy night?" the clerk asked.

The cop exhaled. "Couple fender benders near Paragon. Deer through somebody's windshield on McEwen. Three more hit along Alex-Bell. Folks swear they didn't see them until impact." He paused. "Had a call about a woman walking her dog into traffic. Just staring ahead."

Shirley snorted. "Something in the water."

"Wouldn't surprise me," the cop said. He grabbed his coffee and donuts and walked out looking exhausted.

Shirley turned to us. "Morning, boys. What can I get you?"

Charlie pointed at the case. "Applesauce donut and coffee."

"Sour cream," I said. "Coffee too."

She nodded. "Good choices. Sour cream's still the best thing we make."

She passed us steaming cups and plates. The donuts glistened, golden and perfect. We took a booth by the window.

Charlie bit into his with reverence. "This is why civilization was invented."

I smiled. "That's theology I can agree with."

He gestured toward the counter. "You hear that? More deer. More accidents."

"Yeah."

The coffee tasted off today. Flat. Like everything else.

"Maybe you're onto something," Charlie said quietly. "Think it's the same distortion you felt before?"

"Could be."

I watched traffic inch past outside. Everything looked normal.

"Think Erin could pull data?" Charlie asked.

"She always can." I pulled out my phone.

Erin answered immediately. "You don't call before lunch, James. This is either good or terrible."

"Leaning toward terrible. We've got something strange in Centerville. You at the lab?"

"I'm here." Keyboard clatter behind her. "What kind of strange?"

"Traffic accidents. Deer collisions. People acting off. I need data, recent accident patterns near Grant Park. McEwen, Paragon, Alex-Bell."

"I can do that. Ohio has a crash dashboard. I can pull the last two weeks and map them."

"Good. Check Montgomery County Sheriff's logs too. Maybe scrape the Dayton Daily News traffic feed."

"If there's a spike or clustering, I'll find it." She paused. "You can thank me by coming to dinner tomorrow. Casey's hosting a 5-course dinner with a theme she calls Fire and Brimstone."

I laughed. "Do I have a choice?"

"Nope." She hung up.

Charlie set his cup down. "You think it's him?"

"Who?"

"Arnaut. He vanishes for centuries, shows up right when this starts? That's not coincidence."

Across the parking lot, a woman stepped off the curb and stopped mid-stride. Just stood there. Phone dangling from her hand. A car swerved around her. She never looked up.

"No," I said. "It's not."

Then something moved at the edge of my vision.

Inside Bill's, near the far wall, an old man sat alone in a booth. He'd been there when we arrived, working through a cup of coffee and a plain cake donut. Now he was staring at his plate.

Not eating. Not drinking. Just staring.

His hand moved slowly toward his coffee cup. Lifted it. Held it six inches from his face. Didn't drink. Just held it there, perfectly still, for ten seconds. Twenty.

Charlie noticed. "Is he okay?"

The man set the cup down with mechanical precision. Picked up his fork. Held it the same way, motionless, staring at the tines.

Shirley walked past him, stopped, frowned. "Ray? You feeling all right?"

He didn't answer.

She touched his shoulder. "Ray?"

He blinked hard, looked up at her, confused. "What? Oh. Yeah, sorry. Thought I heard something."

"You've been sitting there ten minutes not moving."

He looked down at his plate like he'd never seen it before. "Have I?" He laughed, but it sounded wrong. "Guess I'm more tired than I thought."

He stood, wadded his napkin and threw it on the table, and walked out. His movements were stiff, deliberate, like someone remembering how to use their body.

Charlie and I watched him get in his car and drive away.

"That," Charlie said quietly, "was not normal."

"No. It wasn't."

We finished our coffee in silence. When we finally left, Shirley waved without looking up.

Outside, the air was too bright.

Charlie started the truck. "Grant Park?"

"Grant Park."

The park was only a few miles south but the drive felt longer. The sun was too bright, making everything look overexposed. Late August air shimmered over the blacktop.

We took Alex-Bell east, turned down Paragon toward Normandy Elementary. The parking lot still showed signs of morning chaos, chalk hopscotch half-washed away, a forgotten lunchbox by a bench. The flag hung limp in the humidity.

Charlie parked under an oak near the playground. "Feels like we've been here before."

"We have. Last time it felt alive. Now it feels like it's holding its breath."

Cicadas droned so loud it was almost pressure. The gate to Holes Creek trail stood propped open with a stick.

We walked down the slope. The moment we passed the fence, the air changed. Suburban noise fell away, traffic, mowers, all of it, replaced by stillness.

Charlie slowed. "You sure we're not trespassing?"

"Everything worth finding makes you trespass."

The trail wound under old oaks and maples, their leaves dusty with late summer. The ground was soft with leaf litter. The air grew cooler. Dense. Sunlight broke through the canopy in narrow shafts.

A hundred yards in, a squirrel darted across the path, froze mid-sprint, and went completely still. Eyes glassy. Unblinking.

Charlie stopped. "That's not right."

I crouched near it. The creature didn't flinch when I moved closer. After several seconds, it blinked once, slow, mechanical, and bolted into the brush, moving too smoothly.

"The Wendigo's domain," I said quietly. "But something's pressing on it."

"Pressing how?"

"The Veil stretches before it tears."

He nodded, jaw tight. "Arnaut?"

"Maybe."

We followed the path down toward the creek. The air was cooler now but charged, like standing in a static field. The smell shifted from summer dust to cold stone. The trees leaned inward, trunks curved just enough to suggest they were watching.

The forest opened onto the creek bed. The same spot where, centuries ago, I'd first met what lived beneath these trees.

Today it felt wrong.

The water moved slowly, confused, like it couldn't remember how gravity worked. Pockets of silt rose and fell in patterns too deliberate to be natural.

Charlie crouched at the edge. "You seeing this?"

"Yes."

"That's not normal."

"No."

He pulled out his camera and started filming. "Looks like an oil slick. Except there's no smell."

"It's not oil. It's memory. The Veil bruising."

He whistled low. "That sounds bad."

"It is."

He filmed the water, zooming in on the reflections. The light bent wrong, refracting in ways physics didn't approve of.

Then we saw them. Along the far bank. Lines carved into flat limestone. Spirals etched deep and clean.

Charlie leaned closer. "Please tell me that's graffiti."

"It's not."

The markings were geometric. Precise. Mathematical. They pulsed faintly, not quite light, just the suggestion of it.

"Whoever did this knows ratios," Charlie muttered. "These aren't random. That curve's logarithmic. And those are perfect ninety-degree intersections."

We crossed the creek on a fallen log slick with moss. The air on the far side felt heavier, like wading through invisible water. The spirals led deeper into the woods, half-buried under roots and ferns.

Fifty paces in, the ground dipped into a hollow where the light went dim. That's where we found it.

A shimmer hanging in midair. Barely visible except when you weren't looking directly at it.

Charlie exhaled. "Heat distortion?"

"Portal residue. Someone used this recently."

He raised his camera, took shots. The lens fogged instantly. "It's rejecting the image."

"Magic doesn't like being measured."

"Great." He lowered the camera. "You think whoever did this is still here?"

"No. It's closed."

He looked around the hollow. "I hate to say it, but this all points to your friend."

"I know. But it doesn't make sense. Arnaut was passionate, fierce, but he always had reasons. I can't figure out why he'd do this."

We stood there, listening to the hum in the trees. The same vibration I'd felt centuries ago in Anglesey. The same taint

Charlie broke the silence. "If Erin's data lines up with this, accidents, deer, all of it, it means whatever's happening is spreading."

"Yes. And someone's feeding it. The Veil's under too much strain." I paused. "I don't sense the Wendigo."

"That sounds bad."

"It is. Very bad."

"You said someone's feeding it. How?"

"Remember the modulation anomalies? The longer that continues, the weaker the Veil gets. But I think someone's accelerating it. Amplifying it."

His gaze drifted back to the shimmer. "And that's making people act strange?"

"Probably. Energy's being borrowed from people and animals nearby."

"Borrowed," he said. "Or stolen?"

I didn't answer.

We hiked back up toward the trailhead. The cicadas had gone quiet, replaced by a distant hum. Traffic maybe. Or something pretending to be.

At the top of the hill, Normandy Elementary came into view above the trees. Yellow buses lined the lot, gleaming and silent. Even the playground felt like it was waiting.

At the truck, Charlie dumped his pack in the bed. "If you're right and Arnaut's tied to this, what's his endgame?"

"That's what worries me. He wouldn't risk revealing himself unless he thought he could control it."

"Can he?"

"He thinks he can."

Charlie watched me for a moment, then climbed into the driver's seat. "Then we wait for Erin's map."

I nodded. "And when she sends it, we see how deep this goes."

We pulled out of the lot. The school disappeared behind us, replaced by trees shifting in wind.

Somewhere beneath the soil, the shimmer pulsed. Rhythmic. Almost like a heartbeat trying to remember its rhythm.

15

Charms, Wards, and the Visitor (Ohio, Present)

The storm rolled in not long after midnight, heavy and slow, the kind that makes the air hum with its own weight. I was in the basement lab, sleeves rolled, eyes still raw from too much reading and too little sleep. The wards along the property line had been restless all evening, thrumming through the floor like a warning from an old bone.

I'd taken that as a sign to stop waiting.

The sword rested on the bench where I'd brought it earlier from its place above the living room mantle. I hadn't handled it for more than maintenance in decades, sharpening, cleaning, the occasional training routine when memory itched, but the world had grown strange again.

It was a good blade, pattern-welded by a London smith before the true masters disappeared into modernity. English steel, folded and tempered by a man who believed work was a kind of prayer. Over the centuries I'd layered it with enchantments the way men add lacquer to wood, one coat at a time, each sealing something older beneath it. Wards of light, counterbalance sigils, binding runes to turn corruption back on itself.

None of it was ornamental. The blade wasn't sacred, but a tool for will.

On the workbench, five small disks of silver lay cooling beside it. Each was no larger than a coin, etched with different marks, one for Erin, one for Charlie, one for Casey, one for David, and one for myself. Charms, not weapons. Simple wards meant to flare warm when danger drew near. I wasn't arrogant enough to believe they'd save lives, but early warning has a value all its own.

I strung each on a narrow leather cord, whispered a phrase into the metal as I tied the knot, and set them aside to let the magic temper. The smell of myrrh and salt hung in the air. I could almost hear the house breathe again.

Then I turned back to the sword.

The corruption spreading under Grant Park wasn't just energy, it had intent. A subtle, slow intelligence that didn't push or strike, but *influenced*. It infected boundaries the way rot infects beams, quietly, patiently, until strength becomes memory.

Most magic resists confrontation unless a person bends it to their will. It likes balance, not argument. But this thing, it didn't follow the rules. It reached through. I'd decided to give it something solid to meet.

I traced my thumb down the length of the blade, sprinkling powdered diamonds on it and whispering the older words, the ones that weren't scripture or song, but closer to breathing. Diamonds are a great ingredient for enchantments of strength given their own sturdy structure. You just need to transfer some of the diamonds essence into the tool you are crafting and the enchantment will hold firm permanently. The steel took them in, the air around me tightening until the lamps dimmed and the sigils on the table smoldered like coals. When I finished, the blade pulsed once.

I felt it, not sound, but resonance, a small echo through the bones of my wrist. A good sign. The enchantment held, though after all these years honing my craft, I knew it would.

The air settled again. The lab smelled of pitch and ozone, as though the storm outside had seeped down through the foundation. I exhaled, wiped my hands, and reached for the small oak box where I kept a bottle of scotch.

That's when the wards in the yard stirred.

It began as a soft vibration beneath my feet, more felt than heard. The outer wards were never meant to block or repel. They were my early warning system, a series of sigils buried beneath the soil, tuned to the movement of energy rather than footsteps. They whispered when someone, or something, came with ill intent.

Tonight, they were whispering insistently.

I froze, hand hovering over the bottle.

The hum came again, steady, deliberate. Something was out there, probing. Not breaking. Not threatening. *Testing.* Like fingers running along the grain of wood, learning where the resistance was softest.

The wards inside the house, enchanted charms in the walls and foundation, answered with a low counter-hum, grounding themselves. They were the physical kind, protection, not warning. They would hold, probably. But whoever was outside could feel them, too. It was meant to give them a sense of danger. It's as if my home had a declaration for intruders. *Not here. Not easily.*

I took up the sword, and climbed the stairs. The air grew warmer as I rose, the storm's electricity brushing against the edge of my consciousness. The basement door creaked open into the kitchen, and I felt the pressure settle over me like a wet cloak.

The hum of the wards tracked movement along the property line, from the side yard to the front.

Then stillness.

I moved through the living room. The house was dim except for the gold light leaking through the curtains from the streetlamp outside. The rain made soft percussion against the glass. The glass on the wine fridge caught a flash of lightning and glowed briefly like molten amber.

Another brush. Closer this time, right at the threshold.

I stopped at the foyer, every instinct older than memory telling me to listen. The wards were trembling, as if confused by the intent of the intruder. Friend or Foe?

I laid a hand against the door. The wood was cold, and beneath it I could feel the vibration of power meeting power, like two heartbeats falling into the same rhythm.

Then it came, muted through the door but clear and unmistakable, cutting through the hiss of rain.

"James, its wet out here. Can you open the damn door."

The voice was low, steady, and as familiar as my own thoughts.

I undid the lock, turned the knob, and swung the door open.

Rain cascaded down from the porch roof in thin silver sheets. At the edge of the light stood a figure half-shrouded by the storm. The face came into focus a heartbeat later, framed in wet dark hair streaked with silver at the temples, eyes like wells too deep for the porch light to reach.

Arnaut.

Thunder rolled like distant artillery.

For a moment, every part of me locked. Shock first, instinctive. Then fear, quick and cold in the gut. Then something else, heavier, the unmistakable ache of recognition. Not joy exactly, but the echo of it, dulled by centuries and disappointment, and tainted by our last meeting at Kramer's.

He stood at the edge of the light, soaked through, hair plastered to his temples, eyes black as the space between lightning.

"I told you we'd see each other again," he said quietly, his voice carrying beneath the rain. "Though I have been watching you for some time."

"The fetchling," I stated.

He nodded. "I have learned to use the tools of the Veil for my own benefit."

"Spying on me, and scaring my friends benefits you?" I asked dryly.

He shrugged, then took one measured step forward. "May I come in, old friend? The rain's colder than I remember, and I'd rather not converse over the thunder."

I hesitated, every instinct sharpening. The wards beneath the floor quivered, responding not to him, but to me. They could feel the tremor in my pulse, the pull between memory and caution.

I stepped aside slowly. "You may enter. As a guest."

As he crossed the threshold, he whispered something under his breath, a single word, low and musical. The rain evaporated from him in a shimmer of air, his coat and hair drying in an instant. A scent of petrichor and desert air lingered.

"Still useful, that trick," he said lightly, glancing down at his now-dry sleeves. "It took me years to perfect it. I was never much good at the more subtle magics."

I watched him closely. The magic had rolled off him like breath, effortless.

For a heartbeat, neither of us spoke. The house's wards hummed low beneath the floorboards, uncertain whether to resist or welcome. My pulse filled the silence.

"You could've just knocked," I said finally.

He smiled, almost sad. "And risk you pretending you weren't home?"

"Old habits," I muttered.

"Yours or mine?" he asked.

"Both."

Something like amusement flickered across his face, and for a moment there was the old warmth and charm he used to exude.

The door shut behind him with a soft, final click. The wards steadied again, low hum settling into uneasy quiet.

He glanced around the room, the sigils in the molding, the glow of the ward-lamps, the shelves of artifacts.

"You've built yourself quite the sanctuary," he said. "I can feel the protections in the stone. They hum like a choir in perfect unison. Your enchantments are as skilled as ever."

"It keeps the peace," I said.

"Peace," he repeated, almost wistfully. "An old luxury."

Lightning flared, catching the glint of the sword still in my hand. He noticed and gave a knowing half-smile.

"You plan to cleave me in two?" he said with a sarcastic smile. He looked at the sword with admiration. "Last time I saw that drawn was Jerusalem," he stated with a far off and painful look in his eyes.

I didn't answer. My throat felt tight, my pulse louder than the storm outside.

"Let's get you warm," I said finally, forcing my voice steady. "And I imagine you'll want a glass of wine."

He chuckled softly. "You still know me too well."

I selected a 1994 Château Margaux, admittedly picking something that might impress Arnaut. The cork eased free with a soft pop, and the room filled with the scent of blackcurrant, truffle, and a breath of violet.

Arnaut closed his eyes as I poured, inhaling deeply.

"Ah," he murmured. "Still faithful to Bordeaux. Good man." He raised the glass to his nose. "Restrained fruit, cedar, a whisper of wet earth. Beautifully melancholic, really. A wine that understands regret. Perfect for an evening like this."

"You know," he said, swirling the liquid, "since I've been back, I've come to love this modern world's refinements. Food, wine, warmth...the senses here are sharper. The Veil starves the palate. But here, everything is excess. The world feasts while its soul decays.

Still, I miss the old roadside taverns. Mud floors, cracked mugs, smoke in the rafters. The ale was terrible, but the company honest. Men lied less when they had nothing to gain. Now the world dines in marble temples and mistakes pretense for virtue."

I half-smiled. "You've developed a poetic streak."

"Or the times have grown dull," he said. "This century reeks of comfort. Even its sinners are soft."

We moved into the living room. He sank into the leather armchair opposite mine, moving like a man who belonged everywhere he went. I sat across from him, glass in hand, and only then noticed the weight in my other, the sword. I had absent-mindedly picked it back up after serving the wine. In one hand, a crystal wine glass, and my sword in the other, knuckles were white on the grip.

He noticed too. "Still keeping old habits close," he said, nodding toward the blade.

"Experience," I said quietly, "isn't a habit."

"No," he said, "but fear is."

For a while, we just sat, the thunder rolling somewhere far off. The Margaux glowed deep red between us, communion and temptation both.

Then he said it: "I came for your answer."

"I didn't hear the question."

"You did," he said. "Rebuild the Watch with me."

I let the words hang in the air. "The Watch died for a reason, and long after

I left its ranks."

"It died because it lost its faith," he said. "Because men like Alaric turned it into a weapon of fear instead of revelation."

"And you want to revive it as what? A ministry?"

"A cure," he said simply. "For the sickness that's devouring this age."

I felt the wards shift again, like they too were listening.

"Speak plainly," I said.

"I see evil sprouting unchecked," Arnaut said, eyes burning in the lamplight. "Not the kind we once hunted, not necromancers or heretics. A quieter evil. Apathy. Faith turned into entertainment. Power used to distract, not defend. Even the Church, the echo of it that still stands, has traded miracles for marketing. It's the story of Noah, and Sodom and Gomorrah all over again. Men are deaf to the divine James. And you know it."

His words landed like an anvil. Because they were true, or close enough to sound like truth.

"You think breaking the world will make men hear God speak again?" I asked.

He smiled, sad and radiant. "Not break. Restore. The Veil isn't a wall; it's a wound. I've seen both sides. It wasn't meant to divide but to protect balance. Ancient men closed it out of fear, locked the divine behind reason. And now the wound festers. You can see it, can't you? In the numbness, the emptiness. The earth wants its soul back."

"And you're the surgeon?"

"I'm the hand willing to make the incision."

"Alaric said something similar back in Rome before you were lost in Jerusalem," I said quietly. "I searched for you for ages after I left the Watch."

He looked up sharply.

"What do you mean?"

"I mean after Jerusalem," I said. "When you vanished. I spent decades trying to find you. Tracing every whisper of energy across the Levant, every disturbance that smelled of your magic. I thought you were trapped. Or dead. I even went back to the Mount, to the Keepers' caverns. They said the Veil had swallowed you whole."

A muscle twitched in his jaw. "I heard you call for me once. I couldn't answer."

"I left the Watch immediately after," I continued. "They blamed me for losing you, and for consorting with the Keepers. Our Oculi said I'd gone native. Maybe he was right. But I couldn't stomach what the Watch had become."

Arnaut nodded slowly, swirling the wine. "I'm not surprised you left. That was coming since Anglesey. You were always the conscience I couldn't afford. At the end I was the anchor that kept you in the Watch."

"And you," I said, "were the zeal I couldn't control."

He smiled. "Perhaps that's why we worked. One to build, one to burn."

"Until you chose fire."

"Fire purifies," he said softly. "It was the only lesson Rome ever truly mastered."

"Grant Park," I said after a moment. "The fractures. The distortions. That's you."

He didn't flinch. "Of course. The first suture must be cut before the body can heal."

"You're going to get people killed. The people in town are already feeling the effects."

"I'm waking them," he said. "They only appear lost because they've begun to listen. You can't hear creation without losing your place in it for a while."

I set my glass down hard. "You're justifying madness with metaphor."

"You always called revelation madness until you saw it proven," he said, voice rising. "Alaric taught me how to use what the magic that changed the ancient oak branch we used in Anglesey. You called it corrupted. It wasn't. The magic was language; divine syntax locked in the grain by the mages in the Vatican. The Church saw its natural form as heresy because they couldn't control it. Alaric found a new magic that manipulated it to the will of God."

I met his eyes. "And now you use the same magic to break the Veil."

"I *understand* it," he corrected. "I can shape its resonance, direct it. The Veil bends when spoken to properly. I can unseal the old boundaries, make the world one again. No more hidden side, no more division."

I stared at him, the same man who once fought beside me in snow and blood, now speaking like a prophet drunk on clarity. "Arnaut, we spent centuries fighting the things that crossed the Veil. You know the dangers to humanity we fought and kept hidden from the world. And what happens to us when you're done? What happens to *humanity* when you tear away its boundaries?"

He smiled. "Then we'll finally see God's plan as He intended, not as we pretend His plans to be." His eyes became like steel, full of resolve and the clarity only a madman possesses.

The wards in the foundation began to thrum, low, urgent, as if they could feel my pulse rising. The house itself seemed to hold its breath.

"Arnaut," I said quietly, "listen to yourself. You're not the Watchman you were. You've become what we swore to stop."

His smile faded. "I expected you to say that, but I held out hope that you would see the truth in my words."

He drained his glass halfway, then leaned forward, voice low, controlled. "You think I'm corrupted. You're wrong. The corruption is in *them*, in this world that worships nothing, that has forgotten sacred beliefs. The divine didn't abandon man, man sealed the divine behind the Veil. I'm only reopening the door."

"And when the flood comes through?"

He looked at me with something like pity. "Then let it wash away the rot."

The silence between us was alive, charged, trembling, fragile. I felt the sword grow heavier in my hand, the old runes pulsing as if it remembered his blood.

He noticed. "You still think it will save you."

I shrugged, "It's you that needs saving Arnaut. This is madness. You are threatening our very existence and inviting chaos into the world."

We stared at each other across the centuries. Brothers, enemies, something in between.

At last, he sighed and stood, the storm-light catching the silver in his hair. "I came to try and make you see sense. You haven't changed in all these years. Still resolute in your piety as ever," he said quietly. "You may not want to join me, but I warn you not to try and stop me. If you do, our next meeting won't be as cordial."

He lifted the Margaux again and took one long, deliberate swallow, emptying the glass. "Magnificent," he said softly. "Blackcurrant, cedar, and sorrow. You always had exquisite taste."

Setting the glass down, he met my eyes one last time. There was regret there, real, heavy, almost human.

"I wish you could see what I've seen, James," he said. "If you did, you'd stand with me. We could finish what we started. But I won't beg. Just stay out of my way, though I know you too well to believe that you will."

He hesitated at the door, rain hammering against the porch roof. "For what it's worth," he added, voice low, "I am sorry. Not for what's coming, but for losing you to it."

Then he stepped into the storm and was gone.

The wards rippled once, like breath leaving a body. The house went still.

I looked down still staring out the open front door watching Arnaut fade into the darkness. I was still holding the sword.

The door clicked shut and the wards fell still, like a chest settling after a held breath. For a beat I just stood there with the sword in my hand, feeling the old weight of it and the newer one Arnaut had left behind.

The oven clock glowed a cold, indifferent 2:47AM The storm was already moving east. Good. I needed the quiet.

I carried the sword downstairs.

The lab met me with a dampness possessed by most basements, and the static of spent magic. I laid the blade on the bench and cleaned it slowly, methodically, letting each pass of cloth pull the tremor out of my hands. The diamonds I'd married to the steel earlier still sang under the edge, steady, grounded.

The five silver discs waited in their pouch by the vice, catching a thin line of lamp light. No more fussing with them, the weave was set. Tomorrow they'd go to Erin, Charlie, Casey, and David with brief, plain instructions, wear it, if it warms, step away from crowds, call me, don't be a hero. The fifth would stay with me.

I turned to the perimeter next.

The yard wards had done their job, warned, measured, endured. I walked their circuit, the buried sigils along the fence, the iron nails sunk at the corners decades ago, the ash line I'd worked into the soil when I built the house. I refreshed their bindings, no new power, just a firming of intent, and threaded a single addition through the whole net, a marker keyed to Arnaut's resonance. If he tested the line again, I wanted more than a nudge. I wanted direction, distance, and intensity.

Inside the house, the protections were already awake, foundation knots, lintel script, the paired glyphs under the stair, the quiet, stubborn little tangle sealed into the fireplace brick. I tightened them too, not to bar him, he'd felt the strength and chosen not to push, but to declare the terms plainly, talk here, fight elsewhere. He would read that truth and accept it, or he wouldn't come at all. Either way, it kept my home protected as best I knew how.

After my rounds, I went back to my lab. On the bench, the sword's runes dimmed to a patient ember. I slid it into its scabbard and buckled it where I could reach it without thinking. There was a time I slept with it within arm's length every night. This would now be my routine again.

I opened the small oak cabinet and set out three simple tools, a brass compass blackened with age, a clay dish etched with a ring of untranslatable marks, and a river stone I'd carried since a mission in Paris. I didn't need a window to feel the park; I let the room go quiet and leaned into the thread I had created on our last visit that ran from my foundation to the Reynolds ruins and back again. As I listened, it came through low at first, a deep, slow throb like an engine idling under water, then lifted, thinned, and quivered at the edge of hearing. The same tremor we'd caught in the creek. The same wrong key.

Arnaut had been careful. He'd modulated the strain so it felt like almost balance if you didn't know the texture of the real thing. I now knew it too well. I listened a while, counting the breath between pulses... four, three-and-a-fraction, four again, then that tiny slip he'd defended as "waking." Not revelation. Shear. He was prying, not healing.

Enough.

I pinched a few grains of salt and a shaving of iron into the clay dish and murmured a short tethering phrase, tying my sense of the park's rhythm to the stone and the compass needle. If the frequency shifted sharply, the stone would heat and the needle would jump. I couldn't be on the trail every hour; this would keep watch when I couldn't.

The lab lights hummed once, then steadied. The air lost its metallic bite. Work done.

I killed the lamps and climbed back upstairs. The house had that kind of dark I like, honest, settled, no angles lying to the eyes. I set the pouch of charms by the front door where I'd remember it in the morning and took the sword with me to bed instead of returning it to the hooks. Small change. Loud message, at least to myself.

I stood awhile at the window, watching the last of the rain bead on the glass and run in slow, neat lines. Somewhere far off a transformer buzzed and clicked. Somewhere nearer, a night bird called once and thought better of it. I listened for the older sounds, the ones under the neighborhood, but the wards were calm now. Whatever echo he'd left at the edge of the yard had bled off into nothing.

The clock next to my bed read 3:51AM.

Sleep didn't come, not really.

16

Faith, Remembrance, and a Ghost (Rome, 1348)

The journey back from Jerusalem was long, but uneventful. I spent the trip brooding and guilt-ridden. By the time I reached Rome, the sun was at its cruelest. Midday in this city doesn't forgive anyone, not the beggars in the alleys, not the merchants shouting in the squares, and certainly not a man like me who hasn't slept in three nights. The road from Ostia was a river of dust, and I carried enough of it on my cloak to pass for a ghost of the Appian Way.

I hadn't planned to stop. My orders, what was left of them, should have taken me straight to the cathedral. The bishop would already know I'd arrived; he always did. But hunger makes its own arguments, and I was too tired to resist. Besides, I needed to collect my thoughts and put something in my belly.

I found my way to the Taverna di San Pietro; a narrow house of wine and smoke crouched behind a mason's yard near the river. I remembered the place, years ago, when the Watch still gathered here after long nights, when laughter meant something different. The street hadn't changed much. Same cracked stones, same ivy choking the wall, same smell of river rot mixed with bread.

The door creaked open under my hand, and for a moment all I heard was the quiet hum of conversation. It felt cooler inside, a relief sharp enough to sting.

The owner glanced up from his ledger. He was much older now, or maybe I'd simply outlived his patience. One eye was still cloudy, the other sharp as glass. Recognition flickered there, though he said nothing. He had owned the place long enough to not ask questions about his Vatican clientele. He poured me wine without asking and I walked toward an open corner table near the window.

I dropped my cloak over the chair, unbuckled my sword, and laid it within reach. The blade hummed as I leaned it on the chair next to me, not sound, exactly, more a subtle vibration I could feel through my fingertips. It had never dulled, not once. The edge was as perfect as the day it was forged thanks to a combination of craftsmanship and my own enchanted additions.

The first sip of wine tasted of dust and burnt figs. I let it sit on my tongue anyway. You learn to accept bitterness after a while.

Outside, the street was loud with merchants, the rhythmic clatter of hooves, and the hollow clang of a bell announcing midday prayer. Inside, the taverna breathed a slower rhythm, low voices, the scrape of wooden cups, a priest muttering something about repentance between mouthfuls of bread.

I'd just started on a plate of stale rye bread and nearly rancid cured meats and felt that pressure in the air that always comes before they appear. My brothers in the Watch.

Four of them stepped inside. That alone made the room lean into silence. The Watch rarely gathered in such numbers unless something was about to happen. There are only twenty of us or so scattered through the world, and we are usually on some errand for the Church.

They wore no uniform. The Watch are supposed to blend, though men with fine swords and quality armor aren't exactly in stealth mode. What marks us isn't clothing, it's the way we move. Quiet, deliberate, as if every gesture is a test of control, honed by years of training, immortality, and too many life lessons to count.

I didn't turn immediately. I kept my eyes on the food, listened to their boots on the floorboards, and waited. Then I heard a familiar voice.

"James."

I looked up. Lucan.

He was broader than I remembered, but his hair was as blonde as the day I met him a century ago. His expression was the same wry mask it had been since the siege at Acre. He gave me a half-smile that let me know he had some inkling of what happened in Jerusalem.

"Didn't think I'd find you in Rome," he said.

"I could say the same."

He gestured to the others, three men I had never met, and had the bearing of new Watch members. The young ones wore the same look I'd seen a thousand times before, confidence without comprehension. They'd heard stories, pieced together fragments of what the Watch once was, tempered by the Church's turn towards intolerance, and imagined themselves part of some holy mystery.

Lucan sat across from me without asking. The others stayed standing, forming a loose half-circle nearby. A show of vigilance, or pride. Hard to tell which.

"You've been gone a long time," he said.

"We were here a few months back. A quick stop through when we were given our mission to Jerusalem. I'd just as soon the city forgot me." I answered.

He laughed softly. "Rome forgets no one. Especially not those who serve her faithfully."

I caught the tone beneath his words, respect, yes, but something else. Weariness. Lucan had always carried too much of the world's weight on his shoulders.

One of the younger Watchmen, if I can call any immortal young, spoke up then, his voice casual but edged. "Word was you stayed east. Some said you'd taken service elsewhere."

I looked at him. "People say many things. I've stopped keeping count."

The man beside him smirked and seemed to test me. "And yet here you are. Back in Rome. Must be important business."

I smiled. "Important? Everything we do is important to the Vatican."

Lucan's eyes flicked toward him in a warning, but he ignored it. The arrogance of the untested. The Watch used to break that out of recruits early. Apparently, the bishop had other methods.

I let the silence grow. In a small room like this the silence carries weight. Eventually, the owner came by with more wine. He hesitated when he saw the company but said nothing. Lucan took the jug, poured for both of us.

We drank without toasts.

He leaned forward. "You've seen the East," he said quietly. "Jerusalem. Arnaut. The reports… none of them make sense."

"They wouldn't," I replied.

"Then help me make sense of them."

I set down my cup. "Arnaut is gone. The rest doesn't matter."

Lucan nodded slowly, eyes studying me. The others exchanged glances, curiosity, and something like discomfort. They didn't understand the name, or maybe they did and wished they hadn't heard it spoken aloud.

After a long moment, Lucan sighed. "The bishop's expecting you."

"I know."

"He's different now. Since the council. Harder. Less forgiving."

"He's always been what he needed to be," I said. "He is the same as most that came before him. It's becoming harder to tell the difference between them over the last few decades. We just accept it and follow orders."

Lucan gave me a tired look, and said under his breath. "Do you still?"

It was an honest question, and that made it worse. I didn't answer. Instead, I picked up my sword and stood. The light from the window caught along my scabbard, a thin shimmer of silver on the leather. The younger Watch stared at it, sensing the hum of its power, uncertain whether they were supposed to be impressed or afraid.

Lucan rose with me. "Please. Don't leave on our account. We'll go," he said.

"I've had enough."

He hesitated, then reached out a hand. I clasped it, a firm grip, the kind shared by men who've buried too many of the same friends.

"Be careful, James," he said. "Things are changing. The Watch too. You'll see."

I gave him a weary nod. "So have I."

When I stepped outside, the sun hit me full in the face, bright and pitiless. The sounds of the street came flooding back, hammers, horses, the call of water-sellers. Rome was awake, alive, indifferent.

I turned toward the cathedral, though I didn't hurry. The bishop would wait. He always did.

For the first time in weeks, I let myself breathe. The air smelled of dust and river stone. Somewhere nearby, a bell tolled again, not for prayer this time, but for something else. A warning, perhaps.

I tightened my grip on the sword. Its hum steadied. Whatever waited beyond those cathedral doors, I would meet it the way I always do now, with open eyes and a cautious tongue.

The Lateran never felt so unwelcoming. Its walls breathed incense and judgment, not comfort. Light slanted through high windows in thin white blades, carving the air into order. Even the sound of footsteps seemed to echo with discipline.

By the time I reached the private audience chamber, the day's heat had begun to fade, leaving the air thick with wax and old dust. A line of sunlight lay across the marble floor, bright enough to show where centuries of knees had worn the stone smooth.

Bishop Severin di Vercelli sat behind the long table, quill in hand, posture exact, every motion deliberate. He was a man who made stillness feel like power. He reminded me much of Alaric, but without the ability to even feign tolerance.

He didn't look up as I entered. "James."

"Your Lordship."

There was a long silence as he finished his writing. He set the quill aside, folding his hands with ecclesiastical precision. "You returned from Jerusalem, I see."

"Yes."

"Alone." He looked around as if expecting Arnaut to walk in any moment. The word was simple, but it carried weight.

"Yes."

His gaze rose. The color of cold stone. "Sit."

The chair opposite him was low by design, the kind meant to force reverence whether one felt it or not. I sat and said nothing.

"The mission was clear," he began. "There was plague in the Holy City, and beneath it, whispers of blasphemy. A healer who summoned false miracles, a contagion that spread faster than God's will allowed. You and Arnaut were sent to uncover the source, to destroy it."

He paused, letting the words settle. "That was the order, yes?"

"Yes."

"And yet here you stand, without your partner." It was a statement, not a question.

I shook my head in acknowledgment, but said nothing. The comment tore at my soul. Despite our growing differences Arnaut was my friend for over three centuries.

His fingers twitched once on the table. "Then explain."

I gave him the truth, nothing more. The false physician. The dead in the streets. The thing that wore a man's face and laughed in none. The pursuit through the markets, the fight near the Wall. Arnaut's charge. The creature's retreat through the shimmering portal. And Arnaut charging headlong into the light without a thought for the implications.

When I finished, Severin's silence was sharper than his voice.

"You lost him," he said.

"Yes," I said while letting out a heavy, and guilt-laden sigh.

"You let him follow the enemy into damnation."

"He made his choice."

"And yet you did nothing to save him."

"I tried."

He rose from his chair, robes whispering like the hiss of a candle. "The Watch is the Church's arm, not its conscience. You were given clear purpose, find the evil, strike it down, leave nothing standing. Instead, you return with nothing but excuses."

"The thing escaped," I said. "We were not prepared for the magic it wielded.

It fled us out of fear and its own preservation."

"You presume to understand it?"

"I've spent my life understanding such things."

He turned from me, pacing slowly toward the window. "Your life, yes. But not your soul."

The words landed like a stone dropped in water.

He went on. "You speak of demons like scholars do of mathematics. You treat the sacred as though it's something to be studied. That is what concerns me most, James. Not failure. Philosophy."

"I don't philosophize," I said. "I survive."

"And that is the root of your sin," he said. "The Watch exists to serve, not merely survive."

I let the silence stretch. The air between us seemed to hum, low and tense, like the moment before a string snaps.

When he finally turned back, his expression had softened, but only slightly. "Tell me about these 'Keepers' you mentioned in your report."

"They call themselves the Shomrei ha'Adamah ha'Nitzchit," I said. "A secret order of Jews who guard the holy ground beneath the Mount. They arrived after the battle, sealed the corruption that creature left behind, and ensured the city didn't fall further into fear."

He listened, but the flicker in his eyes betrayed his discomfort. "You consorted with unbelievers."

"I took help from those who had the knowledge to contain it."

"And implied an authority over sacred ground that belongs to the Church."

"I ceded them nothing," I said sharply. "They were already there, long before Rome."

That last part slipped out harsher than I meant.

He heard it.

"Before Rome," he repeated slowly, the words tasting of poison. "You speak like a man forgetting who he serves."

"I remember," I said with more acid than was prudent.

"Do you?" he asked. "Arnaut remembered. He was flame, dangerous, yes, but pure. He would have burned the heresy clean from that city. And you..."

his voice dipped, low and cutting "...you let the fire go out."

Something inside me twisted. I could still see Arnaut stepping into that light, convinced he could save the world one last time. "He was reckless," I said. "And proud. That's what killed him."

"Faith killed him," Severin said. "He died a martyr for the Church. And yet here you stand with nothing but excuses and blasphemy. At least Arnaut's end will be a catechism for the living"

I met his eyes. "No. Faith didn't kill him. Faith made him blind."

He froze, and the quiet that followed was heavier than shouting.

"Careful," he said softly. "Even your immortality has limits."

I leaned forward slightly. "You sent two of your most experienced men to a city drowning in plague and superstition. You wanted a hammer. You got a grave. Don't talk to me of faith when you measure it in corpses."

He didn't move, didn't speak. Just stared, until the air between us felt carved from ice.

When he finally spoke, his voice was calm again. "You will attend the vigil in two nights' time. Arnaut's name will be read. You will kneel for him. You will remember what obedience looks like."

"I remember," I said.

"Good." His tone softened into mock pastoral care. "Then remember also that the Watch is not finished. Rome will need its hammer again. I will assign you a new partner. One I trained myself in hopes he can bring you back to the fold and temper your independence. And if I sense hesitation in you, even the slightest, I will find someone less... weary."

He turned his back to me, dismissing me without words.

I stood, bowed once, and left.

The corridor outside was long, cold, and empty. My footsteps echoed like accusations. Through narrow windows, the city burned in gold, rooftops, domes, the shimmer of the river. Rome was alive, pulsing, unrepentant.

I walked slowly, not ready to meet the sun yet. The air smelled of candle smoke and stone. My hand brushed the worn groove of the wall, smooth where a thousand men before me had done the same.

I'd carried out orders all my life. Struck where told. Believed as instructed.

Killed when commanded.

And for what?

Arnaut was gone. The demon lived. The bishop saw only disobedience in my grief. And I saw only rot where faith used to stand.

By the time I reached the outer steps, Rome's bells were tolling for evening prayer. I stood under the archway, looking out at the city, the streets alive with heat and dust and the smell of bread from the bakeries.

The sword at my hip was heavy, humming as if it could sense my thoughts.

When the vigil bell rang in two nights, I would stand where they expected. I would bow my head and keep my silence.

But at dawn the next morning, I would be gone.

I knew what that meant. They would seek to hunt me and strike me down as a traitor. Let them. The old guard were my friends and colleagues; I trusted that they would not seek me out. The new watchmen didn't have the skill to find me. When they looked, they'd find nothing to strike.

I would be a ghost, walking out of Rome for the last time.

Night came early in Rome the night of the vigil. Storm clouds from the coast dragged their shadows across the domes, and the streets dimmed to copper and smoke. By the time the bells called the faithful to prayer, the Lateran courtyard was already a sea of torches. Their flames leaned in the wind like listeners.

I stood among the three other members of the Watch in attendance. The three of them were cloaked and hooded, faces half-lit by the wavering orange light. Lucan kept to the back of us, silent and solemn. The new recruits stood in front of me, proud of their posture, eager to prove that Rome's hammer still struck hard.

The bishop's voice carried through the courtyard, smooth and measured. "Tonight, we honor our fallen brother, Arnaut St. Omer, Watchman of the Holy See, who gave his life in service to the light."

The crowd murmured the ritual response, Lux perpetua luceat eis - Perpetual light shall shine upon them.

A censer swung from silver chains, spilling smoke that tasted of myrrh and ash. The scent caught in my throat. Arnaut had always hated incense, said it masked the smell of sin. I almost smiled at the thought.

Severin stood at the dais, his shadow drawn long against the stones. "His sacrifice reminds us that obedience is the highest devotion. Through discipline we conquer chaos, through order we defeat evil."

His eyes found me in the crowd and lingered.

"Let none forget that even the strong will falter when pride replaces faith."

The words were meant for me. The younger Watch turned around to glance at me with unhidden menace. I kept still, eyes forward.

When the chant began, I mouthed the lines automatically. Old habits survive longer than belief. The cadence of Latin rolled through the courtyard, a sound that once steadied me. Now it only echoed hollow.

Lucan was only a few paces behind me. We hadn't spoken since the taverna, but I felt his steady presence. When the prayers quieted briefly, he touched my shoulder lightly.

"You shouldn't have come," he murmured just above a whisper.

"I was ordered," I said.

He studied me, lines carved deep at the corners of his eyes. "Orders break easier than people think."

"I know."

For a moment neither of us moved. Then he said, almost kindly, "They'll turn on you, James. Not tonight, Severin loves his ceremonies too much, but soon. You know how it works. You bury one brother; you hunt the next."

"I've buried enough," I said.

He gave a slow nod. "Then go before they give us another shovel." Dangerous words from a man who should know not to speak such things aloud. It gave me comfort that someone else understood. Comfort from one of only a few people in the world that could truly understand. Perhaps the only person that understood.

The chant swelled again. Torches guttered in a sudden dust; ash spiraled upward like black snow. I watched it fall across the white marble steps and thought of Jerusalem's dust, of Arnaut stepping into the light with the same reckless certainty that had carried him through every battle we ever fought.

Severin lifted his hands for blessing. "May the Watch remain unbroken, the sword unblunted, the will of Rome everlasting."

When the ceremony ended, the torches were doused one by one until only the altar flame remained, a thin blue tongue against the dark. The members of the Watch dispersed in silence with sidelong glances at me, boots whispering over stone. I stayed until the courtyard emptied.

Lucan was gone. So was the bishop.

Only the flame and I remained.

I stepped forward, knelt, and whispered, not a prayer, just a truth. "If you are out there, I will find you brother. I will bring you home."

The flame hissed as a drop of wax fell, and for a heartbeat I imagined it answering. Then it steadied, indifferent as always.

I rose, turned my back on the altar, and walked out through the cloister gate. No guards stopped me; no bells marked my passing. The night air was cool, washed clean by a light rain. Somewhere a dog barked, and the sound carried over the river like a farewell.

At the edge of the square, I looked once more at the Lateran. The great doors were closing, sealing the light inside. The Watch would keep its vigil, its order, its certainties.

I had nothing left to offer it.

The sword at my side was quiet now, its runes dull beneath the rain. I pulled my cloak tighter and started down the hill toward the Tiber. Each step felt lighter, though the world itself seemed heavier.

By dawn I would be beyond the city gates, a ghost moving east through the vineyards, leaving Rome to its own salvation. Behind me, the bells began again, slow, measured, eternal. I didn't look back.

The road carried me through Umbria first, then across the Alps, following trade caravans and plague wagons alike. I kept to the edges of the map, living in the margins of cities that barely remembered their saints.

For years I searched the archives of monasteries and what was left of the old libraries of the east, hunting for traces of Arnaut and the thing that took him. Every clue was contradiction, scholars spoke of a shimmering wound in the air, hermits called it the Gate of Adam, and the desert mystics claimed the stars themselves could bruise when men tampered with divine boundaries. I listened to them all.

When the Vatican's agents came looking, I learned to disappear. I always sensed their coming, though it wasn't often. Change a name, move to another city. For several years I was a nomadic scholar, soaking in everything I could about the Veil. The Church's memory is long, but its eyes are slow and I eventually found peace in my studies and travels.

In Damascus, I found fragments of scrolls burned half to ash, writing that spoke of a living boundary between matter and grace. In Alexandria, an ancient and blind monk whispered that "the Veil hums when the world sins too loudly."

In the ruins of Antioch, I found a mosaic of a man holding a sword to a door of light, his face erased by time. It looked too much like Arnaut for coincidence.

Years bled into decades. I hunted every rumor, every stirring of the unnatural. I tracked down the things that hunt men. A demon in Constantinople, a warlock in Granada, some unholy misshapen beast in Baghdad. I visited the rabbis at the Mount in Jerusalem as often as I could. Each encounter taught me something about what hides beneath the skin of creation. And with each my mission changed from finding Arnaut to understanding the Veil.

And slowly, the shape of truth began to form.

The Veil wasn't heaven's wall, but a seam between order and the unshaped. A living fabric, wounded where hubris and evil had torn it, mended where balance returned. It didn't need devotion. It needed understanding.

That became my new faith.

I built wards, learned new languages, walked with scholars, monks, rabbis, and heretics. Each offered a fragment. Each cemented a new set of ideals and a renewed focus.

I stopped following the echoes of Arnaut's passage. He was always just out of reach, like thunder from a storm I could no longer see and I came to the realization that he was gone and my guilt over it had faded enough that I could move on.

By the time the world replaced myth and legend with science, I had changed and adapted.

The Watch was gone, buried under bureaucracy, immutability, and time.

The Church forgot its hunters.

But I remembered.

And when the hum returned, when the ground beneath Centerville began to thrum with that same wrong rhythm I'd felt in Jerusalem, I knew.

The wound had never healed. Neither had I, but I was prepared.

17

Mimosas, Nerves, and Camaraderie (Ohio, Present)

Dawn didn't so much break as bleed through the edges of the storm. The sky over Centerville wore that washed-out, iron-gray tone that makes the roofs look heavier and trees older. The rain had drifted east sometime before morning, but its memory hung thick in the air, damp, electric, unsettled.

I hadn't really slept. The clock said 6:02, but time had already lost its rhythm. I lay still for a while, listening to the hum of the wards beneath the floor, that subtle vibration between heartbeat and thought that told me the house was still watching the world with me. The sword lay in its scabbard on the chair beside my bed, close enough that I could reach it without rising. I'd slept like that long ago, centuries ago, when sleeping too far from the blade was the same as tempting fate.

Old habits have a way of surviving faith.

Downstairs, the house still smelled of ozone and steel, the residue of last night's work, the tether I'd built in the basement, the charms cooling in their pouch by the front door. The runes in the foundation had calmed since the encounter with Arnaut, but only on the surface. I could feel it underneath, the same wrong key in the soil, the strain in the wards that had begun the moment he stepped across my threshold.

I pushed the blanket aside, stood, and reached for the sword. The scabbard was cool to the touch, the runes along the guard dimmed to a soft pulse. A patient heart, waiting. I carried it downstairs, not because I expected to need it, but because old wars had taught me that readiness was half survival.

The house creaked as I moved down the hall and down the steps. The storm had pulled the warmth out of the wood. At the front door, the pouch of five silver charms rested on the entry table, cords coiled neatly like sleeping snakes. I brushed my fingers over the leather. The enchantments inside thrummed, alive but resting.

I brewed coffee, black, bitter, practical, and sat by the kitchen window. Beyond the glass, the yard was still slick with rain, the grass flattened in small crescents where the wind had circled through. The air held that quiet before sound returns, when even birds seem to wait for the world to decide its next breath.

I pulled out my phone and dialed Eliyahu.

He answered on the third ring. "James."

"Were you awake?"

"I was," he said, and I could hear it, the noise of some anonymous hotel room behind him, television murmuring through thin walls, traffic echoing off glass.

"You're still in the States?"

"For my sins," he said dryly. "I had a lecture last night at Ohio State, so I am still in Columbus. I just need to pack up and I can be there in a couple of hours."

"Great," I said. "I need you here."

"I gathered," he said simply.

I let the silence stretch long enough for the words to settle between us. When I finally spoke, I gave him only what mattered. "Arnaut is alive and he came to the house last night. The wards held, but he didn't test them. He wanted to talk. He's been behind the disturbances in Grant Park. He believes the Veil is a wound, not a barrier, and that he intends to break it, starting here."

Eliyahu exhaled softly, a sound closer to prayer than surprise. "It seems he's become a surgeon of the sacred."

"Nearly his exact words," I said. "He thinks he's restoring balance. He's using an old, dangerous magic. We unleashed it once in Anglesey. The consequences were disastrous."

There was a pause. "Then the pattern in the park isn't random."

"No," I said. "He's building something. Or loosening something. The hum's steady now, but it's tightening, like pressure behind glass. I've tethered it. If the frequency shifts again, I'll know."

"Good," he said, voice quieter. "Let the stone listen when you can't."

"We'll meet here this morning," I continued. "Erin's pulling the data. Charlie's running field models. Casey and David are on support. I want your eyes before we act."

He made a sound of assent, low and certain. "I'll pack now and be to you shortly."

"Thank you."

Then the line went quiet.

I let the phone rest on the table. The rain had stopped. Outside, the light was the color of worn silver, the sky uncertain whether it wanted to clear.

By late morning, the house had settled into the rhythm of waiting. I brewed a fresh pot of coffee, then scrambled some eggs, fried up some potatoes, and set out some fresh squeezed orange juice The smell of potatoes, garlic, and onion filled the kitchen, cutting through the metallic scent of the wards. I looked around and realized the OJ alone may not suffice, so I grabbed a bottle of champagne from the wine fridge as I thought the day may call for mimosas to kick start us.

At eight thirty, I heard the familiar cough of Charlie's old truck outside. The sound was grounding, mundane, and perfect.

He stepped through the door with that broad, weathered ease he'd never lost from the service, blue stripped flannel, worn jeans, sleeves rolled up, and eyes that scanned the room the way pilots check weather even on clear days.

"You look terrible," he said with a warm smile.

"You say that every time."

"It keeps being true," he replied, setting a leather folder on the table.

He eyed the sword where it rested against the wall. "You're armed again."

"Old habits," I said.

He didn't push. "I brought the models we talked about. I ran some simulations overnight, low-frequency resonance patterns based on the coordinates Erin sent. If her data's right, whatever's happening in the park isn't spreading outward. It's drawing inward. Like pressure equalizing around a vent."

"Containment or collapse?" I asked.

He shrugged. "That depends on whether it's deliberate, though I think we know which." I nodded. "Either way, if we don't vent it, it will find its own way out."

I nodded. "Eliyahu's on his way now. We'll decide then."

He gave a small, approving grunt, the sound of an engineer who knows action is at least scheduled.

"Eat?" I asked.

"Depends," he said. "Is it safe?"

"Marginally."

He poured himself coffee and leaned against the counter. "You talked to Erin yet?"

"She's coming by shortly."

"Good. She's the only one of us who still understands how data behaves when it's nervous."

That pulled a smile from me.

Casey and David arrived next. Casey carried a plate with a cloth napkin over the top with images of chili peppers, and presented what she called a "half-successful" tart, still warm. David brought the same nervous energy he brought everywhere, phone clasped so tightly in his hand I thought it might crack.

"Erin will be here in a minute. She is still on her laptop typing furiously," Casey said as she placed her plate on the kitchen counter. Her face lit up then, "Ooh, mimosas!"

They filled the house with noise; a domestic chaos that made it almost feel normal. Casey claimed my kitchen as her own within ten minutes, rearranging utensils and muttering about "the lack of flavors in my spice cabinet." David set to helping Charlie at the table, sorting the maps, labeling coordinates, tracing routes.

The sound of their voices did what my wards could not, it grounded the place.

Erin arrived last. She pushed the door open with her shoulder, hair damp, laptop bag slung crosswise, and that look she got when her brain was already several steps ahead of her mouth. She stopped short when she saw the sword leaning against the wall.

"Oh," she said. "We're escalating."

"You're late," I said with a welcome smile.

"I was chasing data, not time." She pulled out her laptop, dropped her bag, kicked off her shoes, and walked over and unrolled a map across the table as if she'd been living here all along.

"You're also dripping on my floor."

"That's your fault for not having a mat."

Casey gave me a sidelong glance that said, she's your problem now.

We ate. The food was mediocre, the company good. That's balance enough. Casey's tart saved the eggs from mediocrity, and even David, who had the palate of a kindergartner, went back for seconds. We engaged in small talk as we laid everything out and refilled the mimosas.

For a few minutes, laughter filled the kitchen. It felt like a luxury.

When the plates were cleared, the room's weight returned, gently, but unmistakably. Erin opened her laptop, fingers moving fast. "Okay," she said. "Let's see what kind of apocalypse we're dealing with."

She opened a map on her computer, Centerville in soft green and gray, arteries of roads converging around Grant Park like veins toward a heart. She zoomed in, layer by layer, until the fine grid of time-stamped incidents filled the screen, dots in fading reds and yellows.

"Two weeks of reports," she said. "Traffic collisions, medical calls, missing pets, electrical malfunctions, animal strikes, people freezing in place, I pulled everything. Then I filtered by pattern, not category. This is what's left."

She tapped a key. The dots pulsed once and then began to shift, reforming into concentric rings.

"Grant Park is the center," she continued. "Everything radiates inward. Each circle compresses faster than the last."

Charlie leaned in. "Rate of change?"

"Outer ring, every thirty hours. Middle ring, twelve. Inner ring, six. Then… this." She hit another key. The rings blinked once, the core flashing white.

"What's that?" Casey asked.

"Two hours ago," Erin said. "I was late so that I could update these latest data points."

"If I am reading this right, the pattern is holding," I said. "But it's speeding up."

Erin nodded. "That fits. Whatever's happening is accelerating. It's not cyclical, not lunar, not seasonal. It's linear, timed. Like a fuse burning toward the center."

"Which means?" David asked, looking up from his phone.

She glanced at him. "We have three days. Maybe four. But I'm leaning three."

The room went still.

Charlie exhaled. "It's a countdown."

"Exactly," she said. "Each compression line reduces the interval between anomalies. The curve's perfect, someone built it that way."

"Arnaut," I said.

"Whomever it is," Erin said. "It's too deliberate. Even the deviations line up like planned corrections. They are controlling the rhythm."

Casey frowned. "What happens when it hits zero?"

"That's what we're going to find out," I said quietly.

The doorbell rang.

It was nearly 11 o' clock as I made my way to the door.

Eliyahu looked exactly as he had the last time I'd seen him, coat slightly wrinkled from the road, canvas bag over one shoulder, a calm only earned by arguing with both professors and hotel clerks in the same week. His eyes held that old light, humor first, faith second, weariness third, and something older beneath.

"James," he said.

"Come in."

He stepped across the threshold, pausing just long enough to incline his head toward the wards. "Your house hums like it's trying to remember a song."

"It's tired of my company," I said.

"I can relate." He smiled, brief and warm, and shrugged off his coat. "Where are they?"

"In the kitchen," I said. "You hungry?"

"Only for answers."

I picked up the pouch of charms from the entry table on my way to the door. When he walked in, the conversation stopped, but the silence that followed wasn't awkward, but reverence, recognition of gravity.

I made introductions to those he hadn't met. He greeted each of them like equals, Erin with curiosity, Charlie with respect, Casey with kindness, David with the warmth of fellowship.

Then his attention fell on the map. "Good," he said softly. "You've taught the problem to speak."

Erin handed him the printout. "Six points," she said. "We think they align with structural nodes of the distortion. The hollow near Holes Creek, the rise above the trail, the northern ridge, the old foundations by the ruins, the east fence, and the woods behind Watts."

He studied it for a long moment, then drew a fingertip along the center arc. "Six is good," he murmured. "Balance without vanity. Circles invite, squares bind, hexes distribute. We don't want to invite or bind; we want to brace."

Charlie nodded, already sketching. "A load-spreading frame."

"Exactly."

David leaned forward. "And what are we bracing?"

"The wound," Eliyahu said simply. "If we can't close it, we can remind the world how to hold its shape."

They worked through details with the quiet intensity of veterans assembling old weapons. Erin adjusted coordinates. Charlie calculated intervals.

Casey took notes, though I suspected it was more to steady her hands than for record.

I listened. And for a while, the sound of their voices became a strange comfort, the living counterpoint to Arnaut's cold conviction.

When the planning reached a pause, I untied the pouch and spread the silver charms on the table.

"Before we get ahead of ourselves," I said, "these are yours."

The disks caught the light; each etched with a pattern no larger than a thumbprint.

"Jewelry!" Casey beamed.

"Early warnings," I said. "Simple wards keyed to proximity and resonance. They'll warm when danger draws near, not heat, just a pulse. Don't ignore it."

"Effective range?" Charlie asked.

"About thirty yards for direct threat," I said. "More if whatever's coming is loud."

I called each name aloud once, Erin, Charlie, Casey, David, and tied the cords around their necks. The silver warmed instantly against skin.

Charlie didn't react. Erin flinched slightly, eyes widening. Casey smiled in surprise, then blinked fast as though she'd been holding her breath too long. David only nodded once, jaw tight, accepting the weight without question.

The last charm I kept. It belonged to me.

Eliyahu watched the exchange quietly. "Good," he said. "We'll need warning when the line starts to sing."

He picked up Erin's printout again, tapping a line near the park's center. "Tomorrow," he said. "At twilight. The day softens then. The air listens. That's when we move."

Erin frowned. "Tomorrow? We're already running on only three days."

"Three days measured in the human sense," he said. "The pattern follows its own clock. Twilight is when the world balances between saying yes and no. The transition from day to night is when the world is most open to influence."

I nodded. "He's right. The pressure will peak in the final cycle. That's our window."

Casey exhaled, rubbing the charm against her chest. "So, we have one night to prepare."

"One night," I confirmed.

No one argued.

Outside, the clouds began to thin. The light through the windows turned the color of old bone. Somewhere in the distance, a siren cut off mid-wail. The hum in the floor deepened by a note.

The pattern was holding, for a few days more anyway. Evening came early. The sky dimmed without ceremony, the way it does when the air's too heavy to bother with color. By six, we'd run out of things to prepare for. The plan was finished, if you could call it that, a mixture of precision and faith, of Erin's equations and Eliyahu's quiet conviction that meaning held the same weight as math.

Everyone stayed through dinner. It wasn't much, bread, pasta, a couple bottles of a Galilean red that I thought David and Eliyahu would appreciate. The conversation drifted between logistics and distraction; laughter edged with nerves.

Charlie ate like a man who'd learned to chew through waiting. He was the practical one, always grounding us when our talk started floating toward metaphysics. Casey kept things lighter, filling the air with small talk that didn't quite hide the tension behind her smile. Erin sat near the head of the table, the glow of her laptop painting her face in shifting blues. Her fingers twitched against the keys even when she wasn't typing, her mind chasing patterns. David never sat still. He paced, leaned, shifted, fiddled with a cable, checked his phone nonstop, not out of need, but out of nervous energy looking for an outlet. His leg bounced as though it was keeping time with an invisible metronome.

"I can't help shake the thought," David said at one point, "This anomaly, it's... adaptive. Like code rewriting itself while it's running."

Erin looked up. "Which means we can't just cut it. We must rewrite it back."

He nodded, chewing on a thumbnail. "If it were software I could fix it, but this...this whatever it is, doesn't have the same rules as binary code. I recognize some of it, and understand none of it."

Eliyahu grinned. "God created the world with ten utterances... and each one still echoes. Who are we to understand what God has wrought."

Casey smirked. "I'm trying my damnedest Rabbi."

Eliyahu smiled back, a look of paternal patience in his eye, "Be careful with your words young lady, there may be more truth in them than you intended."

The room carried the sound of tired laughter. A shared moment to stave off the nervous energy we all carried. We needed it.

Charlie checked his watch. "We should all get some rest. Tomorrow's going to be long."

Casey rose first, tucking a strand of hair behind her ear. "If I go home now, maybe I can convince my brain to stop rehearsing doom scenarios for an hour."

"I'd recommend bourbon," Charlie said.

"I was going to say optimism," she countered. "But yours sounds more effective."

Erin packed up her laptop, still muttering about algorithms. David helped her with the cords, hands trembling just enough to betray him. When he caught me watching, he shrugged. "I don't sleep much anyway. Too many tabs open."

They left in pairs, Charlie and David first, then Erin and Casey, the soft rhythm of their goodbyes carrying a kind of unspoken understanding, whether we succeeded or failed, tomorrow would change everything.

That left Eliyahu and me. He stood by the window, watching the last of the light die across the neighborhood rooftops. The world outside had that washed, reflective stillness that only comes after rain and before reckoning.

"Strange thing," he said. "How people prepare for what they can't imagine."

"That's what faith used to be for," I said. "Now it's mostly spreadsheets and contingency plans."

He smiled. "You think they're different?"

"I think one used to comfort people."

He turned from the window. "I think both exist in the hopes of learning truth. Modern tools are just the newest way to seek answers. Since humans existed they sought answers to things beyond their comprehension. Faith in a higher power filled in the gaps in understanding of the natural world. If something couldn't be explained, it was HaShem that filled in the gaps. We just have more tools today that have filled in the gaps, and perhaps that is why we move further from faith."

"Profound, but a philosophical debate for another day."

He gave a sheepish shrug and leaned against the table, eyes tracing the grooves in the wood. "Arnaut believes he's restoring balance. That's the hardest kind of heresy to fight, the kind that calls itself healing."

"I've fought enough monsters who thought they were saving the world," I said quietly. "They always start with conviction. End with fire."

Eliyahu studied me for a long moment. "You don't hate him."

"I should."

"But you don't."

I shook my head. "He was my brother. Once. And he's still fighting something real; he's just looking at it from the wrong side of the glass."

He nodded. "Maybe. Or maybe he found something that fills a gap in his own view of the world."

The silence that followed wasn't empty, but full of everything we didn't say. The years, the failures, the weight of too many second chances. Outside, a single car passed, its headlights sweeping across the curtains like a slow exhale.

Eliyahu broke the stillness first. "You know, the Talmud says that before the world was created, God drew back into Himself, a contraction, a pause. Only then could creation unfold. Perhaps tomorrow, all we need to do is make space for that pause again."

"You're suggesting we ask the world to breathe."

"In a way," he said. "Sometimes breathing is all the defense we have."

He turned toward the hallway, the old floorboards creaking under his steps. "You should rest, James. Morning will come too quickly."

"Good night, Rabbi. We will need all the luck we can muster tomorrow."

He stopped at the doorway, glanced back. "Sheyihiyeh b'mazel tov, may

HaShem grant us success."

He smiled, small, tired, and human, then disappeared down the hall to the guest room.

I stayed a while longer, alone in the kitchen. The remains of dinner sat cold on the table. A bottle of wine was half-empty, the light from the window fading into the glass. The air smelled of smoke and rain. I refilled my glass and sank into the couch, reflecting on our discussion and wondering whether Arnaut could be brought to reason. I looked at the sword leaning on the other side of the room, and thought I likely will have need of it soon.

I sat, listening to the quiet, the steady tick of the clock, the distant hum of the world preparing to break or heal.

Tomorrow, everything would move.

But for tonight, the house, and I, were still.

18

Memories, Lessons, and the Master (Rouen, 1067)

Rouen woke slowly that morning, as if the city itself were still deciding what kind of kingdom it now served. Six months had passed since Hastings, and the air still carried the unease of change, the weight of new banners, new masters, new prayers. Mist drifted off the Seine and curled through the narrow streets, clinging to rooftops and chimneys until it burned away in pale ribbons of silver. The cathedral bells tolled, steady and unbothered, as though they alone remembered the world before the conquest.

The garden lay behind a canon's house near the cloister wall. It wasn't much to look at, three small trees, a rectangle of churned soil, and a line of hedges so overgrown they looked like they were trying to keep the city out. The Church called it a place of reflection. Bishop Geoffrey borrowed it for something less holy.

Lothaire, the swordmaster, was already there when I arrived. He stood in the center of the yard, coat off, sleeves rolled, a wooden practice blade balanced easily on one shoulder. His hair was close-cropped and gray, his face seamed by years of squinting into sun and smoke. He'd fought for many lords and cardinals over the years, if the scars along his jaw were any hint, a man whose loyalty had been beaten out of him and replaced with skill.

He looked me over the way a stonemason studies a wall that might not hold.

"You're early," he said.

"I was told to be."

"Good, late men spend more time bleeding."

Behind him, Geoffrey sat beneath a young pear tree, cloak pulled tight, a small book open on his knee. He nodded once in greeting, serene as always, eyes already tracing the margins of thought. Beside him, Arnaut leaned against the wall, arms crossed, half in sunlight, half in shadow, looking like he'd been born there out of stubbornness.

Arnaut had the poise of a man used to surviving things other men avoided, sieges, blasphemies, and conversations with Geoffrey. He'd been in the Watch for years, and it showed in the way he moved, confident and charismatic.

Lothaire tossed me a wooden practice sword. "You've held one before?"

"Enough to know which end kills."

"Every man says that," he said. "And every grave disagrees."

He drew a line across the dirt with his boot. "Stand there."

The blade felt awkward in my hand, too light, too honest. I stepped into position as Geoffrey turned a page without looking up. Arnaut smirked, already entertained, waiting to see how this played out and hoping to be entertained.

"Show me your guard," Lothaire said.

I raised the sword.

He frowned. "You hold it like a farmer gripping a hoe. Too much hand, not enough heart."

"That's strange," Arnaut said. "I've seen him plow well enough in battle."

"Not helping," Lothaire said. "Again."

I adjusted my grip and the swordmaster stepped forward, correcting my stance with the heel of his boot. His hands were rough, his movements economical. He smelled of oil, steel, and fatigue.

"Better," he said. "Now remember, this isn't about strength. It's about weight and balance. Yours, his, and the air between. The sword is a conversation, and if you shout, you'll be ignored."

Arnaut muttered, "Sometimes shouting's the only way people listen."

Lothaire ignored him. "Lift."

I lifted.

"Turn."

I turned.

"Cut."

The wooden blades struck with a hollow clack that traveled up my arm.

"Again," he said. "Until you stop overthinking."

We moved through the rhythm until sweat found my eyes and breath came ragged. Geoffrey's gaze never left the page, but I could feel him listening, measuring. Arnaut watched with the easy grin of someone who remembered being corrected the same way years ago and enjoyed watching someone else endure it.

When the sun crept over the cloister wall, Lothaire dropped his sword point to the ground. "Water."

He passed me a clay cup. The water was cold, brackish, but welcome.

Arnaut leaned off the wall, stretching his shoulders. "He's not bad," he said. "A little slow, but he learns."

"Slow is fine," Geoffrey said, still reading. "It's the ones who learn fast that worry me."

"Because they think they understand," Arnaut said knowingly.

"Because they stop asking questions," Geoffrey corrected.

Lothaire sat on a barrel and rubbed his shoulder. "He's strong enough. His balance will come and the hands are good."

"The head is better," Geoffrey said quietly.

"Sometimes that's the problem," Arnaut replied. "Thinking doesn't help when steel's already moving."

"Thinking," Geoffrey said, "is what keeps steel from moving too soon."

Their voices blended into something familiar, not argument, but ritual. Lothaire rolled his eyes heavenward. "You see what I deal with, James? Priests with sermons."

Arnaut grinned. "It's what keeps him young."

"That, and sin," Geoffrey said mildly.

The swordmaster stood, motioning me forward again. "Enough talk. The Church will still be arguing when the world ends. Lift."

We drilled again, faster this time, short exchanges, light on strength, heavy on timing. He attacked high, low, diagonal. My arms ached, but the movements began to find rhythm. The wood struck, rebounded, found its path again.

"Don't fight the blade," he said. "Guide it."

"That's easy for you to say," I grunted.

"It's easy for anyone who's tired of bleeding," he replied.

By the time he stepped back, my shirt clung damp to my back and my forearms burned.

"Enough," he said. "You're still upright. That's something."

Geoffrey closed his book and rose, brushing dust from his cloak. "Now we need to make him understand."

"Understanding doesn't make him dangerous," Arnaut said. "Practice does."

Lothaire shrugged. "Dangerous comes later. I'm still teaching him to be deliberate."

Geoffrey smiled. "And I'll teach him why."

"Two teachers," Arnaut rolled his eyes. "He'll be twice as confused."

Lothaire snorted, then waved me toward the bench. "Sit before you fall. You'll bruise slower if you rest now."

I obeyed. The air smelled of earth and pear blossoms. Beyond the wall, the sounds of Rouen rose and fell, carts, voices, a dog barking at nothing.

Geoffrey handed me a piece of bread from a small satchel. "You've come far, James. You could have chosen an easier road. Do you still want this? There are easier paths."

"Easier maybe," I said. "But this feels like a calling, something bigger than me."

Arnaut nodded once, approving. "That's how it starts for all of us, a noble reason."

"And how does it end?" I asked rhetorically.

"With a better one," Geoffrey answered anyway. "Or none at all."

"Either way there are always bruises," Lothaire muttered, and drained his water.

We ate in silence for a time. A silence that holds meaning, unspoken agreement that talk would only ruin the peace.

Then Geoffrey said, "Someday, when you take the Oath, remember this day. Not the pain or the drills, this. The smell of spring, the sound of steel learning to speak, the laughter you tried not to show. All things worth defending start like this."

Arnaut smiled. "And end messier."

"True," Geoffrey said. "And that's why we remember the beginnings."

I sat back, listening to them, to the bells beyond the wall, to the wind moving through the trees. I didn't know it then, but these were the last days before the Watch stopped being an idea and became a way of life.

The rest of the day passed slowly, as if time itself had stopped to watch me sweat. The garden grew warmer with each passing hour, the air thick with the scent of damp soil and early pear blossoms. Rouen's bells tolled again somewhere beyond the cloister wall, Vespers already, though to me it felt like dawn had barely broken.

Lothaire had left mid-afternoon, muttering something about dull students and sharper steel, leaving the three of us to talk. Geoffrey stayed seated beneath the pear tree, hands folded neatly over his knees, his book now closed but still resting there like a promise. Arnaut, restless as ever, wandered the garden's perimeter, testing the new fence posts with idle kicks and muttering observations that sounded half like jokes and half like military reports.

I sat my training blade against a bench, content to let silence be the fourth man among us. But Geoffrey was never one to waste quiet when there was a lesson waiting inside it.

"James," he said finally, eyes still half on the sky, "you handled yourself well today."

I shrugged. "If getting hit less often counts as handling."

"Oh, it does," he said mildly. "At least in our work."

Arnaut chuckled and leaned against the wall. "If you can still hold a sword when the day's done, you're ahead of half the Watch novices that I've met."

"Only half?" I asked.

"The other half are dead," he said cheerfully with a beaming smile.

Geoffrey gave him a look of patient exasperation. "You see why I was given this assignment," he said to me. "To balance him."

"I'm very balanced," Arnaut said. "I can drink with either hand."

I couldn't help laughing, which made Geoffrey sigh, a sigh that meant he was amused but unwilling to show it.

"Discipline," he said, "isn't about obedience. It's about understanding why something must be done even when you hate doing it. That's what separates us from soldiers."

Arnaut tilted his head. "No, what separates us from soldiers is that no one ever sings songs about us afterward."

"They sing of kings," Geoffrey said, "not stewards. But kings fall when stewards fail. The Watch exists to make sure the world stays balanced long enough for others to think it never needed saving."

He turned his gaze to me then, calm but piercing. "Our victories go unremembered by design. When we succeed, history stays dull and predictable and that is our burden."

I sat quietly, weighing that. "You make it sound like invisibility is a virtue."

"In our trade, it's survival," Arnaut said, kicking at a pebble. "We keep the world turning while everyone else sleeps through the noise."

Geoffrey's mouth tightened, not in disagreement, but in acceptance of a truth he disliked. "Perhaps, but I'd rather you think of it as stewardship, not noise. The Watch doesn't rule, we guard the edges of things, faith, reason, the evil that doesn't belong in our world. When one grows too loud, the other weakens, and balance must be restored."

He looked down at the closed book in his lap. "Most of us don't live long enough to see what balance truly means."

Arnaut crossed his arms. "Because most of us die while someone's busy defining it."

Their words hung in the air for a long moment. The sunlight shifted, catching in the dust that drifted lazily between us.

"Do you ever agree on anything?" I asked finally.

"Yes," Geoffrey said.

"No," Arnaut said at the same time.

That broke whatever tension lingered, and I found myself smiling again.

Geoffrey gave a shake of his head. "One day you'll see, James, that he was sent to teach you what I cannot."

"And what's that?"

"How to keep faith when faith is no longer comfortable."

Arnaut smirked. "That's the polite way of saying I'll teach you how to fight dirty when God's not watching."

"God is always watching," Geoffrey said.

"Then He's developed a sense of humor," Arnaut replied.

I couldn't tell if their exchanges were rehearsed or instinct. They had the cadence of an old friendship, like men who'd disagreed so often that disagreement itself had become a form of affection.

Geoffrey eventually rose from the bench and brushed the dust from his cloak. "Walk with me," he said, leaving Arnaut to feign insult.

We circled the garden's edge, where the stone wall met the hedges. A small iron gate opened onto a narrow alley that smelled of wet straw and forge smoke. Through the cracks in the mortar, the sounds of Rouen filtered in, merchants shouting, children chasing each other through puddles, the metallic ring of a blacksmith shaping a future he'd never see.

Geoffrey's pace was slow, thoughtful. "When you enter the Watch, you'll be given no heraldry, no family, no name beyond the one you've already borne. You will be told to protect the world from those that seek to destroy it and to obey its keepers. You'll think that means obeying us."

"Doesn't it?" I asked.

He smiled. "Only until you learn that obedience is the first test, not the goal."

We stopped beneath the shadow of the wall. The ivy here was thick, heavy with dew.

"Every member of the Watch must learn where the line lies, not just between good and evil, but between duty and self. We don't fight men, James, we fight what moves through them."

I thought of Hastings, the noise, the horror, the faces. "And when what moves through them wins?"

"Then we record it," Geoffrey said quietly. "And we try again somewhere else."

I looked down at my hands, the bruises darkening across my knuckles. "You make it sound like we lose more than we win."

He didn't answer right away. "Loss is part of the pattern. We hold the line for a season, then others take our place. The world stays whole because enough people refuse to let it break at the same time."

From behind us came Arnaut's voice, echoing lightly across the stones. "That's the sermon version. The truth is, we win by inches and die by miles. But we win enough to keep the rest from noticing."

I turned to see him strolling toward us, biting into an apple he'd stolen from Lothaire's supply.

Geoffrey gave him a weary look. "Do you ever not eavesdrop?"

"Only when you're boring," Arnaut said, taking another bite.

He tossed me the core and I caught it by reflex. "You'll learn both sides soon enough," he said. "Geoffrey teaches the 'why.' I teach the 'how.' And Lothaire makes sure you live long enough to argue about both."

"I'm beginning to think you enjoy being contrary," I said.

"I do," he said without shame. "Contradiction keeps the blood moving."

Geoffrey folded his arms, half smiling despite himself. "You see why he's impossible."

Before I could answer, there was a loud clatter at the gate, followed by a sharp voice that addressed Geoffrey. "Monsieur, by Saint Denis and his donkey, what din is this? Sounds like the Devil's choir rehearsing!" said the guard in Old Norman French.

We turned. A city guard stood just outside the iron bars, one hand resting on the hilt of a short sword, the other gesturing vaguely toward the garden. His helmet was too large, his uniform slightly askew. Behind him, two younger guards craned their necks to see what he was confronting.

"This is private ground," Geoffrey said softly and politely.

The guard squinted. "Private or not, folk been complaining about sword fighting and sermons all morning. We got reports of 'holy combat,' whatever that's meant to be."

Arnaut straightened, eyes bright with mischief. "Holy combat? That's new. We've been promoted."

Geoffrey pinched the bridge of his nose. "There are no disturbances here sir, we're conducting a lesson on church grounds."

"Church or not," the guard said, "folks don't like hearing war drills while they're trying to sell bread."

"Would you prefer we do it in the cathedral?" Arnaut asked.

The guard blinked. "You... what?"

"Never mind him," Geoffrey said quickly. "We'll keep it down."

The man hesitated, clearly out of his depth. "Fine. But if I hear more clanging or preaching, I'll be back."

"Please don't," Geoffrey said politely, but with clear exasperation.

Arnaut waited until the guard and his companions disappeared down the alley before bursting into laughter. "Holy combat," he repeated. "I might put that on my tombstone."

"It would be accurate," Geoffrey said dryly.

"Nah, I plan to live forever. You may never know when the world needs saving and there is no one to help."

"I think the only reason you joined the Watch was that immortality will give you an opportunity to drink and gamble in every tavern built by man," Geoffrey muttered.

"What good is immortality if you can't ride the line between sin and duty," Arnaut argued merely to get a reaction from Geoffrey.

I laughed despite myself, a laugh that comes too easily after tension. For a moment, even Geoffrey smiled, quick, small, but real.

"Come," he said. "Enough interruptions. Let's finish our lesson before the city declares us heretics."

We returned to the center of the garden. The sun had begun to dip, casting long shadows across the dirt. The world felt softer now, the sharp edges of the morning worn down by fatigue and familiarity.

Arnaut leaned on the wall again, chewing on a sprig of pear blossom like a pipe. "All right, Bishop. Give the lad his final revelation. What's the great secret of the Watch?"

Geoffrey looked at me for a long moment before answering. "That there are no secrets," he said. "Only duties we refuse to name."

He stepped closer, placing a hand on my shoulder. "You'll see wonders and horrors. You'll see men burn for things they don't understand and creatures die for reasons that don't matter. You'll confront things not from this world, and are only ever spoken about in whispers or by mothers scaring their children to behave. The only compass you'll ever have is your own measure of right. Guard it. Question it. But don't let anyone take it from you, not even me."

I nodded, only half understanding what I was hearing at the time.

Arnaut straightened. "And when your measure fails?"

"Then," Geoffrey said softly, "you pray that someone else's doesn't."

The last light caught in his hair, turning the gray to silver. For a heartbeat, he looked ancient, carved from the same stillness that filled the garden.

We stood there as the bells of Rouen called the hour again. The smell of hearth fire drifted in from the city. Arnaut stretched, slinging his coat over his shoulder. "Lesson's over, then?"

"For today," Geoffrey said.

"Good," Arnaut replied. "Because I'm starving."

Geoffrey gave a patient smile. "Of course you are."

We started toward the gate, the three of us falling into step. Rouen's rooftops glowed gold in the setting light, and the sound of the river carried through the alleyways, steady, eternal.

For the first time that day, I felt something close to peace. Not the kind that came from certainty, but the quieter kind, the moment between exhaustion and purpose, when both feel the same.

By the time the sun sank behind Rouen's rooftops, the city had folded into itself. Smoke rose in thin gray threads from a hundred hearths, and the streets glowed from scattered torches set in iron sconces. The clang of the smiths had gone quiet, replaced by the low rhythm of taverns and distant voices.

We ate in the refectory hall that night, bread gone hard from the day's air, a small bowl of lentils, and a thin ale that pretended to be beer. Geoffrey gave thanks in Latin, Arnaut mumbled something less polite in what I thought was Old Dutch, and I sat between them pretending to understand both.

"Tell me," Arnaut said around a mouthful of bread, "how long do you think until they let him out into the real world with me?"

"Another year, at least," Geoffrey replied calmly.

"A year?" Arnaut looked at me as if I'd been sentenced. "You'll forget how to bleed properly by then."

"That's the point," Geoffrey said. "If he's still eager to fight after a year of Lothaire's lessons, we'll know he's hopeless."

"I'll take hopeless over holy," Arnaut muttered. "Holy gets you killed slower, but it still gets you killed."

I hid a smile in my bowl. Geoffrey noticed and gave me a look of approval, which I took as permission to exist.

After the meal, we stepped outside into the courtyard. The air was cool and sweet with the smell of rain on stone. Rouen lay quiet beyond the walls, the Seine murmuring like a secret in the dark. A single torch burned beside the cloister gate, throwing just enough light for us to see each other's faces without making the world feel smaller.

Geoffrey folded his arms in his sleeves. "You did well today," he said to me again. "Lothaire said as much."

"That's not what he said to me," Arnaut said.

"I suspect he chooses his words depending on the audience," Geoffrey said.

Arnaut laughed. "Then he's wiser than most priests."

"He's a soldier," Geoffrey said. "He's learned what words buy and what they cost."

"I've learned that too," Arnaut said, "and I'm not half as polite about it."

Geoffrey gave him an admonishing look.

I leaned against one of the cloister's pillars, content to listen. The night had the same kind of peace the garden did earlier, earned, not given. For the first time since arriving in Rouen, I felt like I was standing in the space between who I'd been and who I might become.

"Tell me something, James," Arnaut said. "What do you think you've signed up for?"

"Training," I said, not sure if I was being baited. "Service. Discipline."

He barked a short laugh. "All true. None sufficient."

Geoffrey smiled. "He's not wrong. But neither is he right."

"Well, I am always right," Arnaut said. "The secret is that sometimes you have to figure out how."

Geoffrey ignored him. "You're not training for battle, James. You're training to see. The sword is the easy part. Any man can learn to kill. You're learning when not to."

"That sounds more like your work than mine," Arnaut said.

"It's everyone's work," Geoffrey replied.

I frowned. "And what happens when the choice isn't clear?"

Geoffrey looked at me with the patience of a man who had already heard every question worth asking. "Then you will be judged not by what you chose, but by what you understood before choosing."

Arnaut rolled his eyes. "He's going to fill your head with riddles until you forget which end of the sword to hold."

"It's better than swinging blind," Geoffrey said.

"Blind?" Arnaut grinned. "I once took a fortress at night with one torch and one eye."

"And a dozen men who didn't know better than to follow you," Geoffrey said.

"Exactly," Arnaut said proudly.

The two of them had that way, one building walls, the other knocking them down for sport. I'd seen soldiers bicker and priests preach, but never both at once. I was watching two halves of a story argue over who got to be true.

They fell quiet for a while, watching the torchlight tremble on the wet stones. The bells from the cathedral carried through the night, rich and distant.

"Did you ever think," Arnaut said suddenly, "that Hastings might've gone the other way?"

Geoffrey gave him a measured glance. "Often."

"And?"

"Then the wrong men would still have been dead, and the wrong men would still be in charge," Geoffrey said. "War changes names, not natures."

Arnaut smiled. "See, that's why I like you, Bishop. You say terrible things beautifully."

"It's the only way people will listen," Geoffrey said.

Arnaut chuckled. "True enough."

He turned to me. "Remember this, James, Geoffrey teaches you how to think, but the world won't wait for you to finish thinking. One day you'll have to move before you understand, and then pray you learn afterward."

"That's the lesson?" I asked.

He shrugged. "No, that's survival. The lesson is that you won't always get to tell which is which."

Geoffrey smiled at that. "Perhaps you've learned something after all."

"Don't ruin it," Arnaut said.

The bells tolled again, softer this time. The night had taken on that blue darkness that comes before true black, the kind that promises rain or forgiveness.

We stayed there a while longer, talking about nothing that mattered and everything that did. Arnaut told a story about a monk who tried to bless a cat and lost his thumb for the effort. Geoffrey countered with a tale about a saint who claimed to walk on water until someone pointed out it was winter and the river was frozen. I added nothing except the laughter that came too easily after exhaustion.

When the hour grew late, Geoffrey excused himself to prepare for morning prayers. He left us with a blessing that sounded more like advice. "Rest, both of you," he said. "Tomorrow will not be gentler just because today was hard."

Arnaut and I lingered after he went inside. The torch hissed in the damp air.

"You ever get tired of him?" I asked.

"Every day," Arnaut said fondly. "He's the only man I'd follow into Hell.

Mostly because he'd insist it was a misunderstanding and talk the Devil into leaving."

He pushed off the wall and clapped my shoulder. "Come on, there's wine in the stable loft. The monks pretend they don't know about it. Best we keep their illusion intact."

I followed him, part from curiosity, part from thirst, and part because I didn't know how to refuse him yet.

We found the small cask behind a stack of hay and poured two tin cups. The wine was rough, half vinegar and half blessing, but after the day I'd had, it might as well have been heaven.

Arnaut raised his cup. "To the fools who think they can make the world less broken."

I raised mine. "To the ones who try anyway."

He smiled, and for the first time that day, it wasn't the smile of a soldier or a cynic, but the smile of someone who still believed, even if he'd forgotten in what.

We drank, and for a moment, the world beyond Rouen, the wars, the whispers, the shadows that Geoffrey spoke of, all of it felt far away.

Later, when the candles had guttered and we had our fill of wine, we sat in the hay listening to the river and the rain on the roof. Neither of us spoke.

And though I didn't know it then, that night, the laughter, the stories, the wine, would stay with me longer than most of the prayers that followed.

I didn't sleep much that night, mostly out of reflection. My brain reeling to take in everything from that day. Every time I closed my eyes, the day replayed itself in fragments, Lothaire's voice correcting my grip, Geoffrey's patient silences, Arnaut's laughter cutting through both like a sword finding a gap in armor.

Outside, Rouen's rain had turned steady, the kind that softens every edge it touches. The river carried the sound through the alleys like a hymn half-forgotten. Somewhere a bell rang the last prayers of the night, its echo stretching across the rooftops until it reached me.

I remember thinking that the world felt too big for one man to hold and too fragile not to try.

When morning finally came, the city was silver and washed clean. Smoke rose thin from the bakeries and the soldiers at the gate were stamping their feet against the cold. Geoffrey was already at prayer when I passed his chamber, head bowed, motionless except for his lips. I never heard what he said in those moments, but I came to know the rhythm. The same cadence he used when he spoke of duty or forgiveness, quiet and certain, as if neither word needed convincing.

Arnaut appeared later, rubbing sleep from his eyes and cursing the damp as if it were personal. He looked exactly as he had the night before, perhaps a little older in the light, perhaps not. That was Arnaut's way, he lived in the space between jest and sorrow, moving through it as easily as other men crossed streets.

He clapped my shoulder on his way past. "You look like a man trying to remember his dreams," he said.

"Trying," I admitted.

"Best forget them," he said. "Dreams give false hope, better to be pragmatic like me."

Then he grinned, and the heaviness of morning lifted just enough to breathe.

We trained again that day, and the next, and the one after. The lessons repeated until the bruises no longer surprised me and the ache in my arms became a kind of prayer of its own. Geoffrey's lectures found me in the quiet hours, Arnaut's advice in the loud ones. Between them, I learned the rhythm of the Watch without realizing I was being taught, fight when there's no other way, forgive when you can, and keep moving when you can't tell the difference.

The days and nights in Rouen stretched into a blur. Through it all, Arnaut was there, laughing too loud, drinking too much, always somehow right when I least expected him to be. He had a way of seeing through people that wasn't cruel, just clear. He'd watch the world the way a gambler watches dice, not with hope, but with curiosity about how the game might surprise him next.

I remember one evening months later, standing on the same cloister wall, the city quiet beneath a cold blue moon. Geoffrey had been called away to Rouen's cathedral for some council I wasn't high enough to hear about. Arnaut had fallen asleep in a chair, boots still on, a half-empty bottle balanced on his knee.

The pear tree had gone bare by then. Its branches clawed at the air like a hand reaching for something it could no longer grasp. I thought of the bishop's words, *All things worth defending start like this*, and realized I had begun to understand. Not fully. But enough to feel the weight of it.

We weren't soldiers or saints, not yet and maybe never. We were just three men in a changing world, trying to decide what was worth holding and what needed to be let go.

In the years that followed, I would forget parts of that day, the exact words, the shape of the garden, even the sound of Lothaire's laughter as he scolded me for bad footwork, but not the feeling. That quiet certainty that the world was fragile and worth protecting anyway.

I carried that with me longer than any weapon. I remember wondering at the time, when I was given a choice between morals, duty, and loyalty, would I choose the right path.

19

Stones, Ash, and the Battle (Ohio, Present)

We arrived at Grant Park just before dusk. We parked and unloaded our gear and hiked into the park where we started to lay out our items, a mix of state-of-the-art and the arcane. In an abundance of prudence, Erin, Casey, Charlie, and David had armed themselves. Casey and Erin with their trusty Glocks, David with his new Jericho, and Charlie had a 12-gauge strapped across his shoulder. There was a risk to carrying them this close to a school, but no one was going to take any more chances than they had to, even if the weapons offered little protection against what lay on the other side of the Veil.

The sun set without ceremony, the same way it had since the world was born. There was no color, no fanfare, just a slow erasure of light until the horizon became a bruise and the clouds settled into their own weight. We set up a perimeter of lights to allow us to work in the dark of the forest.

The air felt wrong, too still and too measured. The trees stood in absolute silence, and even the wind refused to play among their leaves. The field in the park's center, a stretch of thin, trampled grass, had become the core of our work. We set up six marked points to form a rough hexagon and snaked copper wire between them like veins beneath skin. It didn't look like much, but aesthetics didn't matter.

Eliyahu knelt at the first node, tapping the soil with the handle of a hammer. The small iron stake caught the stand lights we'd erected, glinting before he set it firm. He dusted the ground with a pinch of salt and murmured something in Hebrew too quiet for the rest of us to hear. He then laid down runic stones at each node in various shapes and sequences that would help focus the feedback and resonance.

Erin crouched nearby, laptop balanced on her knees, the screen glowing an anemic blue in the gloom. Cables ran from a generator to the computer, and then to a narrow case humming beside her, Charlie's homemade field amplifier that he had modified for tonight, a hybrid of engineering and ritual.

"Nodes two and four are stable," she said without looking up. "Three's a little high. It's pulling more than it should."

"Which means?" Charlie asked.

"Means the field is still destabilizing."

Charlie grunted. He was already sweating through his flannel though the evening was cool. He and I were running the main copper, lengths of braided wire cut from industrial reels, wound into arcs between the nodes. His hands were steady, the motion automatic. He'd designed circuits for next-generation military electronics for his entire career. This wasn't much different, except for the way the ground hummed underfoot like a living thing.

"Remind me again why it's copper," Casey said as she unpacked the last coil. Her voice trembled, not from fear but focus.

Eliyahu answered without looking up. "Copper doesn't resist power, it persuades it. Salt dulls, iron holds, but copper listens, you could say it's a diplomat metal. It gives chaos a path home."

"Like plumbing for bad vibes," Casey muttered.

He smiled. "Precisely."

Charlie paused, looking at the copper wire in his hands, then at the group. His expression went distant for a moment, memory pulling him somewhere else.

"You know," he said quietly, "when I was a young engineer, maybe twenty-five, I rerouted a live circuit during a radar test. Thought I was being clever, saving time." He shook his head. "The arc flash damn near killed me. Blew me back ten feet. Second-degree burns on my hands. Couldn't hear right for a week."

He held up his palms, and in the lamplight, we could see the faint scars, white lines across the creases. "One of the senior officers told me I was lucky. Said most people who make that mistake don't get to learn from it."

He looked at each of us in turn. "What we're doing here, with this copper, with these energies we don't fully understand, it's orders of magnitude more dangerous than anything I worked with in that lab. If something goes wrong, if the resonance peaks or the circuit shorts, we won't get thrown back ten feet. We'll…" He stopped, choosing his words carefully. "Let's just say don't cross the copper. Not even close. The discharge won't discriminate who it blasts."

The weight of his words settled over us. David's foot stopped its nervous bouncing. Casey stared at the copper wire like it had grown teeth.

"Understood," Casey said softly.

I walked the perimeter, tracing each connection with my fingertips. The wire vibrated softly, not yet alive but eager, like it was waiting to be used. The air smelled of petrichor and wet leaves. Somewhere beyond the park, traffic moved, a low, distant pulse that felt out of place tonight.

When I returned to the center, Erin had the field map projected on her screen. The copper hex glowed in her model like a mechanical heart.

"If it works," she said, "it'll redirect all the resonance into the center, a pressure equalizer. It should stabilize the field."

"And if it doesn't?" Charlie asked.

I glanced up at the empty sky. "Then we find out what's waiting for us on the other side of the Veil."

No one laughed.

We worked mostly in silence after that. The good kind of silence, the professional kind, each person focused on their corner of the impossible. David handled the monitoring rig, fingers flying over the small keyboard connected to Erin's system. His screen scrolled with live telemetry, jittering with unseen frequencies. His foot bounced without pause, nervous energy looking for release.

Under Eliyahu's guidance Casey laid new lines of chalk along the copper intersections, her motions quick and sure. When her hand slipped and she cursed softly, I could tell it wasn't from fear, but she was angry at the ground for not staying still.

The sky dimmed from gray to black, and the white light from the lamps contrasted with the blue tones of Erin's screen and cast a glow on the copper at each node. The arcs began to hum softly as the circuit absorbed ambient energy. It wasn't bright yet, just a shimmer, like breath on glass.

"James," Eliyahu said quietly.

I turned. He was standing near the center, watching the lines. "Charlie is right. When it begins, don't cross the copper streams. You won't like the results."

"Are you expecting the Stay Puft Marshmallow Man?"

He looked at me a long moment, confused.

David piped in, trying to be helpful. "Ghostbusters. Don't cross the streams."

Eliyahu looked even more puzzled, "But we aren't hunting ghosts."

"Rabbi, when this is over, I think we need a movie night," David responded.

Charlie jumped in, "Can we stay focused? We aren't kidding, we need to be careful."

By the time the last connection was made, the air had thickened to the density of water. The hum of the copper deepened, no longer background but voice. The ground pulsed beneath our feet, heartbeat for heartbeat.

"Array complete," Erin said. Her tone was calm, but her eyes flicked nervously across the readings. "It's stable... for now."

Charlie wiped his palms on his jeans and straightened, lifting the shotgun back across his shoulder.

I looked around at the group, taking in my unlikely crew. A tech geek, a data scientist, a mystical rabbi, a retired military officer, one immortal, and an HR manager. I'd gone into battles with less.

"Remember what the rabbi said," Charlie told everyone. "Once it starts, stay outside the lines. The copper will ground whatever comes through. If you cross it, you become part of the circuit."

No one spoke. They all understood.

The light faded completely. The first stars appeared through the gaps in the trees, dim, cautious, distant. The park went eerily quiet, not night-quiet, not the absence of noise, but a vacuum. Even the sound of breathing seemed wrong, too loud, too separate from the world.

Then the temperature dropped.

Not gradually, but all at once, as if someone had opened a freezer the size of the sky. Our breath came out in clouds. The moisture on the copper wire began to frost over in delicate, spreading patterns.

"Oy vey," David whispered, hugging himself.

The hum in the copper faltered, then steadied again, as if bracing for something unseen. And that's when I felt it, that cold awareness pressing in from the tree line. We were being watched.

At first it was only a shape, a darker shadow among shadows. Then it stepped forward into the light of the nearest node. The Wendigo.

It was thinner than I had ever seen it, skeletal to the point of fragility, skin translucent and stretched taut over wooden bones. Its eyes were hollow coals, luminous, more sorrow than I remembered. The air around it rippled, as though the world had trouble deciding if it was truly there.

Casey stumbled backward, hand flying to her mouth. "What the fuck is that?"

Charlie's instinct was immediate. He swung the shotgun down, thumb sliding the safety off. The copper wires at his feet trembled in warning.

"Don't," I said quietly.

He hesitated, glanced at me and repeated Casey's question. "What the hell is that? Has the Veil broken and we didn't know it?"

"No. It's not here to fight. That's the Wendigo."

Eliyahu stepped closer, eyes fixed on the creature. His voice dropped to a reverent hush. "It's watching," he said. "I believe it senses what we are doing."

Erin's hand hovered over her laptop, uncertain. David wrung his hands and shifted nervously. Once he got over the initial shock, Casey had a look of open awe and a small smile, as if she sensed more than the rest of us of its true nature.

The Wendigo moved with a strange, weary grace. Its head tilted as it regarded us, slow and deliberate, nostrils flaring as if scenting old ghosts. It stopped and stood motionless just beyond the copper perimeter, as if a herald arriving before battle. Frost spread across the ground where it stood, stopping exactly at the copper line. Its eyes met mine, and I felt a deep sense of resignation. It had come here for the same reason we had, to see how it would end.

The hum beneath the copper changed, a new tone threading through it, lower, vibrating through our bones. The air grew colder still. Wind kicked up from nowhere, rattling the stand lights. One flickered. Died. Came back weaker.

The charm around my neck began to heat. It started as a warmth, like sunlight through fabric, and then it intensified, pulsing in rhythm with the copper's heartbeat. One by one, I saw each of my friends touch their own charms, realization dawning on their faces.

"Something's happening," Erin said, looking up sharply. Her voice carried an edge I'd never heard before. Fear.

Eliyahu's eyes narrowed as he searched the tree line. "Where?"

"Everywhere," I said, because it was true. The pressure was building from all sides, pressing in like water against a dam.

David's laptop screen went haywire, numbers cascading too fast to read. "The readings are spiking! All six nodes at once!"

The Wendigo threw its head back and shrieked.

The sound wasn't just heard, we felt it. A physical thing that tore through the air like a spike driven into reality itself. It split the night like glass under pressure. The scream was anguish, rage, and release all at once, shaking the copper arcs and rattling the equipment. Casey covered her ears, crying out. Charlie cursed and staggered. David's laptop tumbled from his knees into the grass, the screen cracking on impact. Two of the stand lights burst in sequence, pop-pop, darkening the scene around us and amplifying the laptop's feeble glow and the first embers of something worse.

Then, as abruptly as it began, the scream died.

Silence flooded in, but it wasn't peace, it was expectation. The air before a lightning strike. The pause before impact.

Then the light came.

A small ember appeared twenty feet away, hanging in the air like a torch glimpsed through fog. It grew as we watched, expanding to the size of a man, then taller, the center flaring white-hot as the air split open. Not with thunder, but with pressure, the sound of the world exhaling wrong. A vertical seam appeared, stretching upward nearly eight feet. The space between shimmered and darkened, folding inward like a wound opening in reverse.

The light stabilized until we could see a figure through it, as if looking through a door into another dimension.

From within the light stepped an all-too-familiar face. Arnaut.

He emerged tall, deliberate, wrapped in the dim aura of shadowed fire. His coat moved as if in wind that wasn't there. His eyes caught the copper's reflection, gold within endless black. Behind him, three wolves that were not of this world poured through, half smoke, half muscle, their jaws dripping shadow like saliva. They moved wrong, joints bending in directions that defied anatomy, eyes burning with cold fire.

The Wendigo didn't move. It bowed its head, trembling, as if acknowledging the inevitable.

Arnaut looked across the field, his gaze finding me immediately, and he smiled. His eyes burned with zeal, wild and sharp.

"James," he said softly, inspecting the clearing. "You came prepared."

I drew my sword. The runes along its edge flared white against the dark.

"When have I ever not been?"

He gave a knowing nod, taking in my companions as if assessing the threat from each. Then he turned back to me and waved a hand forward. The wolves began to circle and the copper hissed around us, the sound of metal screaming under stress.

"You could have stood beside me," he said. "We could have made the world whole again."

"You're still trying to heal it by tearing it apart," I said. "That's not creation. It's decay."

He tilted his head, almost pitying. "You call it decay. I call it mercy."

The charm at my neck pulsed once more, brighter this time, hot enough to burn. I could feel the storm building behind him, pressure rolling outward from the portal like surf at high tide. The field itself seemed to lean toward him, and beyond the copper, the Wendigo's breath turned to frost that crept toward us in delicate, reaching fingers.

Above us, the sky darkened further. Not clouds, but something else, the Veil itself bending under the weight of what he'd done. Stars vanished one by one as if being erased.

The first drops of power fell.

Not rain. Not lightning. Ashes of light drifting down in silence, each one leaving a small scorch mark where it touched grass or copper or skin. Casey brushed one off her sleeve and her hand came away with a red welt blooming across her knuckles. I thought back to Anglesey. To the fires. To the destruction. To the screams. Not again.

"Erin," Casey said, voice tight. "Tell me that's normal."

"It's not," Erin said, fingers flying across her keyboard. "The portal's leaking energy. Raw, unfiltered. There something countering us. If it gets much worse..."

"Then we better work fast," Charlie interrupted, checking the shotgun's chamber with practiced efficiency.

Every person, creature, and plant in the park froze with anticipation. The Wendigo's hollow eyes tracked the wolves. David's hands shook as he drew his Jericho. Casey and Erin stood back-to-back, Glocks drawn, scanning the darkness beyond our failing lights.

The stillness shattered.

Arnaut took one deliberate step into the ring of our work, and the wolves flowed out around him like poured smoke. They spread into the gaps, circling us, low to the ground, eyes gleaming like wet coal. Their growls carried more vibration than sound, a bass note that rattled teeth and chest cavity.

The copper began to glow, not from our power, but from his, reacting to the corruption pressing against it. The lines sang, a high, stressed pitch like wire about to snap.

David's Jericho came up before I could stop him. The crack of the 9mm split the night, clean and too loud in that strange, airless space. The shot hit

Arnaut in the arm just above the elbow.

He staggered half a step. Surprise flashed across his face. Black fire bloomed where blood should have been, spreading across his sleeve like oil catching flame. For one heartbeat he looked down at the wound as if he couldn't quite believe it had happened.

Then he simply flicked two fingers.

The air slammed into David like a wall. He flew backward nearly 10 feet, hit the ground hard, his head cracking against packed soil with a sound that made my stomach drop. The pistol spun away into the dark, lost in the grass. He didn't move.

"David!" Casey sprinted toward him, all tactical awareness forgotten.

"Stay behind the copper!" I barked, but she was already on her knees beside him, hands pressing against his head where blood was beginning to mat his hair.

Arnaut looked down at the smoking hole in his sleeve and smiled, wider this time, genuine amusement lighting his face. "He's bold. I like him." The black fire crawled up his arm, sealing the wound with a hiss like water on hot iron.

Casey's Glock barked twice. Two perfect shots, center mass. Arnaut didn't flinch. Both rounds flattened midair three feet from his chest and fell to the grass like broken teeth, landing with soft thumps that shouldn't have been audible but somehow were.

"Enough," he said quietly, and the word carried weight, a command that made the air itself hesitate.

Charlie stepped forward half a pace, racked the 12-gauge, and fired. The nearest wolf exploded in a blur of black mist, reformed six feet back, and snarled with a sound like rocks grinding together. He fired again, walking the recoil, keeping them back. The shots echoed across the park, too loud, wrong for how muffled everything else had become.

"Buy me thirty seconds," Erin said, low and sharp. She was back crouched by the amplifier case, fingers flying, not looking up even as another wolf circled close enough for her to hear its breath rattling. "I can bleed off some of the pressure he's generating. Just hold them."

"You've got it," I said, and stepped toward Arnaut.

His sword came from nowhere. One moment his hands were empty, the next he held a weapon that looked forged from shadow and hunger. It was long, brutal, a knight's weapon, the kind meant to break shields and cleave armor. Oily light crawled along its edge, bending the air around it like heat shimmer over asphalt.

"Do you remember Acre?" he asked, almost tenderly, taking a practice swing that whistled through the air. "You were faster then. Hungrier."

"I'm still here," I said, raising my own blade. The runes along its edge answered with white fire, clean and bright against his corruption. "And I don't want to do this."

"Then you're already defeated."

He came at me in a storm of power. No grace, no feint, just raw intent channeled through three feet of corrupted steel. The first strike would have split me in half if I'd been slower by a heartbeat. Steel met steel, the impact ringing through my bones, up my arms, into my teeth. The shock of it made my vision blur for a second. I turned his blade aside, stepped off line, and countered, only for him to meet me again, every blow heavier than the last.

Behind us, Charlie's shotgun boomed again. The wolves howled and regrouped. One lunged at Eliyahu. The rabbi threw one hand, holding a glowing stone in the other, shouting something in Hebrew, and the creature hit an invisible wall, rebounding with a yelp that almost sounded surprised. But it didn't stop. It circled, testing, looking for gaps.

"I can slow 'em, not stop 'em!" Charlie shouted, firing again. The muzzle flash lit his face in snapshots, expression grim and focused.

"Working," Eliyahu said through gritted teeth. He stood by the western node, a parchment scroll slowly unrolling in his hands. The ink on it shimmered like dying embers. Sweat ran down his face despite the cold.

Casey pressed down on David's bleeding head, voice cracking. "He's alive, but he's bleeding bad. Crable, he's bleeding bad!"

"I know," I said through clenched teeth, catching another of Arnaut's blows. The impact sent sparks along both blades, white meeting black in cascades of dying light. My arms screamed. The oily sheen on his weapon hissed each time it touched my runes, steam rising where they met. The new enchantments holding back the corruption.

The copper was singing now, a single sustained note that climbed higher with each passing second.

A wolf broke from the pack, faster than the others, a streak of shadow and teeth aimed straight at Erin's back. She was bent over her equipment, defenseless, focused entirely on the numbers scrolling across her screen.

"Erin!" Casey screamed.

The wolf leaped.

Casey launched herself forward, crossing three feet of ground in a heartbeat, putting herself between the creature and her wife. The wolf's jaws closed on Casey's forearm instead of Erin's throat. Bone crunched. Casey's scream tore through the air, high and sharp and human in a way that cut through all the magic and chaos.

Erin spun, eyes going wide with horror. "Casey!"

Charlie's shotgun roared. The wolf disintegrated, but the damage was done. Casey crumpled, clutching her mangled arm, blood streaming between her fingers.

"Erin, I'm okay," Casey gasped through gritted teeth. "Keep working. I'm okay."

But Erin's hands were shaking now, torn between her equipment and her wife bleeding on the ground.

The distraction cost us. One of the remaining wolves lunged at Charlie while he was reloading. He tried to bring the shotgun up, too slow, the creature's claws catching his thigh and spinning him around. He went down hard. The wolf overcommitted and flew by Charlie, unable to capitalize on his fall.

Arnaut pressed his advantage against me, sensing my attention split. He drove in with a crushing overhead that drove me to one knee. The ground jarred up my frame and he pressed, weight behind the blade, trying to grind me into the soil. Oily light crawled along his edge, reached for my runes, hissed and pulled back burned. But he was stronger. Relentless.

"Look around you," he said, voice almost gentle despite the violence. "This is what your mercy buys. Pain. Suffering. Let me end it cleanly."

I could see it all at once. Casey bleeding, her face pale with blood loss but conscious, determined. Charlie struggling to stand, leg giving out. David unconscious in the grass. Erin paralyzed between her equipment and her injured wife. The wolves circling, patient now, knowing we were breaking.

We were in trouble.

The thought hit like a physical blow. After everything, after centuries of survival, after coming so far, we were going to fail. Here. Tonight. In a suburban park in Ohio. I felt a deep sense of despair. These people, my friends, were not prepared for this. I should never have involved them, and I was going to get them killed. Guilt coursed through me, and I couldn't help but remember the same feeling in Jerusalem when I blamed myself for losing Arnaut.

Arnaut saw it in my eyes. Saw the moment I understood.

"I'm sorry, brother," he said, and raised his sword for the killing blow. "I wish you'd listened."

My arms were leaden. My breath came in ragged gasps. The copper's song had become a shriek, overtaxed, about to fail. The portal behind Arnaut pulsed like a heart, growing wider with each beat.

This was it. The end.

Then Eliyahu's voice rose, deep and resonant, cutting through everything.

"Yitbatlu, yidmu, yafuchu l'afar…"

The words weren't just sound. They were structure, reality being reminded of its own rules. Hebrew syllables that predated empires, older than the corruption Arnaut wielded, older than anything except the ground beneath our feet.

The wolves faltered mid-prowl as if a leash had been yanked. Their eyes, whatever passed for eyes, snapped to him. He raised his left hand, palm outward, the parchment across his right arm trembling with the force of what he channeled through it.

"Shuvu el ha'afar asher me'enuv nitzartem. Return to dust from which you were made."

The copper roared like a struck bell.

The first wolf folded, no flourish, no scream, just unmade, collapsing into a drift of gray that the wind didn't dare move. The second staggered, snarled, tried to resist, and came apart along the seams of its shadow. The third leaped at Eliyahu in a last desperate lunge, nearly hitting the copper arc. The rabbi turned his shoulder, voice never faltering, and the thing shattered in midair, falling in a soft hiss that was almost a sigh.

But the energy had to go somewhere.

The third wolf's destruction sent a backlash through the copper array. A wave of spiritual force rippled outward, seeking ground. The nearest copper arc flared white-hot, screaming with more power than it was designed to handle.

The backlash caught the remnants of the third wolf, the pieces that hadn't quite dissipated yet, and hurled them directly into the copper line between nodes four and five.

The effect was instantaneous and horrific.

The shadow-matter hit the supercharged copper and simply ceased to exist. Not destroyed, erased. There was a sound like glass breaking in reverse, a visual distortion that hurt to look at, and then nothing. No ash. No residue. Just a brief afterimage burned into our retinas of something that had been violently removed from reality.

The copper wire where it had made contact glowed cherry-red for three full seconds before cooling back to orange.

"That's what happens," Charlie said, voice shaking, staring at the copper line from where he'd fallen. "That's what I meant. That's the arc flash, but with magic. If any of us touch that wire…"

He didn't finish. He didn't need to.

The blast of spiritual energy rippled through the ground, and for a heartbeat, even Arnaut paused, sword still raised above me.

"The words of God," he said softly, something like respect in his voice. "You stand in a burning house and quote the architect."

"Perhaps," Eliyahu replied, voice hoarse but steady, "but you set the blaze alight."

The momentary distraction was enough. I surged upward, blade flashing, forcing Arnaut back a step. My muscles screamed but I didn't care. Casey was injured. David was down. We had seconds, not minutes.

"Charging at forty percent," Erin called out, her voice shaking but functional. She was back at her laptop, stealing glances at Casey who was pressing her good hand against her mangled arm. "Fifty. The array's stabilizing, but he's pushing back hard."

"What do you need?" Charlie called, limping back into position, blood darkening his jeans.

"Time," she said, the word almost a sob. "And a clear line on node three."

"Working on it," he muttered through clenched teeth.

Our blades met again, white light against black fire. His sword spat dark flame; mine drank it, grounding it through the runes that had been etched into the steel centuries ago, and strengthened by the more recent diamond infusion. Sparks sprayed across the grass, lighting the field in strobing flashes. I could taste copper in the air now, the real kind, from the wires heating beyond their capacity.

"Seventy percent!" Erin shouted. "The field's harmonics are spiking!"

Arnaut raised his sword high, black light crawling along the edge like oil on fire. "You always were stubborn, James."

"Better stubborn than damned," I said, meeting him again.

The clash shook the air. His strength was monstrous, each impact driving me back another inch, but I had patience, and patience had saved me more than once. I parried, turned, let him overreach, and countered with a slash that cut his forearm. He hissed, black ichor spilling, smoking where it touched the grass.

He smiled through the pain. "There's my brother."

The portal pulsed behind him, beating like a dark heart. The Wendigo stood still as stone, watching. For a moment, its eyes flickered toward me, and I felt something, pity, maybe, or perhaps a warning.

"Eighty-five!" Erin's voice wavered. "We're almost there!"

Arnaut felt it too. He drove forward, our blades locking again, faces inches apart. The heat coming off him was like standing near a furnace.

"You can still walk away," I said, knowing he wouldn't.

He searched my eyes, something like grief in his. "So can you."

And for a heartbeat, just one, I saw my companion of 300 years, the youthful Arnaut who laughed too loud, the soldier who sang bad songs on long rides, the friend who had knelt beside me in snow-wet trenches. The man I'd mourned for centuries.

Then the moment was gone and the man before me was only a blade.

He wrenched free and hammered down. I took it on the flat, rode it low, snapped a cut at his knee. He leapt, almost lazy, and answered with a sweep that would have trimmed my scalp if I hadn't ducked.

"Crable!" Erin shouted. "Ninety-two. I need a clear path to node three, two meters. I can't reach it from here because the resonance is dirty. I think the copper is misaligned."

"Tell me where," Casey said through gritted teeth, already trying to push herself up with her good arm. Blood soaked her sleeve to the elbow but she was conscious, alert, still fighting.

"Not yet," Erin said, eyes on the bars climbing her screen. "When I say."

Charlie shifted his stance, put himself between Erin and the portal, shotgun now cradled but ready. He was favoring his left leg hard, face pale. "You tell me if something moves and I'll make it regret it."

The portal pulsed again, harder. Ashes of light fell like slow snow, each one leaving tiny scorch marks.

The Wendigo's ribs heaved, one, two, three, and frost crept another inch toward the copper where it stopped as if at a shoreline.

Arnaut lifted his sword in a two-handed guard I knew too well, a stance we learned from one of our old masters, all attack, no tricks, everything committed to the next strike.

"Last chance, brother," he said. "Don't make me cut you down."

"I'd prefer to not be cut down," I said. "But I can't let you do this."

He came, and I met him, and for a while there was only the old work, step, edge, breath, the small arithmetic of openings found and lost. He was stronger, but I was steadier. He had conviction. I had necessity.

Our swords crossed and held, locked together, neither of us able to gain advantage. The runes on my blade burned so bright they hurt to look at. The corruption on his weapon writhed like living things trying to crawl up my steel.

"Now," Erin said, voice flat with concentration. "Casey, node three. Keep outside the wire. If you cross it, you'll…"

"I know." Casey slid along the copper like a cliff's lip, shoulders brushing leaves, feet sure despite the blood loss that made her weave. She reached the lamp. "Tell me what to do."

"When I say, turn the set-screw one full rotation. Get ready. Three. Two…"

The ground beneath us heaved. Not an earthquake. Something pushing up from below, the Veil itself bucking under the strain.

"Ninety-eight percent!" Erin breathed, fingers white on her keyboard. "Once it tops a hundred, I can push it back into itself, Crable, I need ten more seconds!"

"Got it," I said, and let Arnaut push me, let him think he had me, let him overcommit into that same hungry power that had always been his flaw and his glory.

Ten seconds. An eternity.

Charlie saw what Erin was doing. Saw the numbers climbing. And saw something else, his eyes darted toward the pattern of rune stones Eliyahu had placed near the western node. The ones he'd been adjusting all evening, trying to keep the array stable despite the interference.

His engineering mind made a connection in that moment, the kind of intuitive leap that comes from decades of working with resonant frequencies and harmonic systems. The runes weren't just mystic symbols. They were tuned elements in a circuit. And one of them was slightly off, creating the interference that was slowing Erin's progress.

"Eliyahu," he said quietly, then louder. "Rabbi, your stones!"

"What?" Eliyahu looked up from where he was tending to David.

"The western node…f I just…" Charlie's eyes went distant, calculating angles and frequencies and divine ratios all at once. His hand moved toward one of the stones.

Eliyahu's face went white. "Charlie, no! You don't understand the balance!"

But Charlie was already moving, engineer's confidence overriding caution.

"Trust me," he said, and reached for the stone.

Arnaut bared his teeth, pleased, and drove the long, dark blade forward with everything he had. I was backing up, trying to buy time, but my heel caught a root. My weight shifted wrong. His blade tore across my side, the impact spinning me around, white-hot pain exploding through my ribs.

The world tilted. My knees hit the dirt. Blood, hot and immediate, soaked through my shirt. The copper's hum filled my ears, drowning out everything else.

I looked up. Arnaut stood over me, calm and deliberate. "You should not have meddled, James," he said.

Through the pain and the haze, all I could think to say was, "And you would have gotten away with it too if it wasn't for us meddling kids."

I choked out a painful laugh. Gallow's humor. Somewhere behind me, I swear I heard Charlie groan at the comment.

Arnaut cocked his head, utterly confused. "What?"

I had no time to explain or enjoy my own witty banter. He raised his sword, the black metal dripping light that burned the air.

"Crable!" Charlie's voice cut across the clearing. But he wasn't looking at me. His hand closed around the rune stone.

Time seemed to slow.

Charlie touched the stone. Rotated it. Just a quarter turn, lining it with the adjacent copper line in a way his instincts told him was correct.

"NOW!" Erin shouted, and Casey turned the set-screw.

The world detonated.

Not in flame, but in a massive wave of force caused by the feedback from the magical energy that was both healing and breaking the Veil. The copper flared white, blinding, every line blazing like someone had replaced them with strips of captured lightning. The runes ignited as if carved by fire. A wave of raw energy rolled outward from the stone, through the lines, through the ground, a single chaotic chord of sound and pressure that made reality itself flinch.

Charlie saw it coming. One heartbeat to understand what he'd done. One heartbeat to know he'd miscalculated.

The energy hit him like a freight train.

His body arced backward, every muscle seizing. Blue fire crawled up his arms, into his chest. His eyes went wide. His mouth opened in a scream that had no sound because the air itself had stopped working right.

Then the Wendigo moved.

Faster than thought, faster than anything that skeletal should move. It crossed the distance between the tree line and Charlie in a heartbeat, putting itself directly in the path of the energy blast.

The wave hit the Wendigo square in the chest.

Its body flared like a torch, ice and frost and ancient wood all igniting at once. Its scream joined the copper's roar, two notes of agony harmonizing. The creature's translucent skin cracked, light pouring through the fissures like dawn through breaking clouds.

But it held.

Held its ground. Held the line. Absorbed the worst of the blast that would have killed Charlie instantly.

The energy broke around them both, dissipating into the ground, into the sky, bleeding off into the ether with a sound like a thousand windows shattering.

Charlie collapsed to his hands and knees, gasping, alive. Smoke rose from his singed clothes. The Wendigo staggered back, its body dimmed now, faded, like a candle burning its last. It wavered, nearly translucent, barely holding form. One leg buckled and it sank to the ground, but it didn't dissolve. It remained, weakened but present, its hollow eyes still watching.

But the reset had worked.

The copper dimmed back to orange, stable again. The white fire subsided. The hum settled into something almost peaceful. Arnaut staggered mid-strike, his blade sputtering like a candle in wind. The black fire that clung to him twisted violently, folding in on itself. His balance broke, his knees hit the dirt, and his grip faltered.

"Now!" Charlie shouted, his voice raw. He reached for the stone with shaking hands and reset it back to the original alignment before the system collapsed completely.

I didn't think, I just moved. My sword came up, white runes flaring as I lunged, driving the blade deep into Arnaut's side. The impact sent a shock through my arm, but I didn't stop. I turned my blade, twisting until the black light along his wound hissed and shattered like glass, and blood spilled from the fresh wound.

He roared, both in pain, and in disbelief. I regained my bearing, stepped back, swung again, a clean horizontal slash across his arm. The blade bit deep and his sword clanged to the earth, the oily glow along its edge guttering out like a dying coal. He fell to one knee, gasping, blood leaking from the wounds.

The copper lines held steady, stable again. The white fire subsided, leaving only the smell of fresh blood, burnt flesh, and damp earth.

Erin exhaled like she'd been holding her breath for an hour. "He did it," she whispered. "How the hell did that work?"

Eliyahu's voice, hoarse but steady, carried from behind. "Baruch HaShem," he murmured. "He listened, and we survived."

Charlie groaned, half laughing, half wheezing. "Not bad for a middle-aged skeptic." He tried to stand, legs shaking. "God help me, but this shit is starting to make sense."

Then he saw the Wendigo.

"Oh no. Hey, are you..."

He crawled toward the creature, movements jerky and uncoordinated. The Wendigo lay on the ground, its body barely visible now, like smoke trying to remember its shape. Where it had been struck, its chest showed cracks that leaked pale light, dimming slowly. But its eyes were still open, still aware.

"You saved me," Charlie said, voice breaking. "You didn't have to do that."

The Wendigo's head turned slowly toward him. Its hollow eyes found his face. For a moment, something passed between them, recognition, understanding, acceptance. The creature's hand, more branch than flesh, lifted slightly as if to touch Charlie's face, then settled back to the earth.

The light in the Wendigo's chest dimmed further but didn't go out. Its form held, though barely, like morning mist clinging to the ground before the sun burns it away completely.

Eliyahu limped over, placed a hand on Charlie's shoulder. "It lives," the rabbi said softly. "Weakened, perhaps for a very long time, but it endures. Guardians are not so easily destroyed. It will heal, as this land heals."

"But it's barely there," Charlie said.

"For now," Eliyahu agreed. "But the roots go deep. Deeper than what we see. It will sleep, and in sleeping, recover. The land will sustain it."

Charlie knelt there, one hand hovering over the barely visible form. "I'm sorry," he whispered. "Thank you."

The Wendigo's eyes closed slowly, not in death but in rest. Its form faded further, becoming almost invisible, a whisper of frost and shadow that settled into the ground itself. Not gone. Resting.

Arnaut stared at his ruined arm, then at me. His eyes burned, but beneath the fury there was something else, something heartbreakingly familiar. Maybe recognition, maybe regret, maybe the ghost of the man I'd known for three hundred years.

"You... you could have stood beside me," he said, voice rough and low. Blood ran from his mouth. "We could have remade this world. Healed it."

"You would've burned it," I said, breath ragged. Pain pulsed through my side with each heartbeat. "That's not healing."

He staggered back a step, then another, toward the fading shimmer of his portal. The shadows behind it pulsed, calling to him like a heartbeat out of sync with ours. He looked at me again, not as an enemy now, but as something worse. A mirror.

"You'll see, James. You always do, but always too late."

I raised my sword, stepping forward for the finishing strike. Pain screamed through my side but I pushed through it. This needed to end. Here. Now.

But when our eyes met, my grip faltered.

I saw the man who had once shared my fire, who had laughed in the face of uncountable horrors, and who had fought beside me under banners we didn't believe in. The brother who had disappeared centuries ago into a tear in reality and returned only to wage war on the world he thought he was saving.

The sword felt impossibly heavy in my hands. My arms shook. Not from exhaustion. From something deeper. Three hundred years of friendship doesn't disappear because of centuries of absence. The weight of all that history, all those battles, all those nights drinking bad wine and telling worse jokes, it pressed down on me like a physical thing.

I couldn't do it.

The realization hit like a punch to the gut. After everything he'd done, everyone he'd hurt, the danger he posed to the world, I still couldn't be the one to end him.

My sword's light flickered, faltered, dimmed.

Arnaut saw it. Saw the hesitation. Saw the moment I chose mercy over duty.

He didn't move for a long moment, didn't speak. Just watched me with something in his eyes that might have been understanding. Might have been pity.

Then, slowly, he nodded once. Not forgiveness. Not even acknowledgment. Just an understanding between two old soldiers who'd seen too much and lived too long.

He turned, limping badly, clutching his wounds. Blood dripped from his fingers and left a small trail as we walked. He stepped through the portal.

The seam folded and closed behind him with a sound like a sigh, leaving the smell of ash and lightning and centuries of regret.

For a moment night was still, as we all took a collective breath to regroup. The copper lines sank back into silence, their hum quieting to the rhythm of the earth again. Above us, the stars began to reappear one by one, as if reality was slowly remembering how to be itself.

I sheathed my blade, the metal sliding home with a soft scrape. The runes were cool now, dormant. My side burned where Arnaut's blade had opened me, blood soaking through my shirt in a warm, spreading patch.

"Crable!" Erin called, her voice sharp with professional assessment even as she knelt beside Casey, checking her wife's injured arm. "Let me see. How bad are you hurt?"

"I've had worse," I said, though my body disagreed loudly.

She stood, leaving Casey propped against a tree trunk, and caught my arm, steadying me. Behind us, Eliyahu worked over David, the rabbi whispering prayers while keeping pressure on his head wound.

Casey's voice was tight with pain but steady. "David's breathing is good. The rabbi says he'll be okay once we get him to a hospital. And I'm fine. Going to need some stitches and it hurts like hell, but I'm fine."

Charlie sat in the grass near where the Wendigo rested, pale and sweating, one hand on the earth as if he could still feel the creature beneath the soil. Smoke rose from his clothes in thin wisps. He looked up when I approached, and there was something changed in his eyes. Not broken. Humbled.

"It's still there," he said quietly. "I can feel it. Sleeping."

"Yes," I said, lowering myself carefully to sit beside him. Every movement sent fresh spikes of pain through my side. "It will rest for a long time. Maybe years. But it will heal."

Eliyahu walked over, inspecting the earth where the Wendigo had settled. He knelt slowly, touched the ground with reverent fingers. "The land already begins to remember," he said softly. "The balance shifts back. Slowly, but it shifts."

We sat there for a while in the cooling night air. Around us, the damage we'd caused became more apparent. Scorched earth in radiating patterns from where the energy had discharged. Trees split or bent at unnatural angles. Piles of ash that had been shadow-wolves. The ground itself looked bruised, discolored in patches where the Veil had pressed too close.

"Ray is going to forever wonder what happened in his beloved park when he sees this," I said, managing a weak smile.

That got a small laugh from Charlie, wet and painful, but real.

I looked over at David, still unconscious but breathing steadily. His face was peaceful despite the bruising and blood. I reached out and touched his forehead, muttering a simple incantation under my breath. Healing magic wasn't my strongest suit, but I could manage enough to ease his pain and speed his recovery. I simply didn't have the energy to wake him, but he would be fine once we got him proper medical attention.

"We need to get him to a hospital," I said. "And Casey needs her arm looked at. And Charlie..."

"I'm fine," Charlie said, though the tremor in his hands said otherwise.

"You're not," Erin said firmly, finally allowing herself to check on him now that Casey was stable. "I'm not sure if you are a genius or an idiot for what you did, but it worked."

"My wife used to call me both," Charlie grinned at Erin.

We spent the next half hour mending wounds, packing up everything and cleaning what we could from the clearing. Charlie and I gathered the copper wire, coiling it slowly, neither of us speaking much. Erin collected her equipment with methodical precision, though her hands shook whenever she looked at Casey's bandaged arm. Eliyahu retrieved his sacred stones, whispering prayers over each one before returning them to his pouch.

I walked over to where Arnaut's sword had fallen. It lay in the grass, still emanating a faint oily shimmer. The corruption in it was dormant but not gone. I couldn't leave it here. Wrapping it carefully in cloth from my pack, I stored it with the rest of our gear. Another artifact to lock away, another reminder of what had been lost.

As we finally turned toward the path back to the parking lot, I took one final look at the clearing. The damage was obvious, impossible to explain away. But the park felt different now. Lighter somehow, despite the violence it had witnessed. The oppressive hum that had been building for weeks was gone. The air moved freely again through the trees.

Eventually, the Wendigo rose. It gave us a short glance and slowly disappeared into the woods. I would have to come back soon and see what I could do to help, but not tonight.

"Come on," Charlie said quietly, offering me his shoulder to lean on. "Let's go home."

Home. The word felt strange and perfect all at once.

We made our way through the darkened park, a battered, bloody group of suburban defenders who'd just saved a world that would never know how close it had come to ending. David eventually regained consciousness, and was half carried out by Eliyahu and Charlie. Casey leaned on Erin; her injured arm cradled against her chest. I limped along beside them; one hand pressed to my bleeding side. I almost laughed when I thought about how we would explain all this at the hospital. I could heal myself once home, but Casey's bite would be hard to explain along with David's rapidly bruising body and head wound.

Behind us, the trees whispered in a wind that finally felt clean.

The Wendigo lived, its vigil would continue. The land would remember. The trees would keep watch. And when enough time had passed, when the guardian's strength returned, it would rise again.

That was how it always worked. Guardians endured. The Veil strained and held. The world turned on, ignorant and safe, while a few souls carried the weight of keeping it that way.

As we reached the parking lot, the exhaustion hit me on top of my pain. In a few hours, joggers would run these trails. Kids would play in these fields. Ray would discover the damage and shake his head, trying to make sense of what looked like a lightning strike or maybe some teenagers with fireworks.

Normal life would resume, as it always did, built on a foundation of sacrifices it would never see.

I looked at my friends, bloodied and exhausted but alive, and felt something I hadn't felt in a very long time. Not hope exactly. Something quieter but more durable. Purpose.

We loaded into vehicles with careful silence, each of us lost in our own thoughts. As Charlie's truck pulled away with David in the passenger seat, I saw him looking back at the park in his rearview mirror, one hand pressed against his chest where the charm still hung. On the way to the ER to have David looked at. Erin and Casey to a separate hospital to limit too much suspicion.

I knew what he was thinking. We'd won, but the cost had been high.

I climbed into my own car, every movement an exercise in not gasping from the pain in my side. Eliyahu riding shotgun, quieter than normal. My sword lay across the back seat, wrapped and quiet. Arnaut's blade was locked in the trunk.

As I drove through the silent streets of Centerville, watching the world prepare to wake to another ordinary day, I thought about Arnaut's final words.

You'll see, James. You always do, but always too late.

Maybe he was right. Maybe I would see whatever truth he'd found behind the Veil. Maybe one day I'd understand what had driven him to try to tear the world apart in the name of healing it.

But not today. Today I had friends to protect, wounds to heal, and a guardian to honor.

The Wendigo had given so much to hold the line. The least I could do was make sure that sacrifice meant something.

I pulled into my driveway as the sun broke the horizon, painting Centerville in shades of gold and amber. Somewhere in the distance, a dog barked. A door slammed. The ordinary sounds of life continuing.

Inside my house, the wards hummed their greeting, familiar and steady. Eliyahu said his good nights and made his way to my guest room. I made it to the couch before my legs gave out, collapsing into the leather with a groan that was part pain, part relief.

The sword clattered to the floor beside me. I'd pick it up later. Right now, I just needed to sit. To breathe. To let the adrenaline drain away and feel what we'd done.

We'd stopped Arnaut. For now.

We'd saved the Veil. For now.

And we'd paid for it with blood and pain, but everyone was alive.

The charm around my neck had cooled to room temperature, quiet again. I touched it, thinking of the others wearing their own. Thinking of Charlie kneeling by the Wendigo, both injured in their own way. Thinking of Casey's mangled arm and David's cracked skull and Erin's fear at nearly losing her wife.

They weren't soldiers. They weren't immortal warriors like me. They were just people, ordinary people who'd stood against the extraordinary because someone had to.

And they'd done it willingly. Without hesitation. Without understanding half of what they faced.

That was worth more than any magic I'd ever learned.

I closed my eyes, just for a moment. Just to rest.

The world would keep turning. Threats would rise again. Arnaut was still out there, wounded but alive, nursing his wounds and his convictions in whatever dark place he'd retreated to.

But tonight, we'd held the line.

Tonight, the Veil still stood.

And tonight, against all odds, we were still breathing.

That would have to be enough.

20

Epilogue – Pizza, Gardening, and the Friend

PART 1

The noise of Marion's Piazza hit you like a physical force, a wall of warm, yeasty air thick with the sounds of suburbia at ease. Saturday night, and the place was packed. The thump and clatter of pizza pans from the open kitchen mixed with the hiss of tap lines and the roar of laughter from a table of high school students celebrating something that wouldn't matter in five years but meant everything tonight. Little kids in grass-stained soccer uniforms ran circuits around the tables like it was their personal playground, and nobody seemed to mind. The air itself tasted of baked dough that had soaked into the restaurant so thoroughly it was part of the building now.

This was Centerville's living room. Walls covered with black and white photos of seventies celebrities, most of them dead now, all of them frozen in that kind of Kodak optimism that doesn't exist anymore. Bill Bixby, Rip Taylor, Morgan Fairchild in something sparkly and confident. The kind of place that knew what it was and didn't apologize, good pizza, cold beer, and the company you kept.

We found a table against the wall, under the watchful eyes of celebrities of years gone by. David moved with the careful, stiff-legged gait of a man held together by prescription painkillers and sheer will. The bruises on his face had ripened into a topographical map of purple and yellow, his left eye still swollen half-shut. His arm rested in a sling, stark white against his faded t-shirt. He sank into the cushioned chair with a sigh that was half relief, half pain, the sound of someone grateful to be sitting anywhere that wasn't a hospital bed.

Casey was already in motion despite the thick bandage wrapped around her forearm, visible where her sleeve was rolled up. She moved like a general marshaling troops, compensating for her injury with pure determination and an extra dose of bossy energy. Our number got called at the counter and she conscripted Charlie to help carry the pizzas, pointing with her good hand. She sent me off to grab a fresh pitcher of beer.

When I returned, she was laying out the thin-crust pizzas cut into squares, the Dayton way, using mostly her left hand while her bandaged right arm stayed close to her body. "I've got a pepperoni for Crable. A cheese for David and Charlie, because their palate is as bland as their personalities." She shot them both a look that dared contradiction. "And one Super Cheese for Erin and me." She surveyed our faces, satisfied. "I'd say we've earned our calories. My Fitbit doesn't have an exercise setting for existential terror, but I'm guessing we burned a few the other night."

David managed a lopsided grin that pulled at the bruising on his cheek. "The nurse said I should avoid alcohol with the meds. I told her my existential terror prescription required a beer chaser. She did not look amused."

Erin sat beside him, her gaze doing that thing where she assessed posture and breathing and pain levels without seeming to. "Your head will knit faster with protein and rest, not hops and poor decision-making." She reached over and adjusted his sling strap by a millimeter, the kind of micro-correction that drove Casey crazy but that David found comforting. She feigned seriousness, put on her stern mom voice while pointing a finger. "But the psychological benefits of communal ritual are statistically significant. So, one beer."

"You're all heart, Erin," David said, warmth cutting through the sarcasm.

"I'm all that and more," she corrected, but the corner of her mouth twitched.

Charlie sat beside me, favoring his left leg as he settled in. He still limped, would for another week at least, but he'd turned down the crutches the ER had offered. Too stubborn. Too proud. He surveyed the room with a quiet contentment, eyes crinkling at the corners. "You know, after a week of fighting shadow-monsters and recalculating the cosmic balance, there's nothing like cold beer and hot pizza to soothe the soul."

"Pizza and beer, that's swell," David quipped in a terrible Humphrey Bogart impression.

Casey looked at him, confused. "What? Is your brain working okay?"

David smiled and pointed to a picture of Barry Williams on the wall, Greg Brady frozen forever in faded black and white. "Brady Bunch? Seriously, c'mon."

Erin and Casey both rolled their eyes in perfect synchronization.

David turned serious, ran his good hand through his curly hair. "Um, I just wanted to thank you for taking care of me. I really mean it. You guys are the best." His voice caught slightly. "I don't remember much after going down, but Erin told me what happened. What you all did."

Casey turned to David and gave him a huge hug, her bandaged arm awkward between them. He gasped in pain.

"Oh, my nose!" David yelped. Charlie groaned from across the table.

"No more dad jokes or I'll hug you harder next time," Casey threatened, but her eyes were wet.

David threw his free hand up in mock defense.

For a while, the only sounds at our table were the tear of crust, the clink of glass as we topped off mugs, murmurs of appreciation. Around us, Marion's carried on, oblivious and perfect. At the next table, a couple argued about whether the Bengals had any shot this year. Behind the counter, the manager shouted something I couldn't make out, but might have been encouragement or might have been a threat.

This was the bulwark. Not just the absence of demons, but the presence of this. Laughter in a crowded room. The simple architecture of a well-made pizza. The unspoken bond of people who had faced the abyss together and lived to tell the tale over beer and cheese.

Casey wiped sauce from her chin with a paper napkin, awkward with her left hand. "Okay, so let me get this straight. We fought a thousand-year-old Norman wizard who was trying to tear a hole in reality using tainted magic, and we won because of a rabbi, an immortal, a cybersecurity nerd, a lab rat, a retired colonel, my winning personality, and one mangled arm?"

She held up her bandaged forearm like a trophy. Erin flinched but didn't say anything.

"And a Wendigo," David added, quieter now. "Don't forget the Wendigo. I feel like we don't talk about the Wendigo enough."

The table went still for a heartbeat.

Charlie stared down at his beer, jaw working. When he finally looked up, his eyes were red-rimmed. "To the Wendigo," he said, voice rough.

We raised our glasses. The clink of them meeting was softer this time, reverent.

"To the Wendigo," we echoed.

Charlie drained half his beer in one pull and set it down harder than necessary. "It saved my life. Took the hit that should've killed me. I can still feel where it's resting, under the ground. Sleeping." He looked at me. "It is just sleeping, right?"

"Yes," I said. "Guardians don't die easily. It'll heal. I'll make sure of it."

He nodded, not quite convinced but wanting to be.

Erin broke the moment, her analytical mind already three steps ahead. She looked up at the group, pushed her glasses up her nose. "What do we do next?"

"We?" I asked, the word feeling foreign and wonderful at the same time.

She fixed me with a look that had made junior analysts weep and IT directors reconsider their career choices. "Someone has to apply rigorous analytical principles to the prevention of apocalypses, James. Your current method seems to involve a great deal of waiting for things to go wrong and then hitting them with a sword."

David chuckled, then winced, clutching his ribs. "Don't give her a whiteboard, Crable. She'll have a Gantt chart for sealing interdimensional rifts by morning."

"We could do worse," Charlie said, the ghost of a smile appearing. "I've seen her Gantt charts. They're beautiful. Color-coded. With contingency branches."

"And she labels the axes," Casey added proudly, then winced as she shifted her arm.

Erin reached over without looking and adjusted Casey's position so her arm was better supported. The movement was automatic, protective. Casey leaned into it.

The noise of Marion's seemed to pull back for a second, giving them space. "I'm not sitting on the sidelines again. If we're doing this, if this is what our lives are now, then we do it right. We plan. We prepare. We don't improvise against reality-eating wizards with copper wire and hope."

Casey squeezed Erin's hand with her good one. "We won, babe."

"Barely," Erin said. "And next time we might not have a Wendigo."

The weight of that settled over the table. She was right. We'd won, but the margin had been razor-thin.

"Then we make sure there is a next time," I said. "And we make sure we're ready for it."

David raised his glass with his good hand. "To not improvising."

"To planning," Erin agreed.

"To Gantt charts," Charlie added, deadpan.

We drank to that, and the moment loosened again. Around us, Marion's pulled us back into its noise and warmth. The soccer kids had migrated to the arcade games in the corner, the beeps and electronic music adding to the chaos. One of the staff dropped a tray of pizzas in the kitchen and everyone in the dining room groaned in sympathy.

We stayed until the last square was gone and the third pitcher was drained to foam. The talk drifted to safer ground, work stories and neighborhood gossip and whether the Garden Ninja was secretly wealthy or just committed to her craft at an unhealthy level. David told a story about trying to explain his injuries to his mother that had us all laughing until Charlie's leg started hurting and Casey's arm throbbed and David's ribs protested and we all just sat there.

The goodbyes in the dimly lit parking lot were full of careful backslaps and gentle hugs. The night air was cool, carrying the distant hum of traffic on Far Hills. Streetlights cast orange pools across the asphalt. Somewhere a car alarm chirped off. I watched Casey and Erin bundle David into their Jeep with the focused efficiency of a pit crew, Erin making sure his sling was secure, Casey climbing in one-handed. The Jeep's taillights painted the parking lot red as they pulled away.

I felt a profound, quiet gratitude for the sheer, stubborn normality of it all. For friends who would face down demons and then argue about pizza toppings. For a world that kept spinning despite everything trying to knock it off its axis.

Charlie fell into step beside me as we hopped in my car. He was still limping, trying not to show it. "They're good people," he said, his voice a low rumble in the quiet street.

"The best," I agreed. "The kind you find once in a dozen lifetimes."

"You've had more than a dozen lifetimes," he pointed out.

"Which is how I know."

We drove in comfortable silence. A porch light flicked on as we drove through our neighborhood, motion sensor doing its job. Everything looked so normal, so safe. Like nothing had happened a week ago. Like the world hadn't almost ended in a clearing behind an elementary school.

The house was dark and silent when we arrived, a stark contrast to the vibrant chaos of Marion's. I flipped on a lamp and its glow pooled on the worn Persian rug. The familiar scent of old paper and cedar wrapped around us like a blanket. I went to the cabinet and poured two fingers of Lagavulin into a pair of heavy crystal tumblers, the peaty scent a promise of warmth.

Charlie didn't sit. He stood before the fireplace; his gaze fixed on the ancient sword hanging again above the mantle. The lamplight caught the runes on the scabbard, each one a story I had long forgotten. His reflection in the darkened window behind it showed a man still processing, still carrying weight.

"So," he said, without turning around. "Arnaut."

The name hung in the quiet room, a ghost given voice.

"Arnaut," I echoed. The taste of the scotch and the name were both bitter on my tongue.

He finally turned to face me, his eyes searching mine with an engineer's precision, looking for stress fractures, points of failure. "You alright, Jimmy? I mean, down in your bones. That wasn't just another monster. That was your brother."

I swirled the amber liquid in my glass, watching it cling to the sides, forming legs that ran down like tears. "I am... learning to be," I said, the truth slow to form, slower to speak. "For centuries, I carried the weight of his loss. I thought my caution, my hesitation at that wall in Jerusalem, had killed him. To find him like that... hollowed out and rebuilt into that..." I stopped, searching for words that didn't exist. "It was like losing him twice. The guilt is gone, but the grief remains. It's just a different shape now."

"He made his choices," Charlie said, not unkind, but firm the way only old soldiers can be. "You didn't forge that path for him. You tried to pull him back." He took a sip of scotch, considering. "And in the end, maybe a part of the man you knew was still in there. He could've killed David. He didn't. That has to count for something."

"A moment of grace," I said, staring into my glass like it held answers it didn't. "After seven centuries of darkness. I'll cling to that. I'll remember the friend who walked with me to Rome. But I also need to recognize what he's become." I looked up, met Charlie's eyes. "Somewhere inside him, the old Arnaut is still there. That's why I couldn't finish the fight in the park, Charlie. That's why I let him walk away."

Charlie studied me, his engineer's mind no doubt calculating stress loads on a soul as old as mine, looking for the breaking point. "You're squaring your shoulders again. I can see it. The weight is settling back on you."

"The work is eternal, my friend. This was one frayed thread. The tapestry is vast, and there are always shears in the dark." I set my glass down on the mantelpiece with a soft click. "I need to go to London. I have to see the Green Man for myself, walk the paths at Kew. After what happened here, after feeling how thin the Veil got, it needs a warden's presence. It needs to feel that it's not forgotten."

He nodded slowly, absorbing it. "How long?"

"A few weeks. A month, perhaps. No longer. This…" I gestured around the room, at the evidence of a life I had dared to build, at the artifacts and books and comfortable furniture that meant home. "This is my home now."

Charlie downed the last of his scotch and set the empty glass beside mine with deliberate care. He stepped forward and, without ceremony, pulled me into a brief, powerful embrace. A soldier's hug, all solid strength and unspoken understanding, the kind that says things words can't. It felt like an anchor being dropped.

"You listen to me, you old bastard," he said, his voice low and fierce in my ear. "You are not doing this alone anymore. You have a team. You have a family. We almost died out there, all of us, and you know what kept us fighting? Each other. Not magic, not copper wire. Us."

His grip tightened. "You go to London. You check on your tree spirit. You do what you need to do. We'll be right here, holding the line. But you come back, you hear me? This town needs its weirdest resident."

He released me, hands still on my shoulders, his gaze steady and serious. "And by the way, screw you for making me feel like I'm the old man in the group all these years. As punishment, I've signed you up for AARP. Membership card should arrive in six to eight weeks."

I laughed, and the sound surprised me with how genuine it felt.

He gave my shoulder a final pat, turned, and walked out, closing the door behind him with a quiet, definitive click.

I stood in the silence, the warmth of the scotch and his friendship a potent mix in my chest. The road ahead was long, and the shadows it passed through were deep and old. Arnaut was still out there, wounded but alive, nursing his wounds and his convictions in whatever dark place he'd retreated to. The Veil was stable, for now, but for how long? How many other threats were gathering that I didn't know about yet?

But for the first time in hundreds of years, I knew I wouldn't have to face them alone.

I picked up my glass, raised it in a silent toast to the closed door and the man beyond it, to the friends who'd stood with me, to a guardian sleeping beneath the earth, and to the fragile, beautiful normalcy of a Saturday night at Marion's Piazza.

The first, fragile stirrings of peace settled in my chest.

Not the peace of an ending, but the peace of knowing that whatever came next, I wouldn't face it alone.

PART 2

The park looked worse in daylight. I stood at the edge of the clearing where we'd fought Arnaut, hands shoved in my pockets, surveying the damage. A week had passed since the battle, long enough for the scorch marks to settle into the grass like old bruises. The copper wire was gone, packed away in my basement, but the pattern remained, six circles of dead grass where the nodes had been, connected by lines where nothing would grow for months. Maybe years.

Ray had cordoned off the area with yellow caution tape and orange cones, the kind the city used when they pretended to fix potholes. The official story was a lightning strike, which wasn't entirely wrong if you counted magical lightning. A crew was scheduled to come out next week to assess the damage, which meant Ray would spend the next month deflecting questions he couldn't answer about why lightning struck in a perfect hexagon.

I walked the perimeter slowly, checking. The air felt different now, cleaner, like a fever had broken. The oppressive hum that had been building for weeks was gone. Birds were back, sparrows and cardinals moving through the branches. A squirrel scolded me from an oak, annoyed that I was disrupting its morning routine. Normal sounds. Good sounds.

But underneath, if I listened with more than ears, I could still feel the Wendigo.

It was there, deep in the earth, a presence so faint it was almost imagined. Like standing over a grave and feeling the weight of what's buried beneath. Not dead. Sleeping. But the sleep was profound, the kind that comes after exhaustion too deep for dreams.

I knelt where it had fallen, where Charlie had knelt a week ago with tears on his face. The frost circle was still visible, a perfect ring of grass that had died from cold in the middle of August. I pressed my palm flat against the ground.

The earth was cool, cooler than it should be. I could feel the Wendigo's presence like a slow heartbeat, barely there. One beat per minute. Maybe less. It was alive, but barely holding form. The energy it had spent saving Charlie, absorbing that blast, had nearly unmade it.

"How do I help you?" I said quietly to the ground. "What do you need?"

The earth gave no answer. Guardians didn't work that way. They weren't conversational. They were old, elemental, more force than personality. The Wendigo had shown me things over the centuries, memories, sensations, warnings, but never words. It communicated the way stone communicates with water, slowly, through pressure and time.

I sat back on my heels, thinking. The Wendigo was tied to this land, to the limestone and the creek and the old stories that had once been told here. The Miami and Shawnee had known how to tend it, how to feed it with ritual and respect. But that knowledge was gone, scattered west with the people who'd carried it.

What I knew about healing guardians could fit in a thimble. Each guardian was its own theology manifested over centuries.

"Time," I said finally. "That's what you need, isn't it? Just time."

The ground beneath my hand seemed to settle, a fractional easing of tension. Not agreement, exactly. Acknowledgment.

I stood, brushing dirt from my knees. The clearing would scar, but scars heal. The trees would grow back. The grass would return. And beneath it all, the Wendigo would sleep until it remembered how to wake.

Movement caught my eye, a flicker of black at the tree line.

I turned, hand dropping instinctively toward where my sword would be if I'd been stupid enough to wear it to a public park. But I'd left it at home, hanging over my mantle. My fingers found only empty air.

A woman stepped from the shadows between the oaks.

She wore black, as always. Long-sleeved shirt despite the heat, black yoga pants, sensible shoes that made no sound on the leaf litter. No straw hat today, just a dark headscarf tied back. Her hands were bare, and I could see calluses across the palms, the permanent kind that come from decades of working soil.

The Garden Ninja.

She moved with a precision that wasn't quite military but wasn't civilian either. Each step placed deliberately, weight distributed, balanced. She stopped ten feet away, close enough to talk, far enough to run if she needed to.

We stared at each other.

"You're quieter than I expected," I said finally.

"I'm a ninja," she replied, deadpan. "It's in the job description."

"Uh, you know about that?" I asked.

"Honey, I know about a lot of things."

Up close, I could see her face properly for the first time. Sixty, maybe sixty-five, though she moved younger. Weathered skin, the kind that comes from sun and wind and not caring about either. Green eyes, sharp and clear. The kind of eyes that noticed everything and judged quickly.

"How long have you been watching?" I asked.

"Long enough." She glanced at the scorched grass, the dead circle, the trees that had been split by raw power. Her expression didn't change, but something in her posture tightened. "You made a mess."

"Um, we saved the world."

"You made a mess saving the world," she corrected. "There's a difference."

I almost smiled. Almost. "Are you here to file a complaint?"

"I'm here to help." She took a step closer, and I noticed she was shorter than she seemed from a distance. Maybe five-one. Rail thin, but not frail. "The land is wounded. The spirit is barely holding on. Left alone, it could take years for either to heal. Maybe a decade for the Wendigo to regain even half its strength."

"You know about the Wendigo."

It wasn't a question, but she answered anyway. "I've tended this ground for thirty years. Of course I know. The trees tell me things. The soil remembers." She paused. "And I've seen it, once. Years ago. At dawn, by the creek. It watched me for a long time. I think it was deciding whether to trust me."

"Did it?"

"I'm still alive." She shrugged. "That's usually a good sign with spirits of winter and hunger."

We stood there while a breeze moved through the clearing, rustling leaves, carrying the smell of creek water and damp earth. Somewhere a crow called, harsh and mocking.

"My name is Elaine," she said.

"James."

"I know." She smiled, thin and sharp. "James Crable. Drives a black BMW that's too nice for the neighborhood. Drinks expensive wine. Keeps odd hours. The kind of neighbor who's polite but never really there."

"You've been watching me."

"I watch everyone." She shrugged. "It's what I do. But you, I watched more carefully. Because you have magic, and magic near a guardian is either protection or threat. I needed to know which."

"And now you know."

"Now I know." She knelt beside the frost circle, placed both hands flat on the ground. Closed her eyes. For a long moment she was perfectly still, and I could feel something shift in the air around her. Not magic exactly, or not the kind I was used to. Older. Quieter. Like watching roots find water.

Her eyes opened. "It's deep. Deeper than I thought. The damage goes right to the core." She stood, brushing her hands together. "But I can help. I can heal the land, and through the land, feed the spirit. Give it strength to recover."

"How long?"

"Months instead of years. Three, maybe four, if I work every day." She looked around the clearing, assessing. "The soil here is traumatized. The trees are confused. The water table has been disrupted by all that magical energy. Everything is out of balance. But balance can be restored if you know how to ask nicely."

It then hit me, "You're a druid."

She met my eyes. "What's left of one. My order is scattered, small, careful. We remember what happened when we weren't careful. When we drew attention."

The weight of Anglesey settled between us like a third person.

"We remember the Watch," she continued, voice flat. "We remember groves that burned and druids and children who died because Rome decided our magic was corruption." Her eyes met mine. "When an immortal moved into the neighborhood, I stayed hidden. I tended my garden and watched the park and hoped you'd move on eventually. I didn't know if you were still Rome's creature."

"I'm not," I said. "Haven't been for a long time. The Watch is long dead, and the Church has moved on from trying to bend the world to its will."

"I know that now." She glanced back at the scorched earth. "Watching you protect this place, that told me enough. You're not serving the Church anymore. You're serving something else."

"The balance," I said. "That's all. Just trying to keep the world from eating itself."

She nodded slowly. "Then maybe we can work together. The spirit needs more than time. It needs tending. And I can do that, but I'll need access. Ray is going to have questions if he sees me working here every day."

"I'll handle Ray," I said. "Tell me what you need."

"Mostly time and privacy. I'll need to work the soil, plant specific herbs, sing the old songs. Rebuild the relationship between land and spirit." She looked at me directly. "It won't be fast. It won't be flashy. It's the kind of magic that looks like gardening to anyone who doesn't know better. But it works. The land will remember how to be healthy. The water will remember its path. And the spirit..." She paused. "The spirit will remember how to be strong."

"Four months."

"Give or take. Depends on how badly the Veil scarred when it nearly tore. Depends on whether that man you fought comes back and undoes my work." She crossed her arms. "And depends on whether you can keep curious teenagers and well-meaning park rangers from trampling my plantings."

"I can manage that."

She reached into her pocket and pulled out something small, wrapped in cloth. "I brought you something. A peace offering. Or maybe an apology for not trusting you sooner."

She unwrapped it. A seed, dark and perfectly round, no bigger than a marble.

"Oak," she said. "From a tree older than either of us. Plant it here, at the center of the frost circle. Let it grow over the sleeping spirit. Oaks are patient. They'll stand watch long after we're both gone."

I took the seed, felt its weight. Heavier than it looked. "Thank you."

"Don't thank me yet. That tree will take fifty years to matter. A hundred to be strong. We're planting for a future neither of us might see."

"I've planted for futures before," I said. "It's the only way anything grows."

She smiled, and for the first time it reached her eyes. "Then maybe there's hope for us after all."

She turned to leave, moving back toward the tree line with that same deliberate quiet.

"Elaine," I called.

She stopped, looked back.

"I'm going to London tomorrow. There's something I need to do. But when I get back, let's talk. Really talk. About the Wendigo, about what's coming, about how we protect this place."

"I'll make tea," she said. "You bring the expensive wine I know you have."

"Deal."

She vanished into the trees, and I was alone again with the scorched earth and the sleeping guardian and the seed heavy in my palm.

I knelt and dug a small hole at the center of the frost circle, right where I'd felt the Wendigo's heartbeat strongest. The soil was cold and damp. I placed the seed carefully, covered it, pressed the earth flat.

"Grow strong," I said. "You've got a long watch ahead of you."

The wind picked up, moving through the clearing like breath. Somewhere beneath me, too deep to hear, the Wendigo's heartbeat pulsed once. Then stillness.

I stood, brushed the dirt from my hands, and walked back toward the trail.

Tomorrow, London. Tomorrow, Kew and the Green Man and the work that never ends.

But tonight, I had a seed to tend and a guardian to honor and the strange, unexpected comfort of knowing I wasn't alone in the work anymore.

The next day, I left for London. I had long ago created portal stones from my home in Centerville to the one I still had in Kew. It allowed me to go back and forth instantly rather than deal with airports and delays. Once in Kew I hopped in my car and went on a road trip.

After five hours, I stood on the windswept coast of Anglesey, salt spray sharp against my face. The modern world had layered itself over the old, but the bones were still there if you knew how to look. I found the grove by feel more than memory, following a sorrowful hum in the earth where power had been wounded centuries ago.

The oaks were old here, gnarled and twisted, branches reaching like arthritic fingers. Ivy climbed everything. The ground was soft with centuries of leaf fall, and the smell was all damp earth and rot and growing things.

I stood for a long time, letting the ghosts settle. Arnaut's zeal. Alaric's certainty. My own blind obedience. We'd come here convinced we were doing God's work, and we'd burned people who'd only wanted to tend their land and honor their dead.

Elaine's decades of vigilance made more sense now. Hiding from me made sense. Trust, once broken that badly, takes lifetimes to rebuild.

I'd brought a shovel from a hardware store in the village. The clerk had given me a strange look when I'd paid cash and refused a receipt. I didn't care. Some work needs to be done without paperwork.

I dug at the base of the oldest oak, the one that had probably seen the burning. The one that remembered. The soil gave way easily, as if the ground wanted this found. Two feet down, my shovel struck something that rang like a bell.

A small silver coffer, tarnished black with age.

I pulled it free, brushed the dirt away. The hinges protested but opened. Inside, wrapped in waxed cloth that had barely held together, was the relic. The splinter of oak bound in silver wire, the relic of obedience that Alaric had given us to carry into the grove like a weapon. It had not decomposed in these many years. It still looked like it did the day it was given to my care.

It still hummed, but softly and with purity. It was weak, for sure, but the corruption was washed clean, whether by the years in the grove, or through our use of its magic that night. I lifted it carefully, and for a moment I swore I could feel the tree it had come from, its anger, its sorrow.

"I'm sorry," I said to the grove, to the ghosts, to the oaks that had witnessed. "For what we did. For what I was part of. I can't undo it. But maybe I can make it mean something now."

The wind moved through the branches, and if I chose to hear forgiveness in it, that was my business.

I wrapped the relic carefully in fresh cloth and placed it in my pack. Then I walked back to my car for the long ride home.

My business in London was quick. The Green Man was tired but holding, the gardens breathing steadily around it. I walked the paths, checked the old protections, felt its gratitude in the movement of leaves and the warmth of sunlight through the canopy. It was good to be back, nostalgic even, but it wasn't home anymore.

Home was Ohio. Home was a house on a nondescript suburban street and friends who fought demons over beer and pizza. Home was a sleeping guardian under frost-touched ground.

The moment I returned to Centerville, I went to Elaine's house.

She was in her garden, as I'd known she would be. Kneeling by a bed of lavender, deadheading spent blooms with small, precise cuts. She didn't look up as I approached, but her posture shifted, awareness without alarm.

"London treat you well?" she asked the lavender.

"Well enough."

"And Anglesey?"

I stopped. "How did you know?"

"You have the smell of ancient oak on you. And grief." She looked up finally, green eyes measuring. "You went back to the grove."

I pulled the small box from my pack and held it out.

She set down her shears, wiped her hands on her pants, and took the box.

Opened it. Went very still.

"This is…" Her voice caught. "This is from *the* tree. The one felled by the ancient Romans."

"Yes."

She lifted the relic with both hands, cradling it like something newborn and fragile. Tears tracked down her face, and she didn't bother wiping them away.

"They took this from my people," she said quietly. "Bound it. Corrupted it. Used it to silence our magic, to make us forget how to speak to the land. It is now clean again." She looked up at me. "And you're giving it back."

"It's time," I said. "The old feud needs to die. We don't have the luxury of old grudges anymore. The world is fraying, Elaine. We both know it. Whatever's coming next, we can't face it as enemies."

She closed the box carefully, held it against her chest. "My order will want to know about this. They'll want to meet you."

"Good. I'd like to meet them."

She stood, brushing dirt from her knees, and surprised me by reaching out and gripping my shoulder. Strong grip, callused hand, the touch of someone who'd worked hard their whole life.

"Thank you," she said. "For this. For the park. For standing when you could have walked away." She paused, looked down at the box. "This will help. With the healing, with the Wendigo. Old oak knows how to talk to wounded spirits. I can use this to speed the recovery. Maybe cut the time in half."

"We stand together now," she said. "There's work to do. A lot of it. And we're going to need all the help we can get."

She smiled, and it transformed her face from stern to something almost gentle. "Then I suppose I should start making that tea. And you can bring that expensive wine you promised."

"Tomorrow," I said. "Tonight, I need to sleep for about sixteen hours."

"Tomorrow then." She clutched the box tighter. "We'll plan. We'll prepare. And maybe, just maybe, we'll be ready for whatever comes next."

I walked home as the sun set, painting Centerville in shades of orange and gold. Somewhere behind me, a guardian slept. Somewhere ahead, threats gathered. But for tonight, the balance held.

And I wasn't holding it alone anymore.

235

COMING SPRING 2026: Book 2, Chapter 1 – Fog, Messages, and the Disbanded (Brentford, England 1899)

A hard winter fog rolled in from the Thames that night, thick enough to swallow the sound of carriage wheels on Brentford's streets. The fog turned gas lamps into dim halos and made a man question whether the ground beneath his boots was truly solid. December had come with a vengeance, bringing frost that clung to the cobblestones and made each step crack faintly under my weight.

I walked from Brentford Dock through streets that felt more ghost town than living city. The warehouses loomed dark and silent on either side, their brick facades slick with condensation. Coal smoke mixed with the river smell, that particular combination of industrial waste and low tide that marked London's western reaches. The Grand Union Canal lay somewhere to my left, invisible in the murk, but I could hear water lapping against stone and the occasional groan of a barge settling against its moorings.

Brook Road South appeared out of the fog like something conjured. The street was residential here, narrow houses pressed together with their windows shuttered against the cold. A dog barked somewhere, muffled by the weather. A woman's voice called out briefly, then silence returned.

The Griffin stood at the junction with Braemar Road, a corner pub with a distinctive tower-like structure that caught what little light escaped the gas lamps. The building itself was Fuller's, built some fifteen years earlier with that solid Victorian confidence that declared permanence. The polygonal corner treatment gave it an unusual profile, angular and severe, like something cut from different geometric shapes and forced together.

Above the entrance, carved into the stonework, a griffin watched the street with blank eyes. The brewery's symbol. Fuller's had owned the orchard that once stood here, and the pub bore their mark like a brand. The creature looked pale and stiff in the icy gloom, frost gathering along its wings and beak.

The pub's windows glowed with warm amber light that made the cold outside feel sharper by contrast. Smoke from the hearth drifted through the glass in slow curls, and the silhouettes of patrons leaned toward the fire the way men do when they cannot remember the last time their bones felt warm. I stood outside for a moment, letting the cold settle deeper into my coat. The fog pressed close, patient and hungry.

Then I pushed open the door and stepped inside.

The world changed. Heat hit me first, the blessed shock of warmth after the brutal cold of the streets. The fire snapped loudly in its grate, battling the winter air that crept in each time the door opened. The smell was thick and immediate: coal smoke, wet wool, spilled ale, tobacco, and beneath it all the yeasty scent of bread from the kitchen. The smell soaked into wood and never quite left.

The interior was all dark wood and brass fittings. An L-shaped bar sat to the back of the room. Behind it, bottles gleamed on shelves, and the brass taps caught the firelight. There were various tables tucked into corners and some benches running along the walls where working men could sit and nurse their pints in relative privacy.

Coats steamed slowly where they hung near the hearth, dripping condensation onto the floorboards. A few men stood at the bar with their hands wrapped around pints as if they feared losing the heat. Others sat hunched over tables, speaking in low voices that mixed with the crackle of the fire and created a background hum that felt almost alive.

Gas lamps hung from chains, their mantles glowing steady and warm. The whole place felt like a refuge, a pocket of civilization carved out of the winter darkness. A place where a man could forget, for an hour or two, that the world outside was cold and hostile.

I chose a corner table away from the draft, settling into a chair that creaked under my weight. The wood was worn smooth by use, and someone had carved initials into the armrest. J.M. 1887. I wondered who J.M. had been and whether he was still alive.

I pulled off my gloves and rubbed warmth back into my fingers. Despite never aging, my hands looked old in the candlelight, calloused from work that spanned centuries. I let the heat from the candle on the table soak into my skin. The flame bent each time a gust rattled the windowpanes, dancing and recovering, dancing and recovering.

Around me, the pub conducted its evening business. A group of dockworkers occupied a table near the fire, their faces red with ale and heat. They spoke loudly about wages and foremen and which tavern girl would give them the time of day. Near the window, an older man sat alone with his pipe and his thoughts, staring into nothing. Two younger men played cards at a side table, slapping down their hands with theatrical flourishes. They went about their business, drinking and laughing and arguing, secure in the delusion that the world was safe and reasonable and governed by natural laws.

I envied them their ignorance.

Lucan arrived a few minutes later. He stepped in from the cold with frost on his coat and tension in his jaw. As he entered, he scanned the room, found me, and made his way through the press of bodies. He moved like a soldier, economical and aware, always conscious of exits and potential threats.

He looked more troubled than when I'd last seen him. Three years, perhaps four. He had not aged in the hundreds of years I had known him, not in the way mortal men do, but he had a look of strain and a tiredness that comes with the weight of eternity. He shook the chill off like a man returning from a long march rather than a short walk through Brentford's streets.

"You look frozen," I said as he sat.

"Frozen and tired." He pulled off his gloves with stiff fingers. "And neither seems to be improving."

I flagged the barman, a thick-armed man with a scarred face and the look of someone who'd seen his share of trouble. I ordered two pints of mild along with a bottle of whiskey. The prices were chalked on a board behind the bar:

twopence for mild, threepence for bitter, sixpence for a measure of spirits. Working man's rates.

When the drinks arrived, Lucan held his glass close, letting the heat seep into his fingers before taking a drink. He closed his eyes briefly, savoring the warmth.

"Thank you," he said quietly. "I had almost forgotten what warmth felt like."

"You wrote as if the matter was urgent."

"It is. And growing worse." He set down his glass and leaned forward, lowering his voice. "Three deaths in Brentford. All near the river. All drained of blood. Have you heard anything? I know you live just across the river."

Around us, the pub noise continued. Someone laughed, high and a little tipsy. The fire popped as a log shifted. The dockworkers started an argument about football, voices rising.

"No, but I have been travelling. When?" I asked.

"First one was six weeks ago. A dockworker, found behind one of the warehouses near Brunel's old dock. Second was a prostitute, three weeks later. Third was just five days ago. A merchant's son."

"That last one will cause trouble."

"It already has. The police are asking questions. The father has money and connections. He's demanding answers." Lucan drank again, deeper this time. "But the police won't find anything useful. They're looking for a human killer. They don't understand what they're hunting."

"And you do?"

"Not entirely. That's why I need help."

Before he could continue, the door opened again. A sharp gust of winter air rushed in, carrying fog and the faint smell of the river. Two figures emerged from the doorway, both brushing frost from their coats as they stepped inside. The other patrons barely glanced at them. Just more cold souls seeking warmth and ale.

But I looked. Old instinct. Always note who enters a room.

The woman entered first. Tall, more than five and a half feet, with dark hair damp from the fog and pulled back in a severe style that emphasized the sharp angles of her face. Beautiful in a predator sort of way. She moved with economy, no wasted motion, scanning the room with green eyes that missed nothing. Her coat was well-made but practical, designed for movement rather than fashion. She carried herself like someone who knew how to handle trouble. There was something in the way she assessed the room, not the casual glance of someone seeking a seat, but the calculated sweep of someone cataloging exits, threats, and tactical advantages. It reminded me of a sniper selecting a position.

Behind her came a man with the unmistakable bearing of an American. Thin, broad shouldered and corded muscle. He had a swagger that warned of danger, wearing a coat with the collar turned up against the cold. He stomped frost from his boots before scanning the room like a soldier entering unfamiliar ground. His face was weathered, his jaw strong, his eyes the pale blue of winter ice. His right hand stayed near his coat's opening, hovering over what I suspected was a weapon. Even in an ordinary pub, his body was coiled, ready.

Lucan rose, lifting his hand in greeting. They spotted him and made their way through the tables.

"James, this is Corisande Valencourt," Lucan said as they approached.

She extended her hand. Her grip was firm, her palm rough. The hand of someone who'd trained with weapons. "A pleasure," she said, "and please, Cori is fine." Her accent was educated, the Queen's English spoken with a cadence that said she didn't spend much time in aristocratic circles. "I have heard your name for years."

Her green eyes held mine for a moment longer than courtesy required, and I had the distinct impression I was being weighed and measured against some internal standard. Whatever her conclusion, she gave no indication.

"Only the flattering stories, I hope."

She smiled faintly. "Flattering stories are rarely the ones worth telling."

The American offered his hand next. "Ezekiel Whitmore. Call me Zeke."

His grip was crushing, the handshake of someone who'd grown up in a place where physical strength mattered. "Lucan tells me you're the real deal," he said, his American Southern drawl warm and genuine. "Hope he ain't overselling, because we surely need someone who knows their business."

"We'll find out."

They settled around the table. The barmaid appeared, a tired-looking woman with graying hair and knowing eyes. She took their orders without writing anything down. Two more pints, another whiskey. She returned quickly, collected her coin, and disappeared back into the crowd.

Cori held her hands near the candle, letting the warmth touch her fingers. Zeke wasted no time pouring himself a generous shot of whiskey. He downed it with a satisfied nod and immediately poured another. "Now that's proper," he said. "English winter'll freeze a man's soul."

For a moment, we sat in silence. The pub noise swirled around us, a cocoon of ordinary human activity that felt surreal given what we were about to discuss. The fire cracked. Someone dropped a glass and cursed. The dockworkers' argument about football escalated into friendly shoving.

Lucan leaned forward again. When he spoke, his voice was barely above a murmur.

"The Watch is gone. Rome dissolved it in September. Pope Leo signed the papers himself. After twenty-two hundred years, they decided we were no longer necessary."

Cori's jaw tightened, but she said nothing.

Zeke muttered something that sounded like a Texas curse, low and creative.

"It only lasted this long because of people like you and your dedication to the original mission," I said.

Lucan's expression hardened slightly. "Our mission doesn't end because we have no bureaucracy to support us. The Watch has been slowly dying for years and a few of us saw it coming." He spread his hands to include Zeke and Cori. "For the last two centuries most of the few new members that have been admitted have been different. Many have shown signs of aging, and their powers are weaker. But we're not here to mourn the past."

Lucan pulled a notebook from his coat. The leather was worn smooth, the pages dog-eared. "We've chosen to carry this work forward, with or without the Vatican's blessing. Which brings me to you, James. I need your experience on this."

He opened the notebook to a marked page. The candlelight caught sketches and notes, all in Lucan's precise handwriting. Maps of streets. Drawings of footprints. Dates and times.

"This is no common predator," Lucan continued. "We've been tracking it for six weeks. It hunts at night, obviously. Prefers victims who won't be missed quickly. Dockworkers, prostitutes, vagrants. People the authorities don't care about."

"Until it killed the merchant's son," Cori said quietly. "A miscalculation. Which suggests either growing confidence or deteriorating control."

"Exactly. That was a mistake. Too visible. Too important. Now there's pressure to solve the case, which means more police presence, which makes investigation harder. It is reminiscent of a vampire, but I don't think it is."

"What makes you think it's not a vampire?" I asked.

Lucan turned to a page showing sketches of wounds. Two puncture marks, precise and clean. "The wounds. A vampire feeds messily when hungry, carefully when cautious, but it is never precise. These wounds are surgical. Perfect punctures, exactly the right depth and placement to drain a body in minutes."

"Could be an old one," Zeke suggested. "Vampire with some real control and finesse."

"I considered that. But there's more." Lucan flipped to another page. A symbol, roughly drawn but clear. A circle with three intersecting lines, each ending in a different shape. Square, triangle, spiral.

I felt something cold settle in my chest. I'd seen that symbol before. Long ago, in a different century, in a city that no longer existed.

"That was found near the third body," Lucan said. "Scratched into the wall of the alley. Fresh. Probably done the same night."

I reached for the notebook, studying the drawing more closely. The proportions were different from what I remembered, but the basic structure was unmistakable. I leaned in and studied it closely.

"This looks familiar," I said.

Cori leaned forward, her focus sharpening. "You've seen this before?"

"Something like it. Different configuration, but the same principle.

We called it a binding mark. Used in ritual magic to contain or control supernatural entities."

"Control specifically how?" she asked. Her tone was precise, demanding exactness rather than generalities.

"That depends on the ritual. Could be summoning. Could be banishing. Could be binding a creature to a specific task." I looked at Lucan. "If someone's using binding marks, they're working with real knowledge. Not the superstitious nonsense most people think is magic."

Zeke leaned back in his chair, the wood creaking. "So, we got something powerful killin' folks in Brentford, leavin' mystical signs at murder scenes, and Rome disbands us right when it starts up?" He shook his head. "That stinks worse than a Texas slaughterhouse. Someone knew this was comin'."

"You think Rome knows," Cori said. It wasn't a question. Her voice held the cool certainty of someone who'd already reached that conclusion and was waiting for others to catch up.

"Rome always knows more than they're tellin'," Zeke said, bitterness creeping into his drawl. "They decided we were more trouble than we're worth, and whatever's happenin' in Brentford ain't their problem anymore."

Lucan closed the notebook and tucked it away. "Which brings us back to my question. Will you help?"

The fire popped loudly in its grate. Outside, the fog pressed against the windows like something trying to get in. The pub felt suddenly smaller, the warmth less comforting. Somewhere in this city, something was hunting. Something that combined the efficiency of a predator with the knowledge of a sorcerer. And we were four people with no support and no authority to stop it.

I looked at my old friend. We'd fought together in Damascus, back when the world was younger and the threats more straightforward. He stood by me when I decided to leave the watch after Arnaut disappeared. He was the only member of the Watch that I still spoke with, and the only one I have trusted for over 400 years.

"You know I will," I said.

I motioned to Cori and Zeke each, "I assume you are part of this as well?"

"Hell yeah." Zeke's response was immediate and fierce. "Been at this near 50 years. Ain't about to let some papal decree tell me when I'm done."

Cori's smile was cold and elegant, her green eyes sparkling in the candle-light. "I didn't come to London for the weather, Mr. Crable." She lifted her glass in a salute. "Something this interesting deserves proper attention."

I found myself noticing the precise way she moved, the controlled economy of every gesture. When she lifted her glass, there was no wasted motion, no unconscious flourish. Everything deliberate. It was oddly compelling.

Lucan smiled, though it didn't reach his eyes. "Good. We need your experience, James. You've seen more than any of us, and this thing," he tapped the notebook, "this requires someone who studied runes and binding marks."

"This thing is smart," he continued, his voice taking on the tone of a commander briefing his troops. "It varies its hunting grounds. It never uses the same approach twice. It leaves no witnesses and no clear pattern except the bodies themselves."

"And the symbols," I added.

"And the symbols. Which suggests purpose beyond simple feeding." Lucan drank the last of his whiskey. "One person couldn't track it properly. Two might get lucky. But four of us, working together, we have a chance."

"What's the plan?" I asked.

Lucan pulled out a larger map, unfolding it on the table. It showed Brentford and the surrounding areas, the Thames a thick blue line running through the center. Red marks indicated the three murder sites. They formed a rough pattern along the river's edge.

"I've been mapping the kills," Lucan said, tracing the marks with his finger. "Trying to predict where it might hunt next. There's an area near the docks, here, that fits the pattern. Old warehouses, minimal foot traffic at night, easy access to the river."

"You think it uses the river," Cori said.

"For movement, perhaps. Or escape. The fog's been heavy all month, and the water muffles sound. It's perfect hunting ground."

I studied the map. The marked areas clustered near the industrial heart of Brentford, where Brunel's old dock connected the Thames to the railway network. Warehouses and loading yards, mostly empty at night. Dark alleys between buildings. Plenty of shadows for something to hide.

"When do we start?" I asked.

Lucan's tone shifted, becoming more commanding. "Tomorrow night. Meet here at dusk, he pointed to a spot on the map in the dockyard. "Bring whatever weapons you have." He looked at each of us in turn, making it clear this wasn't a suggestion. "And be ready for anything."

"We went out two nights ago," Cori said quietly. Her fingers traced the rim of her glass, then she seemed to catch herself and stopped, her hand going still. "The frost showed prints for a few minutes before the fog erased them. We found tracks near one of the warehouses. Human-shaped, but wrong. The stride was too long. The depth too even."

"Each print was exactly the same depth," she added, her analytical mind clearly still working through the details. "No variation for weight shift or gait. As if it glided rather than walked."

The words hung in the air between us. Around us, the pub continued its oblivious business. Men drank and laughed and argued about things that didn't matter. They had no idea what walked in their streets at night. No concept of the darkness that lived alongside their ordinary lives.

We sat in silence for a while, each lost in our own thoughts. The fire burned lower. The candle on our table guttered and reformed. Outside, the December night deepened, and the fog grew thicker.

Finally, Lucan stood. "Tomorrow at dusk. Don't be late."

We left separately, a precaution from old habits. Cori went first, pulling her coat tight against the cold and disappearing into the fog. As she passed, she caught my eye briefly, and something unspoken passed between us, an acknowledgment, perhaps, or a challenge. Then she was gone.

Zeke followed a few minutes later, clapping Lucan on the shoulder with enough force to make a mortal man stagger. "Tomorrow then," he drawled. "Time to show this thing what real hunters look like." His broad shoulders hunched against the winter air as he pushed through the door with characteristic directness.

Lucan stood and we clasped hands. "It's good to see you old friend." And with that he turned and walked out.

I was last, stepping out into a night that had grown even colder. The fog was so thick now that I could barely see the building across the street. The gas lamps were just dim suggestions of light, barely strong enough to illuminate their own posts.

The cold hit me like a physical blow. My breath rose in thin plumes, lost as soon as the fog closed around them. Ice crunched under my boots. Somewhere in the distance, a dog howled, the sound lonely and haunting.

I stepped out from the Griffin's warm haze and turned east along Brentford High Street, the cobbles slick. Past the shuttered shopfronts and the silent wharves of the Thames, I kept to the road that bent toward Kew Bridge. The gas lamps threw weak halos against the fog, and the river's dark breath followed me as I crossed. Beyond the span, the lanes narrowed, leading me through quiet cottages and the shadowed edge of the gardens. The world was hushed, every hearth-bound family tucked away from the chill, leaving only my footsteps to mark the way back toward Kew.

I thought about what Lucan had shown us. Three deaths. Bodies drained of blood with surgical precision. Binding marks scratched into walls. Something tall and fast that moved through the fog like it was made of it.

And all of it happening after Rome disbanded the Watch.

The timing felt wrong. Too convenient. Too neat. Like someone had been waiting for exactly this moment, when we were scattered and disorganized and without resources.

But who? And why Brentford? I thought about Kew Gardens and the Green Man and tried to find a connection.

The questions followed me through the fog, unanswered and troubling.

I reached my house, a block from the gardens, its brick front softened in the summer by ivy but now browned by the winter cold. The glow of a gaslight spilled from the fanlight above the door. Inside, I lit the lamp in the hall and let the familiar warmth wash over me. The polished oak floor gleamed beneath a Persian runner, and the scent of cedar drifted faintly from the paneled study to the left. Through the doorway I glimpsed my shelves lined with books, a heavy desk scattered with papers, and the quiet promise of work yet to be done.

I opened a secure trunk marked with sigils and examined its contents. Priceless and dangerous items I'd collected over centuries. I removed my old sword. The sigils on the scabbard glinted in the lamp light.

I drew it carefully. The blade was marked with more runes and sigils, and sharper than when it was newly forged. I carried this since I was a newly admitted member of the Watch. Now the Watch was gone.

I cleaned the blade and checked for any imperfections I already knew wouldn't be there.

Tomorrow night, we'd hunt.

Four members of a disbanded order, without authority, tracking something that had already killed three people and would certainly kill more if we failed.

I smiled grimly in the lamplight. This was familiar ground. Despite the time that had passed, this was what I knew.

I thought about my new companions. Lucan, steady as always. Zeke, all swagger and instinct. And Cori, precise, controlled, with those calculating green eyes that seemed to see straight through pretense to the truth beneath. It had been a long time since I'd worked with anyone who moved with such lethal grace.

I lay down on the narrow bed and closed my eyes, but sleep was slow coming. My mind kept returning to the symbol Lucan had shown us. The binding mark. This was no amateur conjurer we were dealing with. Lucan was right to seek my help.

If someone was using binding marks in Brentford, they were playing with forces they didn't understand. Or worse, they understood perfectly and didn't care about the consequences.

Either way, it needed to stop.

Outside, the fog pressed against the window. The temperature dropped further. Frost formed on the glass in delicate patterns, beautiful and foreboding.

Somewhere in this city, something was waking up. Getting ready to hunt. Choosing its next victim from among the thousands of souls who had no idea danger walked among them.

Tomorrow night, we'd be waiting.

None of us would need to do this. Immortal members of the watch had lifetimes to accumulate wealth and comfort. We did it because someone needed to stand against the dark.

That was a mission I could get behind.

I drifted into restless sleep, dreaming of fog and blood and symbols drawn in darkness. Dreaming of the work that never ended, no matter what Rome decreed or the world believed.

The night deepened. The fog thickened. And in the darkness beyond my window, something moved through Brentford's streets, hunting.

About the Author

Jack Calder grew up in Ohio, spent several years living in London, and now resides just outside Washington, DC, proof that he can thrive in everything from Midwestern winters to British drizzle to Beltway chaos. He spent most of his adult life in corporate strategy and M&A, with more than two decades of global experience, he has spent an impressive percentage of his life in airports. His work has taken him across Europe, the Middle East, and Asia, giving him a front-row seat to the cultures, histories, and odd coincidences that inevitably find their way into his fiction.

A devoted world traveler and unapologetic lover of food and wine, Jack insists that every new setting in his stories should be researched thoroughly, which usually involves a good meal. When he's not writing or working abroad, he enjoys life with his wife and their three college-aged children, who still love having their parents hang out with them.

The Veil Chronicles is his debut series, blending historical fiction, urban fantasy, and the dry humor that only a nearly empty-nest dad can fully weaponize.

You can connect with me on:

https://x.com/Jack_Calder1

https://www.facebook.com/jack.calder.440235